THE
CAREGIVER

A NOVEL

SAMUEL
PARK

Simon & Schuster

New York   London   Toronto   Sydney   New Delhi

Simon & Schuster
1230 Avenue of the Americas
New York, NY 10020

First Simon & Schuster hardcover edition September 2018

SIMON & SCHUSTER and colophon are registered trademarks of Simon & Schuster, Inc.

For information about special discounts for bulk purchases, please contact Simon & Schuster Special Sales at 1-866-506-1949 or business@simonandschuster.com.

The Simon & Schuster Speakers Bureau can bring authors to your live event. For more information or to book an event, contact the Simon & Schuster Speakers Bureau at 1-866-248-3049 or visit our website at www.simonspeakers.com.

Interior design by Carly Loman

Manufactured in the United States of America

10   9   8   7   6   5   4   3   2   1

Library of Congress Cataloging-in-Publication Data
Names: Park, Samuel, author.
Title: The caregiver : a novel / Samuel Park.
Description: First Simon & Schuster hardcover edition. | New York : Simon & Schuster, 2018.
Identifiers: LCCN 2017044640| ISBN 9781501178771 (hardcover) | ISBN 9781501178795 (softcover) | ISBN 9781501178788 (Ebook)
Subjects: LCSH: Mothers and daughters—Fiction. | Family secrets—Fiction. | Domestic fiction.
Classification: LCC PS3616.A7436 C37 2018 | DDC 813/.6—dc23 LC record available at https://lccn.loc.gov/2017044640

ISBN 978-1-5011-7877-1
ISBN 978-1-5011-7878-8 (ebook)

For my parents

This at least of flame-like our life has, that it is but the concurrence, renewed from moment to moment, of forces parting sooner or later on their ways.

> —WALTER PATER,
> *The Renaissance: Studies in Art and Poetry*

I pray you, in your letters,
When you shall these unlucky deeds relate,
Speak of me as I am.

> —SHAKESPEARE,
> *Othello*

Bel Air, California

The early 1990s

Mara, age twenty-six

Prologue

THE ROADS OF LOWER BEL AIR, DURING THE DAY, WERE full of beat-up pickup trucks and old cars of dubious colors. They belonged to the army of gardeners and maids who charged up the driveways and manicured the plots of roses and poppies that did not mind the California heat and cleaned the rooms that were already clean because they'd been cleaned the week before. There was often quite a bit of traffic, since the denizens of the San Fernando Valley sometimes used Roscomare Road as a shortcut between Westwood and the Valley, to bypass the ever-clogged, always-under-construction 405 freeway. They flew over the bumps, zigzagged over the winding, vertiginous cliff-side roads, and tail-gated me so much that sometimes I pulled over to the curb for a moment just to let them pass. I didn't like being rushed, but I also savored these moments of quiet, being outside and looking in, before my workday started.

I was officially a caregiver at Mrs. Weatherly's house on Ros-comare Road, but my duties also included cooking and cleaning.

My routine upon arriving was always the same: I parked my car in the most visible corner of the street, wheels practically kissing the curb. Last time I'd left my vehicle vulnerable to the incoming traffic in the narrow road, my side-view mirror had been shattered.

Today, to my surprise, as I came in, I ran into my employer's ex-husband, Mr. Weatherly. He was busy at the task of putting on his shoes, which back in my native Brazil was either an afterthought or a nonissue. I, for one, never understood how putting on shoes could be a task of its own, rather than a subset of another, or why it involved a piece of furniture, like a chair or a bench, or how it could possibly take more than three seconds. I glanced at Mr. Weatherly from the corner of my eye as he rose to his full size from the chair. He had that kind of imposing height that made me aware of where he was in any room in the house. He made little noises in tandem with his nose and his mouth, not grunts exactly, but sounds that suggested his satisfaction in the deed he'd just accomplished.

"Oh, good, Kathryn was just asking for you," said Mr. Weatherly, on his way out. "She can't find her nausea medication."

"It's on the nightstand. I'll go help her."

Kathryn Weatherly was a tall, blond woman in her early forties. She dressed almost exclusively in white, beige, or cream. All of her outfits had a lightness, an airiness to them. When I first met her, I assumed she was an actress. Not a famous one whose work you'd know, but someone who needed to be looked up, someone with an asterisk next to her name. The way I used to imagine people glanced twice at my mother, an actress of sorts, before their gaze moved on.

Kathryn once told me that she had lived in Bel Air all her life and attended elementary school at John Thomas Dye, where she'd been classmates with Ron Reagan and Aissa Wayne, the cowboy's daughter. Nearby, at the Bel Air Country Club, Kathryn's father would play golf on the challenging course while her mother would watch from the restaurant, where the food was not really that good, to be perfectly honest, she said. At the Hotel Bel Air up the street, there was nearly always a wedding, especially in June, especially on Sundays, and Kathryn wondered why there were people taking photos at what was, to her, like a local diner.

Kathryn shuttled back and forth between those two places for most of her childhood and teenage years, and though there was often talk of going somewhere else, it also didn't make much sense to break her familiar routine. When she got older, Kathryn got a kick out of passing by Elizabeth Taylor's house, maybe spotting Liz herself in a pink caftan and silk scarf, heavily made up in lavender, eyes drooping from either sleepiness or drugs. Or passing by the Reagan estate, a sighting as exciting and inevitable as Loch Ness for a Highlander.

Now, dying of stomach cancer, Kathryn rarely left her bedroom unless it was to go to the UCLA hospital down the street.

I saw no shafts of light escaping from under Kathryn's door. Bright suns everywhere in the kitchen and the living room, but the master bedroom remained a stubborn Neptune.

"Kathryn, it's Mara," I announced with a knock. "I'm here."

"How do you expect me to leave you this house if you're not here to anticipate all my needs?" she bellowed.

I couldn't help but roll my eyes a bit. She'd said this before, and often repeated it. Inside, her room was completely dark, full of stagnant air. Scarlet drapes bunched up on the ground, an abundance of Mulberry silk. Above the dresser hung a painting of ocean and pinery, like an open window, the view pristine. Kathryn sat up in the bed, a sea of creased, lumpy blankets keeping her moored.

"You're not going to leave me this house. You're just saying that so I won't leave."

Not that the idea was entirely far-fetched. Kathryn was only forty-four years old, had no children, a now-ex-husband, and her parents were already dead. She had no inclination for charity, not even cancer research.

"Of course I don't want you to leave. You're an excellent care-giver and the only person who cares about me," said Kathryn. I could see that she'd found her Zofran, the bottle lying next to her on the bed, the glass of water half empty.

I busied myself opening the curtains. "What about Mr. Weatherly?"

"He just came to give me sex," said Kathryn, awaiting my re-action. When she saw I looked properly appalled, she continued, "But don't worry, we're not getting back together. He says it's the last time. So for sure I'm not leaving him the house. And I didn't fight tooth and nail to keep it in the divorce only to hand it to him from beyond the grave."

"You're not going to die, Kathryn," I said, as I removed the pillowcases to wash them.

"How do you know? Did you find a cure for cancer over the weekend?"

"No, but I'm a witch," I said with a grin. "I have powers."

Kathryn nodded in appreciation. "Okay, then find your broom and get thee to Bel Air Foods. Nelson said he was planning to stop by there on his way to work." While she said this, Kathryn handed me a tie that I figured he must've forgotten. "If you leave now, you'll probably still catch him."

I didn't want to catch him. "He'll probably come back once he realizes he forgot it."

Kathryn shook her head. "He won't realize until he takes his first bathroom break, at eleven. I don't want him to spend all morning looking like a hippie. I don't want him to look slovenly in front of his patients. Be a helpful one, please."

Nothing made me feel more like an American than being in a supermarket. So much choice, so many different ways to fill yourself up. My first week in America, I'd marveled at the brightly lit, gigantic, air-conditioned Ralphs, with its wide aisles. Like an amusement park. Bright colors everywhere, the buoyancy of the products on the shelves, the neatly arranged rows of shiny fruits and vegetables. The Muzak turned up so high it could hardly be called background. I had been hypnotized by the sound of the scanner at the checkout, used as I was to clerks punching in numbers by hand. For many of my first years in America, I'd take a trip to the supermarket whenever I felt sad. Even if I didn't buy anything, walking down the aisles gave me a sense of belonging. The task of perusing the products distracted me in ways nothing else could. Going to the supermarket was free; there was no admission price. Nobody questioned my right to be there. It was the most democratic institution in the city.

Bel Air Foods was not a typical grocery store, though. One of the few nonresidential buildings in the area, it was the smallest grocery store I'd ever been to. I could see practically all of it from the entrance. The aisles were narrow, wide enough for only one person at a time. There were none of the brands I was used to, but different ones, organic or all-natural, and in packaging resembling cosmetics, jewelry. There were entire sections devoted to spices, olive oil, and salad dressing, at prices that seemed mildly offensive. The produce section was actually the most bountiful, gleaming with bright red tomatoes, corn in mint green husks, and only fruits and vegetables that were in season, none of them packaged. Like a fancy farmer's market. The store had a considerable wine section, located right in the middle, and unlike the Ralphs in Westwood, none of it was under lock and key—even the bottles that cost fifty, a hundred dollars. Bel Air Foods was so low-key the cashiers didn't even wear uniforms, and there were no conveyor belts at the checkout stand.

I spotted Mr. Weatherly by the fresh meals area, presumably buying his lunch for later. He wore his white coat, in spite of the heat outside, and had his head slightly bent, studying the ingredients of a fussy-looking turkey sandwich. It was always a shock to see him exist outside the confines of his former house.

"Mr. Weatherly?"

He looked up. Before he could say a word, I held up his tie and said, "You forgot this."

Mr. Weatherly reached for his collar, noticed the missing item. He shook his head in appreciation of his own absentmindedness. He took the tie from me and instead of putting it back on in his car in front of the rearview mirror, as I expected him to, he rested his chosen sandwich back on the refrigerated counter and started putting on the tie in the middle of the store. He didn't have to think about what he was doing; his hands just moved on their own, making a knot, pulling it in. I watched him, feeling a little embarrassed to see him perform something so private in front of me.

"*Obrigado*," he said, when he was done.

He'd said "thank you" in Portuguese. I said he was welcome in Portuguese, too. I thought it was sweet that he remembered that I was Brazilian. I hadn't had more than one or two conversations with him in the past.

"I know '*obrigado*' and '*por favor*' in a number of languages," said Mr. Weatherly. "You can get pretty far anywhere with just 'thank you' and 'please.'"

I thought about that for a second. "Especially if you use different intonations. Like, '*Por favor*, don't kill me,' or '*Por favor*, give me a discount.'"

"Yes," said Mr. Weatherly laughing, a sound that I found amusing. Americans laughed even when you weren't that funny, but just to keep you company. It was part of their bigness, their largesse, part of what I liked about them.

Mr. Weatherly leaned closer to me, his eyes now serious, and said, "Listen, that was kind of awkward this morning, me leaving, you arriving. But, I want you to know that I'm not . . . taking advantage of her. I just . . . don't know how to say no to someone in her condition."

I didn't know why he was telling me that. I hadn't noticed any awkwardness at all. Awkward for me was the way he was sharing this detail of his relationship with Kathryn. It would never occur to me that he might possibly feel judged by—of all people—the caregiver. So they were divorced. So they were having sex. Who was I to comment?

"I think she was happy that you visited," I said, it being the only thing I could think of to say.

"I know. And that's the problem. She's happy, I'm not," he said, moving away from me, as though disappointed that I didn't understand, as though disappointed that this minimum-wage-paid stranger hadn't offered him the correct and necessary solace.

I wanted to tell him that if that was the case, he should stop leading her on, but I said nothing.

"Thank you," he finally said, with a hint of dismissal. "For the tie."

I felt relieved, and turned around to go. When I got to my car, a selfish and conniving voice inside me asked what made it more likely for Kathryn to leave her house to me—if she were to continue sleeping with her ex-husband, or if she were to stop doing so. As soon as the thought occurred, I shooed it away, and chastised myself for even allowing it.

Back at my apartment, I helped my roommate Bruno circumvent the laws of the land and perform his clandestine video operations. Bruno ran a bootleg video store sharing pirated American movies, and after midnight was when he really got going. He had a sudden burst of energy and could go on for hours transferring video to VHS tapes. The store had a lot of members, most of them grateful, but some of them left messages complaining of video quality. Bruno would respond by cursing them. I offered to respond to customers for him, but Bruno said he liked letting out his aggression. More than that, though, I think he felt a real sense of pride in his work—in Rio, he'd dreamed of being a music video director—and took pleasure in calling the complaining customers "parasites."

His business model was simple: Bruno paid his friends to go to the first screening of a movie on opening weekend, carrying a small but high-quality camcorder with them. I helped sometimes, though I found American movies a bit dull and sexist. The trick to getting a usable recording, I learned early on, had to do with where I sat.

I had to sit as far away from people as possible, so the mic would not pick up their sounds, and God forbid someone near me got up to use the restroom. The success of a recording depended on erasing all traces of the manner in which it was obtained, so the viewer would have the illusion of unmediated access to the images on the screen.

"Isn't this stealing?" I initially asked. Bruno told me that the African and Latin American immigrants who came to his store didn't have money to go to the movies and American culture—with all the ideals that went with it, individualism and freedom and the pursuit of happiness—belonged to everyone, regardless of their income level or country of birth.

"That is bullshit," I replied.

"Which is not the same as horseshit," Bruno agreed, scratching his blond-dyed crown.

Our third roommate, Renata, was also Brazilian, but unlike Bruno and me, she had a Green Card. She'd married an American man with the understanding that it was solely a business transaction, but he had other ideas in mind and wouldn't let her alone. By Brazilian standards, he was pushy, but by American ones, he was a rapist. Renata had put up with it for a harrowing two years because she needed her Green Card and the day after she got it, she promptly moved cross-country from Florida to California. Renata worked as a manager in a Brazilian restaurant off Hollywood Boulevard, and though she was thin, she had the prominent belly of someone whose national cuisine included baked desserts for breakfast and deep-fried flour in everything.

Her restaurant was like Humphrey Bogart's bar in *Casablanca*. All the Brazilians in town eventually made their way there, where they momentarily sated their homesickness with warm cheese breads fresh out of the oven and hearty portions of beef stew and fried pastries filled with hearts of palm. Bruno sometimes worked at the restaurant for extra cash, and came home with a newfound contempt for Brazilians who hadn't been in America for as long as he had.

Of the three of us, I thought Renata missed Brazil the most. I could hear her sing popular Brazilian songs in the shower every morning, and she'd dated a string of Brazilian men who invariably went back. She decided to give her future American children Brazilian names, the reverse of the trend in Brazil of giving Brazilian children American names.

Renata actually made enough money to live on her own, but she was saving so she could have her own business someday. She looked up to the Mexican Americans who owned their own auto shops and restaurants and stores in Boyle Heights and Highland Park. Because Renata was the only one with pay stubs and a credit history, the apartment was rented in her name. She sent in the checks, and Bruno and I gave her cash for our respective shares.

Our apartment was a two-bedroom in the not-so-nice part of Hollywood, closest to the 101 freeway. There was a small dining table decorated haphazardly, covered by a cheap tablecloth with alternating white and red squares. Initially, I was struck by Renata's silverware; it was strikingly similar to my mother's. I'd searched for the same style for months upon my arrival here. Why had I assumed I could ever find again the same spoons?

My room had a bed and a desk, Renata had told me cheerfully when I moved in. It seemed obvious that the previous tenant didn't want the bed anymore but hadn't bothered to haul it to the trash. The desk was made of unfinished wood, an exercise in carpentry in need of paint and laminate. The carpet had some stains in it, and a few dust bunnies gathered near the door of the closet. The room was barely large enough to fit the twin bed and the desk.

But then I saw the view. It was only a partial view, a blocked view, but I could see a hint of sky, and the canyons beyond, from the canyons to the hills.

Bruno had screened off part of the living room where he slept on a twin bed. He didn't mind the discomfort because he was in America, and he could run into "Weird Al" Yankovic in the grocery store. Renata had the master suite that she kept locked, which I found unfriendly. My own room had no lock. One day I noticed money missing from my own desk drawers. I was sure Bruno had taken it, but didn't say anything because I didn't want him to stop lending me his computer.

Ten years before, I had walked out of Los Angeles International Airport with only three hundred dollars and sixty-seven cents to my name. I didn't know where to go, me and my bag, and I couldn't even ask the cab driver for help, my English was that bad. The caramel-skinned old man kept staring at me through the rearview mirror. He left me in front of a sign saying "For Rent," and I hesitated before ringing the doorbell. I only did so when I spotted some brown kids playing inside the complex, figuring they seemed too happy to be witness to malevolence.

The woman who answered sized me up, offered me a room in a two-bedroom apartment on the fifth floor, and told me that if I needed work, I'd better lie about my age. She said all this in Spanish, which was close enough to Portuguese. When I asked what kind of work I could do, the woman, without hesitation, suggested being a caregiver.

After a few years, I liked to play a game with myself in which I imagined the woman suggesting something else. Seamstress. Welder. Dance hall hostess. Waitress. And then, according to this game, I pictured myself, for the last ten years, doing that work instead. Two strangers—the cab driver and my landlady—had decided the most important aspects of my life: where I'd live, and what I'd do for a living. Later I'd move, but my job would stay the same.

Though I've been here ten years now, I'm surprised by America in new ways each day. When I first got here, I remember noticing how much of it was free: The doggie bags at the restaurants. The clothing catalogues. The public bathrooms. What else I noticed: The old and the disabled got checks every month from the government. Everyone drove cars, and they exchanged them for new ones more than once in a lifetime. Women were not allowed to be beaten by their husbands and it was okay if they didn't cook every night. Sometimes they were even allowed to cheat. The women who were single were free to be friends with the women who were married, and sometimes the latter even introduced them to their husbands. The men worked, and instead of the women staying at home to cook and clean, they got jobs, too, so their families could live in houses instead of apartments. The men who were gay did not necessarily dress like women, and were not all prostitutes. The women who loved other women were not called "women with big feet." They had their own special name, referring to an island that none of them came from. Nobody had servants. When hunger struck, a white man in a red uniform arrived with a square, flat box. Americans ate at mini-factories where the open layout allowed customers to see the assembly line. Everyone, not just the rich, went to restaurants, where they could pick and choose ingredients.

Americans were not all white, though it was hard not to use those terms interchangeably. Americans were black and brown and yellow and even orange. Some were considered *hicks* or *ghetto*, which surprised me because everyone looked expensive. Everyone had accents, and the white ones, the ones who didn't know that they had accents, were the hardest to understand. Americans did not refer to each other as "my dear" or "my love." They did not bring food to each other's houses unless it was an event designated for that purpose. Grandparents did not live with the grandchildren. Doctors did not live above their offices. A doctor's wife did not work as his receptionist. There were only two political parties, and neither was the Communist Party. Black hair for women was associated with malevolence in cartoons. No one ever opened their windows and everyone preferred canned air.

In America, there were no metaphors. If a woman trusted her partner, she didn't say that she would set her hand on fire. When a woman had all the power, she didn't say she had a knife and a piece of cheese in her hands. When she didn't like an offer, she didn't tell it to go back to the sea. A smart man didn't have an ass made of iron. An awkward man didn't stick his feet over his

hands. A flirt didn't sing. A shortcut wasn't a parachute. An unde-
sirable wasn't a leftover. A whore wasn't a creature of adventure.
An awkward situation did not imply a tight skirt. A frugal man
didn't have the hands of a cow. A tattletale didn't have hard fingers. A rubbernecker wasn't waiting for the circus to catch fire. A
lucky man wasn't born with his behind turned toward the moon.
A fragile person wasn't melted butter. No one said that it was bad
to complain with a full belly. Or that a pathetic man looked like a
mutt that fell from the moving truck. Or that lying down with pigs
meant waking up in the pigsty.

The Americans didn't have a name for someone who took advantage all the time. They had words that came close, but without
the right sting. Or a name for someone who had no shame, or
had a lot of nerve. Or for someone who missed someone else very
much. There weren't appropriate labels, only approximate ones.

In America, I was constantly asked questions that weren't really questions. "How are you?" "Were you able to find everything
you wanted?" I was surprised to learn that I couldn't knock on my
neighbor's door and expect a cup of coffee. I had to walk faster on
the street. I had to wait for the glowing white flash of a stick figure
in order to cross the street. The people I met sounded nothing like
the English-language tapes I'd studied. The commercials were
slick and clever and full of noise. There were no ads for condoms
or sexual lubricants on TV. The boys did not congregate on the
street to play soccer. No one, in fact, congregated on the street.

In America, I liked to ride escalators, elevators, walk past au-
tomatic doors. The rooms were enormous, the sidewalks generous. In parking lots, I liked to watch the kind and guarded couples
coming out of their starship-sized vehicles, their obedient children

in tow, wearing clothes specially purchased for the season. They glided over the blacktop, their minds on things lovely and sweet, utterly sure of what the next day would bring.

In America, I'd lie in bed at night and think of Brazil. I'd think about how much I wanted to talk to the woman I'd lost there, my own mother. I wanted to call her on the phone, but I knew she wouldn't answer and she wouldn't call me back.

In America, there weren't ghosts everywhere.

It was all so different from what I'd left behind.

Rio de Janeiro, Brazil

The mid- to late 1970s

Mara, age eight

chapter one

THE FIRST INHABITANTS OF COPACABANA WERE NOT THE fishermen, or even the Indians. They were the two whales that washed ashore in the closing days of August 1858. No one knew how they ended up there. Some said they were beached whales, stranded, victims of rough weather and poor navigation. Others said they were free, healthy visitors, just resting on their bellies. Either way, hundreds of people pilgrimaged to see them, including the emperor and his retinue, braving the rough paths that led to the ocean. The emperor didn't wear his crown and mantle, just a simple sooty tailcoat with trousers and a cravat. Some say he brought his wife, others his mistress. I would like to think he brought both.

Following closely behind, the members of Rio's high society rode past the brushwood onto the beach, in horse-drawn carriages. They set up tents so the sun wouldn't wrinkle their faces. Others came on horseback. Many on foot.

After two days, the whales disappeared. It is said that those who came to see them and missed them stayed anyway, and embarked on a long picnic that lasted three days and three nights. The views after all were magnificent, the beach fortressed by moss-covered granite hills on one side and infinity on the other. The white foam of the seawater bubbled and blistered, rose and fell, the rhythm as even and soothing as that of a mother rocking a crib. The sand mirrored the sun, gold-speckled powder. The breeze tasted of sea salt.

This wasn't the last time the beach had unexpected visitors. In 1941, four fishermen from the drought-ridden Northeast, men of the humblest ilk, got on a simple raft and sailed for sixty-one days along the coast, without a compass or a map. They wanted to get to the capital and speak to the president. They wished to explain how unhappy they were that they had to share their catch with the owners of the rafts and the middlemen who sold the fish to the markets. As they crossed the length of nearly the entire country, a good 2,500 kilometers, the fishermen fought off storms, waves, and sharks. Only the stars guided them; only their patron saints guarded them. When word got around of their story, other boats began to follow and circle them as they neared Guanabara Bay, turning their arrival into a procession. Hundreds awaited them at the beach. They were greeted as heroes. Their raft was lifted onto a truck like a royal heirloom, as the crowd applauded.

Back in the 1970s, when I was eight, I knew of Copacabana only as my home, not a resting place for mysterious whales or fisherman on a political pilgrimage. I read these old stories in the library at school, but was more concerned with knowing the city itself. I knew how long it took for me to get to the subway station. Which *padaria* had the most flavorful café con leche. Which restaurant would give me a stomachache afterward, and just to be sure, I religiously took the pills that my mother gave me to prevent tapeworms. I knew which section of the promenade I could go to without running into one of the bullies who liked to pick on me. I didn't set foot in the ocean for weeks or even months at a time. Its reminders were only the old men in tight swim shorts strolling down the avenue, true Don Juans, and the tanned teenagers dragging folding chairs on the scalloped limestone asphalt. It didn't compute that someone, somewhere in America had written a song about a nightclub named after our neighborhood.

During the school year, which began in February and ended in December, I went to Getúlio Vargas Municipal School, where that year I was a studious and eager second grader. There was a single classroom, with the teachers coming in and out to lecture us. My favorite subject was Portuguese, because we got to talk about stories during class time. In the warm months, our classroom got as hot as the inside of a mitten. During our short breaks, the more nimble of us raced to the narrow counter of the cafeteria, where we waved our bills at the workers hoping to get their attention before the sodas ran out.

My best friend was a girl named Debora Amaral, and because we were seated alphabetically, she was always one desk behind me, Mara Alencar. I spent half of my classes turning my head so she could whisper in my ear, and not five minutes would pass without me feeling the tip of her pencil poking my back.

After school ended, at noon, we went to each other's apartments to do our homework and once we were done, we watched American cartoons: the *Jetsons*, the *Flintstones*, and *Scooby-Doo*. We longed for the same American toys for Christmas and Children's Day: the Easy-Bake Super Oven, a ballerina music box, the

Girl's World life-sized styling doll head that came with roller curlers, a plastic comb, eye shadow crayons, and hair color applicator pens. We often engaged in long debates as to whether the doll's hair would grow back if we cut it. We never found out the answer, since neither of us had the money to buy one. When school was not in session, Debora went with her parents to visit her grandparents in the distant suburbs of Rio, three hours away, and because I didn't have many other friends, I either played by myself or tagged along with my mother when she went to work.

My mother did many things for work—cleaning, waitressing, and temping as a receptionist—but then, she was largely working in the movies. Or rather, her voice was working in the movies. Inside a foam-covered, soundproofed booth that smelled of cigarettes, my mother dubbed the voices of American actresses into Portuguese. Our fantasies and daydreams came from that country, sometimes in color and sometimes in black and white, and they required a tribute to our essential differences.

The man who did the male parts had a paunch and too little hair, but his voice was that of a handsome man—a mellifluous instrument—and he knew just how much breath each syllable deserved. My mother and the man never looked at each other, their eyes bound to the phantom people on the screen in front of them, and I thought of how hard it must be to be in two places at once, inside that booth and inside that screen.

As my mother juggled different inflections and intonations, voicing women and girls, I wondered how she knew to match their lips. She had uncanny timing, and knew exactly when to begin speaking and when to stop. Within a single scene, my mother's silken voice turned throaty or nasal, adulterous or matronly. All these people lived inside of her and took turns emerging from her throat. I was caught between being proud of her and being sad that no one watching the movie later would know who owned that laugh, who owned those cadences. They might even laugh along, not knowing who they were laughing with. My mother was talented, and for the talented mother, a child feels pride. But fear, too.

At the end of one session, I heard my mother talking to the sound engineer. He had long curly hair and wore a necklace made out of small bones. He wasn't making eye contact with her, instead focusing on putting the earphones and microphones away. The other actor had already left.

"I'm starving, Raul. You can't say no to me," she said, standing next to him, in a voice so quiet she must've thought I couldn't hear. "It's my money, anyway. It just hasn't made its way into my pocket yet."

Raul brushed his knuckles against his beard and shook his head. "I can't. You're going to have to wait until the end of the month."

My mother wouldn't let up. She straightened her back, as if needing to make herself bigger, and crossed her arms. She wore a puffy bright neon yellow jacket, and a heavy, thick red bracelet on her left arm. On her cleavage hung a pair of sunglasses—giant round ones, meant for funerals and dramatic expressions of grief. She'd recently gotten a perm—thick black curls chasing down her round face.

"Did I do a good job or did I do a good job?" she asked.

Raul sighed. "You did an excellent job. As always."

"And we finished early," said my mother. "Don't think I don't know you pay for the booth by the hour, so I'm pretty sure I saved you some money today."

"Ana . . ." He was already crumbling a little.

My mother shrugged her shoulders. "Well, you can hire some other girl next time, who'll take twice as long and cost you twice as much."

I knew my mother was bluffing. I'd heard her say how much she loved this job and would never let someone take it from her, and how much better it was than anything else she'd ever done. But Raul wouldn't know that from looking at her face, a careful mosaic of confidence.

"All right, all right," said Raul, shaking his head. He reached into a drawer and pulled out a pad. He wrote down a receipt for the cash advance, keeping a carbon copy for himself. At that rate, I knew my mother's payday at the end of the month would be tiny, but what other option was there? Raul took ten five-cruzeiro bills and handed them to my mother.

Afterward, my mother and I sat victorious in a *padaria*, eating *coxinhas*. My mother ate ravenously, practically attacking the poor little chicken strips battered in crispy flour. I ate more slowly, savoring my food, gulping my Guaraná soda. My mother got one for me, but not one for her.

The night was a vinyl record, dark and full of scratches, in perfect sync with the needle of God. But in the *padaria*, our bodies were lit up too much under the fluorescent lights, as if none of us had earned the tenderness of shadows.

"Mom . . ." I said, getting her attention. "What if that man hadn't given you the money? What would we do for supper?"

My mother looked up from her *coxinha*. "Have I ever let you go to bed without food in your belly?" she asked, with a hint of woundedness in her voice.

"No," I lied, already regretting having asked. But when you live so close to the cliff, you wonder what resides at the bottom of it.

My mother pushed away her plate and stared straight into my eyes. "I will always take care of you. I don't care what I have to do, and I can think of a degrading thing or two." And at this, she made the sign of the Ghost and the Holy Spirit, "but you'll always have a roof over your head and food in your belly."

"I know that," I said, embarrassed, wishing I hadn't said anything.

"I may not have money or an education, but I'm not ugly, and I'm not dumb, and I have a big mouth and big ears, and that's always served me well."

I turned back to my *coxinha*, not entirely reassured. She reached for me and brushed her fingers against my hair. She smiled, pressing her cheeks against mine. My mother's touch had a way of reaching into my heart and letting it beat more tranquilly, a musician turning a metronome.

"Drink your Guaraná," she said gently. "You need sugar in your blood."

I gulped from the bottle; it was only half empty, but I asked if I could have another one.

She did not hesitate. "Of course, girl, of course." She waved grandly for the waiter, as though ordering at the Ritz-Carlton. "Everyone has a peak, and mine's about to start," she said with a grin. "Nothing beats the combination of skills and luck."

On our way home, we walked hand in hand down the boardwalk of Copacabana. My mother strolled casually, taking in the breeze from the ocean. The beach at night wasn't like the beach during the day; it slept, cocooned, a different kind of endless. Just because you couldn't see it didn't mean you couldn't feel it—its throbbing, its breaths. Streetlights reached far up into the sky and lit our path like a thousand mini-moons. In front of us, we followed the quartz stones made to resemble waves, their sinuous lines making us move forward. The bodies around us walked slowly, the men with their big bellies and the women showing off their tans. The air smelled of beer and fried foods.

When we reached the driveway of the Copacabana Palace, my mother stopped and pointed to a group of tourists getting into a van. They were in town for Carnaval. They looked American, with their yellow hair and sunburned skin, their tight shorts and cameras around their necks.

"You know who they are?" asked my mother, lowering her head toward mine, our cheeks brushing against each other's. She pointed at them. "They are from America. Everyone there is rich. Even the poor people. When you arrive in America, they hand you a magical plastic card that lets you buy anything you want."

My mother grabbed my hand and we continued walking. She held me firmly, as though I were something that a pickpocket could take away from her.

"But don't worry, my girl, one day I'm going to be rich, too, and live in a big house. A psychic once told me so."

"What's a psychic?"

"A psychic is a woman—or a man, I suppose they could be men—who tells you what you want to hear in exchange for money," she said without hesitation.

I laughed, though I wasn't sure I knew why that was funny. I never knew when my mother was being serious or not. When she was imparting a lesson or just thinking out loud. Either way, from early on, I believed my mother to be special. I suppose every daughter believes her mother to be special, somehow, but when I compared my mother to my friends' mothers, or to mothers on TV, she really did seem a little different. She didn't keep secrets from me, she swore in front of me, we shared everything. I knew she was beautiful because of the way men on the street turned to stare at her, making me feel that I wanted to hide her, to keep her for myself. She didn't always feel like a mom to me. Sometimes she felt like an aunt who let me get away with things, or a friend just visiting for the weekend, one you could be really intense with because you knew they would soon be gone.

"But who needs money, anyway," said my mother, looking at the beach. "How much do you think those tourists paid to come here?"

"A thousand cruzeiros?" I guessed.

My mother nodded. "Counting airfare and hotel? That sounds about right. Now how much did *we* spend to check out this view?"

"Nothing."

"That's right. A sale is good, a clearance is even better, but nothing beats free."

When we arrived at home, I sat on my mother's lap.

What better place was there? Where else wafted such fragrant air, filling my nostrils with the scent of azalea and jasmine? How large and constant and strong she seemed, though she was only five foot five, really not that much taller than me. She always seemed capable of handling my weight, my bones, my moods. Her legs never fell asleep, her feet were never ticklish. If I went to bed on her lap, she rocked and cradled me, and sometimes when I woke,

I found her eyes fluttering, she returning from the same depth of sleep, the same place where I had been.

From as far back as I could remember, and I could remember pretty far back, she liked to nuzzle against the crown of my head and tell me, in a sing-songy voice, "I love you in the morning. I love you in the afternoon. I love you in the evening. I love you in the spring, in the winter, in the summer, in the fall. I love you when you're good. I love you when you're naughty." And she would pause there, as if I needed time to fit all that love inside me. I could feel her breath linger behind my ears, the slight rocking of her body forward. To this day, when I think of my mother's love, it is from behind me, it is from the parts of my own body that I cannot see: The corner where the lobe of my ear gives way to the jaw. The inches that separate the nape of my neck from my shoulder. She is there, always, whispering, singing, delivering prophecies and incantations.

Carnaval was a good distraction for our money issues at home. During Carnaval, which generally took six days, our neighborhood was flooded with strangers. The lines were long even at the pharmacy and the butcher's shop. At the *padarias*, every inch of counter space boasted an elbow or an arm, with people squeezing against one another as though their bodies were accordions. No one believed in orderly lines when they were thirsty. The boardwalks, which were pretty narrow to begin with, became as claustrophobic as tunnels. To make it harder, some people chose not to walk, but instead to stand around to drink and have conversations. They did so with the same sense of entitlement as the lampposts. We had to go around. We had to go around.

Everywhere we went, we could hear music, even if we were kilometers from the Sambadromo, where the parade actually took place. Every *padaria*, every store, every corner vibrated with percussion, either from a live band, or a TV airing the parade. In our apartment, that's how my mother and I watched the show. On the Globo channel, we could see, for hours and hours, performers wearing elaborate costumes doing what I could only describe as dance-walking. Shaking, shimmying, then stepping forth, upper bodies swaying from side to side. I wondered how hard it was, to dance and walk at the same time. I could only hear two instruments—tambourines and steel pans. The women wore gigantic feathery headpieces that would put peacocks to shame and in some cases, *were* peacocks. On their bodies they essentially wore bikinis, but these were the sparkliest and most colorful bikinis I'd ever seen, studded with bijoux and beads, and strings hanging from them. The men wore bright, flowing pants and shirts decorated with glitter and sashes. Float after float went by, many of them featuring enormous statues and monuments of foam and papier-mâché.

A lot of tourists didn't know this, but Carnaval was a contest. A contest amongst different schools in Rio that taught samba. I tried to watch enough of each school's presentation to see if I agreed with the judges at the prize ceremony. I never did. The school that won never had, in my opinion, the best costumes or the best floats or the best themes. I liked the floats that were inspired by people we'd learned about in textbooks like the martyr-dentist Tiradentes, or the black courtesan Xica da Silva, who was deemed the most powerful Brazilian woman of the eighteenth century. Or characters in books I'd read as a child, like Emilia, the rag doll that came to life in the Yellow Woodpecker's Farm. Or Saci-Pererê, the mischievous boy with one leg who never let go of his pipe. But I suppose if you've seen those characters before, they lose their novelty. Which is why the unexpected floats inspired by the *Star Wars* movie or the Watergate scandal garnered so much attention, even though they had nothing to do with us, or with our country.

At first the parade dazzled us, but so much of it was the same, and it took so long to find out who won, that my mother usually changed the channel. But one person who really loved Carnaval was our next-door neighbor Janete. Janete was a *travesti*. I knew what a *travesti* was because, like most other Brazilians, I knew of the fashion model Roberta Close and her famous Adam's apple. Roberta Close was always on TV, or on the covers of magazines. If I didn't see her, I could hear her ubiquitous song in the speakers of the stores my mother and I went to. Everyone thought of Roberta Close as one of the most beautiful women in the world, except for Janete, who really hated her—a very personal and deep kind of hatred—and I wouldn't have been surprised if Janete told me that Roberta had once killed every member of her family. But I appreciated Roberta Close, not least because it was through her that I understood Janete. And I understood that Janete was a man who was able to be as beautiful as a woman, a man who was going out of his way to add some glamour and exoticism to everyone else's lives. Even my second-grade self understood what was probably implicit about the *travesti*—and about Carnaval itself: that it was one of those things that allowed us to understand who we were, even if that distinction had come by accident, not design.

Janete often came by to borrow sugar or makeup, transactions that should have taken five minutes, but then she'd stay for hours.

My mother loved Janete. They had met when my mother was working at a women's clothing store. Janete came in as a man—a rather imposing, tall black man with a 100-kilowatt smile. She was awkwardly trying to figure out if a dress was her size without being able to try it on. When the owner wasn't looking, my mother snuck Janete into a fitting room. When the owner of the store, who was Armenian, like all the owners of all the stores, found out, he fired my mother. He couldn't believe my mother would let a *travesti* into the fitting room. My mother didn't care; she liked Janete. It was Janete who later told my mother about the vacancy in her apartment building.

In our living room that evening, my mother was putting makeup on her as though she were a giant living doll.

"You sure I can't convince you to come?" asked Janete.

"To a Ball G? What am I going to do in a Ball G? I don't have a *pinto*."

"They don't check at the door!"

"Janete, imagine the guy's disappointment if he reaches down my skirt and finds nothing there. He would be really upset. Some men don't like holes and I have a hole. Two holes, in fact. Three, if you're really counting."

"But most parties are not G during Carnaval. You know that."

"No, I'm going to go to bed early. I have to rest my vocal cords. Otherwise they'll wonder why Katharine Hepburn sounds hungover for the entire movie, and you can tell by the looks of her, that woman is no fun."

Janete gave my mother a disapproving tap on the knee. "Do I need to remind you that Carnaval is only once a year? And it's our most important holiday? Home on a holiday is for wilted flowers."

My mother laughed. "Do I need to remind you that I have a little girl?" My mother pointed at me on the sofa. "She's small, but she's not invisible."

"Mara is old enough to stay home by herself," said Janete, glancing over at me, smiling. "Aren't you, my love?"

I nodded.

My mother shook her head. "I've had my share of Carnavals in the past. And I already get my share of being groped on the bus every other day of the week."

She sat back on the sofa and lit a cigarette. I looked around for an ashtray before my mother made one herself. She could make one out of any piece of paper, like origami. She preferred white paper, the kind my homework was often mimeographed on, so I had to be vigilant. I'd shown up to school more than once with black burn marks where my answers should be, and though my mother always apologized profusely, she never stopped doing it.

"How do I look?" Janete asked, twirling for our admiration. She really did look as beautiful as Roberta Close, or even more so. Although I probably felt that way because Roberta Close was far away and Janete Éclair was right there in front of us, and sometimes admiration is just a matter of distance.

"Beautiful. Delicious. You're going to make a lot of money tonight," said my mother, between puffs of her cigarette. She let out the smoke slowly, like the women in the old black and white American movies she dubbed. I could see in her eyes a glint of envy. If it weren't for me, chances were my mother *would* be going out with Janete.

"Maybe we could drop off Janete wherever she's going?" I suggested.

My mother squinted. Maybe I'd been wrong to believe she wanted to go out. I was filled with a feeling I'd had before, realizing that I'd acted after reading a person wrong, and then being stuck both with the person's puzzled reaction and my own surprise that there could be more than one reason for a look, for an expression.

Janete dropped her head in an exaggerated manner, her eyes smiling from temple to temple.

"Your daughter's a genius. And I could use the help. Navigating all those steps in this dress and these heels is not going to be easy."

The dress was green and sparkly, molding to her hourglass silhouette. Janete made a quick show of stumbling in her too-tight dress, but I knew she was faking it because she always had exceptional balance, and I'd seen her run after a bus wearing tighter outfits.

My mother looked over at us and she scoffed. Not in a contemptuous way, but in a way that let us know she found us silly and ridiculous. Then she kept her gaze upon us quite intensely, as though she weren't just seeing us, but seeing her thoughts reflected back to her. I sometimes noticed this faraway glance in her eyes, when I could tell she was thinking of something or someone who wasn't there in the room. Who else did she need to consider, when we had each other?

"All right, let's go," she finally said, smiling. "Afterwards we'll take advantage of everybody being out to go moonbathing."

"What's 'moonbathing'?" I asked, knowing, but wanting to hear my mother explain it.

"It's like sunbathing, but you don't need to put on sunscreen and your skin doesn't peel off the next day. And unlike the sun, the moon doesn't have to share space with the shade because it *is* the shade."

My mother reached into her closet and pulled out a short dress stamped with swirls, floral patterns, and every color of the rainbow. It had a scooped neck, flowy sleeves, and came with a matching headband. She took off her clothes quickly and put the dress over her, in a single move.

"You look beautiful, Mom."

"You are correct in your assessment," said my mother, reaching into the closet again for something for me to wear. There were really only two options—she chose the turtleneck with an embroidered red bib and ruffles on the neck and sleeves, and matching polyester pants with flared legs—the set had been one of my mother's most extravagant purchases.

"We have to make you look good, too," said my mother, under Janete's approving gaze. "After all, I can only be as beautiful as the company I keep."

I took off the orange nylon shirt with lace-up shoulders I always wore and put on the turtleneck. "And being beautiful means putting on good makeup and nice clothes, right?"

"Of course. When God gives you a canvas, it is a sin not to paint it," she replied.

"Like Michelangelo and the Sistine Chapel."

"That's right," said my mother, proudly, stroking my chin. "My smart girl. I'm glad I never talked down to you while you were a baby. You were listening to Tchaikovsky when you were two. You could tell a Portinari painting from a Lasar Segall when you were three. You knew what a *travesti* was when you were four."

✿   ✿   ✿

In the bus, the music was in people's heads. Everyone dressed like they were on their way to greet it, dance to it, be moved by it. A lot of samba, heavy on percussion, that music that sounded like confetti falling, batons twirling, feet shuffling. I couldn't actually hear the music—just a lot of loud talking, some laughter—but the notes hung from the low-cut dresses and plunging cleavages, from the bright shirts left unbuttoned by the men, their pants as loose as those of circus clowns. The bus did not feel like a bus full of strangers, and if we were strangers, that was just a momentary phase.

My mother hung her arm around my neck and shoulders, as though she'd turned herself into a coat and draped herself over me. I repositioned so we had the same view. Janete stood—by choice, really—as though she were on display, and needed to be standing to achieve the fullness of effect. She wore a very realistic black wig, paid off in five installments. We'd once heard a scream through the walls and when we came to check on her, we found out she'd spilled water on it. The dress was all asymmetrical lines, a diagonal V revealing her right collarbone and glittering sleeves of different lengths covering each arm. I thought she looked grand, and though there was some snickering, and though I distinctly heard the word *bicha*, I knew Janete was enjoying herself and our company.

"Janete, I'm going to do your voice," said my mother. I glanced over at her and she smiled back. "Next time they ask me to dub a movie, I'm going to give your voice to one of the characters."

"You're talking nonsense," said Janete, with a contradictory

grin. "Like when you're doing that American black servant girl, in
Gone with the Wind?"

"No," said my mother, shifting a little, so I had to lean forward for an instant. "When it's some *lady*, from a British movie." My mother thought of British movies as the most exotic thing in the world, what with their posh accents, ornate costumes, and damp-looking castles. "Like Joan Fontaine."

"I don't think you can imitate my voice," said Janete, practically daring her.

"You don't think so?" my mother echoed, having the vowels and consonants bump into each other and adding an extra flair to the last two words in the sentence. She was imitating her almost perfectly. "You don't think I can imitate your voice?"

Janete threw her head back and laughed, a throaty laugh that tickled every bit of air around me. "Again!" Janete shrieked. "Do it again."

The woman in the seat in front of us turned around and, for some reason I couldn't fathom, gave my mother a dirty look. My mother winked at the woman, and when the woman turned back around, my mother shrugged her shoulders and smiled at me.

"One day I'm going to watch your work," said Janete, showing us her palms as though that was indicative of truth.

My mother's movies aired late at night, around midnight, after the news shows ended. She sometimes had me stay up late with her and watch. I'd fall asleep before they were over, listening to my mother profess her love to different men, the anguish in her voice lulling me, her words a series of declarations that made less and less sense as my eyelids fluttered and I sat on the edge of sleep. I knew she wasn't talking to me, but as she confessed all her feelings and desires using those heightened words, it was hard not to hope for her to find peace at the end.

As the bus started moving again, my mother's expression had suddenly changed. She looked nervous—a look that I rarely saw, one she never allowed me to see. I'd only seen her like that when she was having a bad dream, and then I'd stare at her deciding if I should wake her. I followed the direction of her gaze, a line that was as clear as though it'd been painted, so that my eyes landed on a man at the front of the bus. He was tall, wore an ill-fitting shirt that looked like it might be silk, but was too shiny to really be so, and his black hair had been gelled back unevenly, so some parts had more volume than others. He looked out of place, and had the distinct alertness of a person from out of town. Though he was separated from us through several layers of bodies, I could tell, quite distinctly, that he was the source of my mother's fear.

"What's wrong?" I asked.

She reached for my arm, saying nothing, and began to get up from her seat. Janete's nightclub was in Catete, and we were still a long ways from it. Without taking our eyes off the man, we stood up. There was no room for us to move. My mother reached for Janete, who looked surprised to see us getting up as though to leave.

"I have to go," my mother said.

Janete looked puzzled.

My mother began to push past Janete, who wasn't going to be left behind without more of an explanation.

"Where're you going? This isn't our stop," said Janete, loudly, a touch of irritation in her voice.

"I have to go," my mother repeated, trying to squeeze past the people around us. They were forming a solid wall, not a centimeter to be spared. I kept asking where we were going and what was wrong, but she wouldn't answer me. The people around us, unsure of why we were moving to the back of the bus, were unwilling to make way. Somebody actually cursed at my mother. I could feel my mother's palm getting clammy in my hand. She looked back, right past me, and I mimicked her, shadowlike, and saw that the man, who hadn't noticed us before, was now looking in our direction. The expression on his face changed, and if before he looked merely tired, now he looked alert and angry, as though my mother had picked his pockets when I wasn't looking. In that bus, in that moment, my mother and I no longer seemed anonymous, and I was surprised to realize how much of a friend anonymity was, how much of a comfort.

"Out of my way, out of my way, please," my mother kept saying, as she fought against the current. She was openly panicking by now, squeezing herself by force through the crowd. Several people gave her dirty looks, and some others let out short expressions of complaint. But my mother was a pit bull. When I looked back, I saw that the man was coming after us. I had never before felt such a gallop in my heart. My mother's body was the barometer that allowed me to measure the amount of joy or pleasure to be had, or, in this instance, fear.

When we reached the turnstile, the fare collector shook his finger No, but my mother ignored him and crouched on the floor, squeezing under the metal bar with her skinny body. I did the same. Once we got up, we were greeted by what felt like a thousand stares, from passengers both sitting and standing. Their big, round, accusing eyes, locked on to us, reminded me of owls in the night, perched at ease in their own element.

"Next time you *must* exit through the front," I could hear the fare collector fuming.

Finally, after what felt like an impossibly long time, the bus stopped. The doors opened in front of us with a loud, yanking noise, and before the new trove of passengers could board, my mother and I rushed down the steps. As we did so, our linked fingers felt like too-tight knots.

As we stepped away from the bus, my mother seemed to dip into enough safety to allow us to look back. We saw, through the window, the man stopped by the turnstile. He was taller and heavier than I realized, with deep-set eyes and thin lips. The fare collector was standing now, physically restraining him. They looked like they were having an argument. The man pointed to my mother. He kept pointing, more angrily each time, in the direction that we'd gone, and the fare collector kept shaking his head.

The bus started moving again. The last thing I saw, though, was Janete, in another window, looking out at us, her eyes forlorn, misbegotten. Left by herself, under the lights of the bus, she still looked grand and glamorous, but there was a sadness about her that I'd never noticed before. It was so clear now, seeing her among strangers, with the rectangular frame of the window flattening her, telling me what to pay attention to. It wasn't the sadness of my mother and me leaving her, I was stubbornly sure. I sensed something generous about her sadness, an outward trajectory. As though it came with a need to provide solace to us.

"Why did we have to leave?" I asked my mother, as we watched the bus drive away. "Who was that man?"

My mother took a deep breath, still recovering.

"I hate Carnaval," she said, simply. "It washes off all the scum onto the beach."

We took the 219 bus back to Copa, and the entire time my mother kept glancing over her shoulder. But back in our apartment, she seemed at ease as we sat in front of the glowing television, waiting to see who'd won Carnaval that year.

"It's all corrupt," my mother said, the most loquacious she'd been since we got home, her legs on top of each other on the couch. She had pretty much clammed up after we'd left Janete, answering my queries with monosyllables or non sequiturs. I left her alone, because when you grow up with a moody mother, you learn and relearn the futility of wanting things to make sense.

"What do you mean?" I wasn't asking for the meaning of the word *corrupt*, which greeted me from every newsstand from the time I was able to read. But I was happy to hear her voice, and I wanted more of it.

"They never give it to the school that did the best job," my mother explained, as the winners were about to be announced. "They always give it to the school that provides the most money to the association. It's not really fair to the dancers. Or the artists and designers, who work so hard all year. The government wants to put on a good show for the rest of the world, and they meddle in Carnaval the way they do everything else."

My mother rarely spoke of the military regime, and I found it strange that she would bring it up so suddenly. "Do the dancers get paid? How do they get chosen to work on the floats?" I asked, changing the subject, watching as a middle-aged man in a tan suit—who looked nothing like Carnaval—stood at the podium, accepting the prize.

"I don't know. But it's time to go to bed," said my mother, as though we'd been up just to find out the winner, and not because the bus ride with Janete had taken the wind out of our sails and we needed time to recover. She turned the knob to shut the TV off, and the man on the podium shrank down to a single line and then disappeared.

It was understood that on nights like this, when it was likely to be noisy outside, with fights breaking out and drunks hollering, that my mother would let me share her bed instead of me sleeping on my own twin on the other side of the room. I climbed under the blue mosquito netting hanging over her bed, being very careful not to lift the netting too high, just in case there was an insect nearby waiting for a chance to sneak in. Years later, I would take for granted that if I were awakened in the middle of the night by hysterical laughter outside the window, or the sound of sirens, or a woman screaming, I'd be able to bury my ear into her shoulder and fall back asleep.

chapter two

I THINK THE MOMENT THAT CHANGED MY MOTHER'S
life—though she did not know this at the time—began when Raul
explained the laws of subtraction.

We were standing in his sound booth once again. I stared at the
tape, which usually moved clockwise, then counterclockwise, and
was now dormant.

My mother wanted what was her due.

"There must be a mistake," she said, counting the cash. "This is
not what we agreed to."

Raul took off his headphones and sat back in his chair. It was
the first time I noticed that his chair had wheels, and it was hard
not to ask him if I could take a turn.

"We agreed on thirteen hundred cruzeiros," my mother continued. "There's only four hundred here."

Raul then explained to her something I had learned and mas-
tered a year earlier in math class: the laws of subtraction.

"You've been taking cash advances at pretty much every single session," he said patiently.

"Of course. I have to eat, and my daughter does, too," she said fiercely, gesticulating an arm in my direction.

Raul sighed and pulled out from a drawer a receipt book with alternating white and pink pages. He flipped through the front and began subtracting the amounts noted on each page. The numbers added up. I knew because I did the math in my head. It was easy to, because she always cashed out pretty even amounts. Fifty here, ten there, five on a day when she felt disciplined. I just had to ignore the last two zeros and hop two houses to the left and subtract.

"Understood?" Raul asked.

"How am I supposed to live on this?" my mother asked. "I mean, could *you*?"

Raul looked out at the black sea in front of him. He took all the levers in one corner, and, with a single stroke of his hand, pushed them all down to 0. I thought it must be fun to have a job that gave such power to your fingers.

"I don't make much more than you, Ana. The difference is, I pack my lunch," he said, pointing to the tin container sitting on the spare chair; some of the leftover beans still swam in their own juice.

I suddenly felt guilty about all the Guaraná sodas I had ordered at the counters during our lunches.

I really wanted to leave, but, to my surprise, my mother took the chair next to Raul. He had to rush to move his leftovers or she would've sat on them. She stared at him directly.

"I want my salary. The full thirteen hundred," she said, crossing her arms and legs, as though locking herself into place.

Raul looked at her, bewildered. The sound room was so

cramped and their chairs were so close to each other that their knees were almost touching. I wondered if Raul was trying to figure out how to get rid of my mother without losing her forever.

"You're turning *your* problem into my problem," said Raul, a touch of anger creeping into his voice.

"That's right. And you know what goes really well with a problem? A solution."

My mother started to impatiently shake her right leg, which sat propped on top of her left knee. Her face turned to steel, and no look from Raul could chip it. I crouched on the floor, my bum on my ankle, like a frog, making myself small, and almost disappeared into the wall.

"Look, if you want to make more money, I may have something for you," said Raul.

"My daughter's sitting right there, Raul," my mother said, waving her arms in my direction. "And her ears may be smaller than yours, but they work just fine."

Raul shook his head, staring at the ground. "It's nothing like *that*. You know I respect you." He hesitated for a moment, as if struggling with some decision. "Although, maybe you should have her step outside for a moment."

"Leave her outside by herself? I can tell, my friend, that you don't have children," said my mother. Though she admonished him, I could hear her voice warming a bit. "If it's not dirty business, you can say it in front of her. She's very mature."

Raul glanced at me and then back to my mother. He spoke more quietly, as though he'd pushed down one of the levers on his sound board.

"It's acting work, but it's a little dangerous." Even whispering, he sounded hesitant. "You'd have to pretend to be someone you're not. But not in a movie. In real life."

My mother looked intrigued, a small smile appearing on her face. She stopped shaking her leg and sat forward, almost folding her body into Raul's.

"I think of myself as a very good actress."

"I think so, too," said Raul. "And in this situation, the ability to improvise, to stay in character, no matter what happens, would be very important."

"I'm interested."

Raul leaned back on his chair and shook his head.

"I said it may be dangerous." He was warning her, but I couldn't tell if he was doing that to protect her or to protect himself.

"Being hungry scares me more."

Outside, after being in the darkened booth, it took a while to adjust to the sun. My mother, too, took a moment to compose herself. I realized the self-assurance in front of Raul had been an act, as I saw her rest her hands on her hips and exhale two, three times, slowly, as she did sometimes after scenes. The sun beat down on her, making her translucent—as though I could almost see her insides. I watched her breathe and waited. A steep hill awaited us, a reminder that we *cariocas* have chosen to lay our asphalt over igneous rock. Below, the street unfurled like a stairway with a thousand steps. Above, the slope stared at us dauntingly, without offering a hand.

I didn't know much about my mother's life before she had me, but I knew she was born in a tiny town in the desert Northeast. In her home, when she lived with her parents and her two brothers, they had no electricity and no running water. They lived in a hut, their property separated from their neighbors' by long strings nailed to the soil. For windows there were empty square spaces in the walls that allowed in a constant stream of dust and sand. My grandmother apparently spent most of her time with a broom in her hand. My grandfather worked as a cane-cutter in some nearby sugar fields, and because he owned his own machete, and didn't get a machete rental fee taken out of his paycheck, he brought home more money than his coworkers, enough even to pay for a pound of meat once in a while. My uncles joined him as cane-cutters as soon as they were tall enough to chop the stalks. My grandmother stayed home and cooked corn bread and sweet potatoes.

My mother was the only child in her family who didn't work. That was decided when she was six years old, when it became clear that she was unusually beautiful. She took after neither of her parents, though she bore a strong resemblance to her maternal grandmother. My grandparents recognized some potential in my mother's features, and decided that they would raise her to marry off to a well-to-do man. My mother, therefore, was allowed to go to school instead of going to work. She was not even expected to help my grandmother around the house, for fear that it would make her rough.

My mother never discussed why she left the Northeast, and though she did so before I was born, I never asked. Around the time I became aware of her origins, the Globo TV network began airing a public drive to help the Northeast, asking for donations. So I understood the Northeast to be troubled and worthy of charity, the kind of place anyone would leave if they had the chance.

I knew what my grandparents looked like because of some photos that my mother had kept. In one of them, my grandfather sat smiling on a wicker chair, in what must've been their home. My grandmother perched on the arm of the chair, looking dour and surprised. Their teenage children wrapped themselves around them, all three of them peering at something beyond the frame. My grandparents did not look like mean or vicious people, but their visages offered no clue as to their relationship with my mother. When I asked her why they never wrote to her, she said that they didn't know how to write, and that was that. When I asked her why she never went to visit them, she said that it cost too much, and it took too long to take a bus all the way north, which, indeed, required crossing the entire country. When I asked her if they ever wanted to meet me, my mother told me, matter-of-factly, that they didn't know that I existed.

They didn't know that she'd kept me, she said, using these exact words. I asked no more questions.

She had left, I was sure, for the same reason everyone else left and moved to the south: for opportunities. It never occurred to me that my presence in her belly had anything to do with it. It never occurred to me that when my grandfather found out, he kicked her out of the house with only the clothes on her back, and told her never to return.

When she first got to Rio, my mother worked as a live-in maid, a caretaker of sorts, in a small apartment in Copacabana. Her employer, a woman in her fifties who had no husband and no children of her own, didn't mind that my mother was raising a child. My mother and I slept together on a twin bed and had our own bathroom, which ran only cold water. On Sundays, we went to the beach and built ambitious sandcastles. For each of my birthdays, my mother treated me to a piece of *goiabada*, my favorite dessert.

Then, around the time that I turned four, my mother left her position and found us an apartment of our own. I was considered old enough to stay at home by myself, and that let her take an odd job here and there, answering the phone in a dentist's office one week, cleaning toilets in a nearby school the next. All her life, she was used to these jobs being elusive and temporary, and I supposed that was what made her open to meeting with the guerrillas when Raul offered, even though most people would've said no.

The three men arrived at our apartment two hours after they were supposed to. They were all roughly the same age, in their early twenties, not that much younger than my mother. Their faces looked unshaven, though no more than the average man in the street. They were light-skinned, and wore white-collar shirts of the cheap kind, the kind bus drivers and waiters wore.

I was not supposed to see them. I was not supposed to be awake. But I opened the door to our bedroom a couple of centimeters, and because that corner of our apartment was so poorly lit, no one noticed. My mother had put me to bed earlier, looking slightly nervous, but once she'd seen me close my eyes, she'd probably thought she could put me out of her mind.

I watched them as they came in, catching glimpses of my mother, who was sitting down, and the men, who weren't, chose to stand in three separate corners of our small living room, surrounding my mother. I wondered if they didn't sit because of the tears in the fabric of our sofa, and I suddenly became self-conscious of the dust on our floor.

The bedroom door was cracked just enough to see a bit and

hear them fairly well. I wasn't observing out of idle curiosity; men never came into our home.

"This is Pacifier, that is Single L, and I'm Octopus," said one of the men, who had his back to me. His authority clearly showed he was their leader.

"You really expect me to use those names?" my mother asked.

"You don't need to know our real names. The less you know, the better," Octopus retorted.

My mother scoffed. "So you're doing it for my benefit? How thoughtful. You know *my* name and you know where *I* live," said my mother, in that sardonic manner of hers. "You want some coffee?"

"No," said Octopus. "Is there anyone else home?"

"No, there's no one home," my mother said, glancing slightly toward my door. But she said it so convincingly I believed her myself.

They either believed her or didn't really care.

"What did Raul tell you?" asked Octopus. He shifted and I could see part of his face, and I silently edged down to the foot of the bed, where I could look out at a better angle. His eyelids were slightly droopy, making him look tired. The corners of his mouth dug in slightly, suggesting a perpetual bemusement. He had long-ish hair and a beard. He reminded me of Jesus Christ if Jesus had been the lead singer of one of those rock bands on TV. His eyes were a deep shade of cobalt blue, a bit of a shock amidst the pitch darkness of his hair. He had a hooked nose and a square jaw, and I sensed that if he cut his hair and shaved, he would be beautiful and boyish, but he'd chosen a look of dark mystery instead. It wasn't his looks that drew attention, though, but the intensity of his manner. The expression on his face suggested he was always thinking;

he came across as not wasting words, as not wasting anything, for that matter. As though he alone knew what lay beyond the ravine, what remained behind once the fog cleared off. He was the kind of man whose approval you desired, almost by instinct.

"Very little," my mother said. "That you need an actress."

He nodded. "It's an important role. A role that we're having trouble casting. Can you improvise? Can you stay in character even if something unexpected happens?"

"Yes and yes."

She nodded at him and he nodded back at her. They seemed to be falling into sync.

"I can do all that," she repeated. She'd never improvised before, as far as I knew. She always had time to rehearse when she dubbed the Hollywood movies. In fact, I wasn't sure I'd ever seen her act outside of the sound booth. "What is this show? Who will I be doing it with? Raul said it's 'real life.' What does that mean?"

The man introduced as Pacifier looked over at Octopus, as though they were communicating telepathically. They seemed to be making some decision. Pacifier crossed to the other side and I could no longer see him, even if I moved my head.

"You'd be performing for a single audience member. A very important man," said Octopus.

"Like players acting for the queen?" asked my mother.

Octopus traded glances with Pacifier. Pacifier shrugged his shoulders. "Is that a chess reference?"

My mother answered his question with a quick shake of her head and asked, "Who is this important man?"

"He's a Police Chief at a station in Ipanema," said Octopus. "The 13-DP."

"And what would I be performing for him?" my mother asked. I could hear in her voice the same skepticism she'd shown when Raul had first brought up the job.

"You're going to tell him a story that's going to keep him out of the station for a couple of hours," said Octopus.

His body stopped shifting, became a column, his back to me always. He never put his hands in the pockets of his pants. His legs never rested against each other.

"What kind of story?" my mother asked.

"A very good story. A story that me and my colleagues have devised."

My mother thought for a second. "And my job would be to make him believe that the story is true?"

"If he does not believe you, the whole plan falls apart," said Octopus.

"The whole plan?" asked my mother.

"You can use whatever it is you actors use—an accent, tears. The Police Chief must be so convinced by your performance that he will follow you out of the station and leave it unsupervised."

What if she refused? They were giving her so much sensitive information. I wondered if everyone in that room knew my mother would end up doing it.

"What are you and your men going to do while I keep him away from the station? You have people being held in that jail?"

Octopus hesitated, and traded looks again with the others. They hadn't smiled once, as far as I knew, since their arrival. There was still time, I wanted to tell my mother, to make them leave.

"You don't need to worry about that. What you don't know, you can't give away," said Octopus, pacing around my mother. "I do have an important question for you, though. Something I always ask people who are new to the group."

A group? Raul had said only that this was a job.

My mother sounded skeptical. "What is it?"

"Do you have any dependents?"

"Dependents?" my mother echoed nervously, as though to buy time.

"A sick father who needs care. A child. Someone who wouldn't survive without you." Octopus looked away, then added, "In case something happened to you."

My mother looked down on the floor. Through the flutter of my eyelids, I could tell she'd grown uneasy. Her face betrayed the churning and burning going through her stomach. My mother had always seemed strong to me, and never more so than in that moment, alone at night in a room with three strange men. I thought of my grandparents, and what they would think if they could see her now. Would she be confirming their prejudiced exhortations? Would this just reaffirm their distance? Or would a forgotten part of them kick in, a primal, evolutionary part that still wanted to protect their offspring?

I crept back up the bed, leaving the scene that had been playing out in front of me.

I heard her silence for a moment and then she said quietly, "No. No, I don't."

chapter three

I RARELY GOT TO RIDE IN CARS, SO THE DRIVE FROM OUR apartment to the farm in Santos was a thrilling treat. We were in the back, my hands buried deep into the crook of my mother's arm. Pacifier drove with a man I hadn't seen before in the passenger seat. Neither Octopus nor Single L came this time.

Several times my mother whispered to me, "Are you all right?" and I nodded that I was. Each time I said this, she closed her eyes and shook her head slightly, as though I'd just lied to her, even though I hadn't. With our hands linked I could feel her sweaty palms.

I couldn't quite figure out why she was bringing me with her. But there was, first of all, the fact that no one—none of our neighbors, none of her friends—was willing to watch me for the relatively long period that she was expected to stay at the farm—three full days. Janete couldn't do it; she had picked up work at a nightclub and was out at all hours. And there was the fact that she couldn't leave me alone in the apartment for those three days.

In the week since the men had been to our apartment, my mother never brought them up except to say she'd received a new job opportunity. She didn't know that I'd eavesdropped and I didn't tell her that I had—that was a milestone, our first serious lies to each other. When she told me she needed to go to a farm in Santos to rehearse for a play, I begged her to let me come along. She had no choice but to tell them that she did indeed have a child. I don't know exactly how they reacted to her admission, but I was allowed to come. Ana couldn't help but brag to me that Octopus had confided that her skillful lying had convinced him that she was the woman for the job.

As we drove, I looked out the window as the gray sky chased us. A car could go fast in a way that a bus couldn't. I watched as the familiar views of Copacabana gave way to the colorless, leafless suburban areas. Identical, morose midrise buildings blocked one another like standing dominoes. Clotheslines hung from every balcony, shirts and pants flapping in the wind like flags of every country. No sign of trees, none of the nature Rio was famous for. In the horizon, the favelas stretched over rolling hills. The makeshift houses, with their varying shades of plywood, concrete, and even brown brick, jutted and abutted with no rhyme or reason. They were like matchboxes that had been poured carelessly over fragile, unstable land. Driving fast, we overtook several buses. The people inside were standing, and having trouble doing so. Every other car was a Beetle: a round shell, their headlights shaped like eyes. The passing drivers had their windows down, not wearing seatbelts, the ones with radios blasting as a form of bragging.

Before we arrived at the farm, we passed by a row of several adjacent lots with elaborate, painted signs warning us to keep out.

Each sign spoke of a different danger. Each gate was high enough to intimidate. Our destination had a green gate, and was void of hysterical placards. But their gate was more secluded than the others, shrouded by dense vegetation. I heard the gravel of an unfinished road rolling under the tires as we approached.

My mother and I waited while Pacifier got out and undid the metal noodles of chains and locks at the gate. While I watched her, I thought of how hard it was to say no sometimes, to turn back on a decision. It was so much easier to glide forward, to acquiesce. My mother put her arm around my back, as though the more of my body she held, the more I'd be protected. She stared nervously at the gate opening, a man inside waving us on. Pacifier got back in the car, and my mother tensed, and I thought that she wanted to stop all this. But she didn't want to do it herself. She wanted another person to intervene, or maybe even God himself, through an earthquake or a mudslide. So that while my mother and I extricated ourselves, we could apologize to these men and hold in our heads a version of ourselves as polite, appreciative, and obedient. We were not like that on our own, but in front of these men who'd offered my mother money, who had something she wanted, we felt the need to be.

Pacifier drove onto the narrow path. Trees stood like sentinels on both sides, creating the impression of a tunnel. Their large, paddlelike fronds brushed against the windshield, making a slapping noise. Below us, the gravel grew noisier, too, as the tires made the rocks trample and roll over one another, their protests like the gritting of teeth.

The first thing I noticed, upon our arrival at the house, was that there was a police van parked next to it. When I got out of the car, though, and I could see the other side of the vehicle, I realized it wasn't really a police van. It was a regular van that a young man was painting green and yellow, using a large acrylic mold to write on. It was the size and shape of police vans I'd grown accustomed to seeing on the streets, carrying officers to dangerous shootouts. The man crouched on the ground, a brush in his hand, his clothes splattered with paint. He said a quick hello to Pacifier and his friend and smiled at my mother and me, as though he knew who we were.

Pacifier, now that he had fulfilled his job of driving us there, seemed to completely forget about us. He and the other man, who never said a word to us for the entire ride, went ahead into the house and disappeared. My mother and I stood awkwardly for a moment, unsure of what to do. The house was one of the largest I'd ever seen, surrounded by lemon trees and heavy banyan leaves. The front had a deep awning that created a porchlike space presently occupied by a volleyball net and some empty cans of paint. Half the wall was covered in tile, a deep blue pattern cross-sected by the white lines of the grout. The painter, noticing our hesitation, pointed toward the house.

"Go in," he said. "There're people inside."

The house smelled like sausages. My stomach growled, and I would've been embarrassed if I hadn't heard my mother's growl even louder. We hesitated by the foyer, adjusting to the coolness of the house. The living room had hardly any furniture, just stacks and stacks of chairs folded against the wall, and a yellow couch dwarfed by a bookcase overflowing with piles of old magazines. The couch had holes in it, holes that looked like scabs someone had picked.

My mother and I waited for someone to appear. My earlier

feeling of dread was now replaced by confusion. As though we'd been invited to a party, but showed up on the wrong date, or at the wrong place. Finally, my mother walked toward the voices, past a hallway that was nearly as wide as the living room itself, and we found ourselves in a large kitchen with dark, concrete floors. In the far corner, a young woman was stirring the largest pot I'd ever seen, making *feijoada* in an industrial quantity. Next to her, a short man stood on an empty box of produce so he could reach the sink. He was washing scallions. Both of them glanced at us, then went back to what they were doing.

"Upstairs," the woman finally barked, her face momentarily covered by steam.

We turned back to the living room and walked up the stairs, doing so with purpose, now that we had the permission of the cook. Some of the steps creaked, like piano keys, that my mother's feet hit first, followed by mine.

Upstairs, my mother led us toward a bathroom. I didn't even wait for her to lock the door before I pulled down my underwear and sat on the toilet. I'd been holding it in for the last hour and it felt good not to anymore.

My mother waited until I was done and then we traded places. While she peed, she leaned forward, putting her elbows on her knees, and her hands over her forehead, muttering something to herself. I looked over again at the second toilet, trying to figure out how it worked. I turned the faucet on tentatively and water began to stream upwards, like a little fountain, though not really far up enough for me to comfortably wash my hands. I turned it back off.

"I shouldn't have brought you here," my mother said, looking at me. "I shouldn't have come."

"Are they going to feed us?" I asked.

"That *feijoada* smelled good, didn't it?" my mother said. "You could tell she soaked the beans for a long time, like you're supposed to."

She wiped and pulled up her underwear.

I washed my hands on the actual sink. While I did this, my mother put her hands on my shoulders and stared at the mirror, as though taking a picture of herself. Her gaze looked distant, almost sad. To me, my mother was always smiling, because when she looked at me, she *was* always smiling. I hadn't given much thought to what she looked like when she wasn't looking at me.

When we came out of the bathroom, a dour-looking man was waiting for us. He beckoned us with a wave of his hairy hand, and led us into a room where some people were chatting. In the room, which was quite large, there was a foosball table against one wall, and a Ping-Pong table against another. Both were covered by maps. The room must've been right above the kitchen; the smells floated in freely through a window on the far side. It was one of those windows that opened outward instead of upward, held in place by a folding hinge. There were men and women here, most if not all of them college age, gathered around in a semicircle, sitting on metal folding chairs. Two of the chairs had been placed right into an empty area in the middle of the room, facing each other. The stage, so to speak.

When my mother and I came in, there was a sudden silence. I recognized Octopus from the other night, even though I'd barely seen his face at the time. He had a certain aura around him that made him hard to miss, not just because of the way he presented himself, but by the way everyone else angled themselves in relation to him. He smiled at my mother, a hint of gratitude in his eyes, as though he hadn't been sure that she'd come. Someone handed my mother a piece of paper and led her to the chair in the middle. A man stepped forward and took the chair across from her. He introduced himself to my mother as Carlos. A kindly woman with short, boyish hair led me toward an empty chair.

With the lines in front of her, something about my mother shifted. The woman trembling in the bathroom vanished. The confident woman from Raul's sound booth took her place—the woman who spoke Portuguese for Katharine Hepburn. She studied her lines, nodding slightly once in a while. Everyone watched— my mother had complete control over the room.

After a few minutes, she put the sheets away and, making eye contact with her scene partner in the opposite chair, she began.

"Thank you for seeing me, Chief Lima," said my mother, adopting the manner of a woman more docile than her.

"My men said that you had information to give me. What is this referring to?" asked Carlos, in character, as committed to the role as my mother. It was easy to see he wasn't trained, though. He was doing too much. Moving his head, his hands, more than necessary.

"The terrorists, of course. Everyone in Rio knows how hard you're fighting them," said my mother, sitting quite still, not in the absence of energy, but the repression of it.

"I'm not sure I know what you're talking about, but if you know anything, I'm willing to listen," said Carlos. There were tiny pauses, as each of them thought of what to say next. Neither he nor my mother checked their pages—I realized then that they hadn't been given actual lines, only the situation.

"I came to you because you're what's keeping those communists from ruining our country," said my mother. When she said *communists*, the word was met with smiles, even clapping from someone in the back. "When you fight them, you fight them on behalf of all of us."

"Thank you. But that's enough flattery, even for me, *mocinha*. What did you come here to tell me?"

My mother nodded slightly and then glanced over at Octopus, as though anticipating his reaction. He watched my mother with intensity.

"I live in the favela Rio das Pedras. I have the lower unit in a three-floor shanty. Honest, hardworking people. But about a month ago, a new element moved in upstairs. Suspicious-looking, wearing imported shoes. They don't spend the night, just gather for a few hours during the day. Students from Federal, I could tell. I've taken out the trash in those classrooms."

I looked over at the audience and wondered if the many young people in the room were students at that very school.

"Last week, I was watching my soap during lunchtime and I couldn't pay attention to whether the protagonist figured out that his new lover was really his old lover in disguise because the conversation upstairs was so loud. I heard male voices, and female voices." She looked down at her lap and twisted her hands together, a nice touch. "And I heard them talking about bombs, about bombs they would use against the police."

Then she stopped, with a look on her face that meant she wasn't sure what to do next. You could run out of words like you could run out of money. Her scene partner was no help. He'd gone from actor to observer and seemed afraid to jump in, as though even her silences were too good to interrupt. My mother glanced over at Octopus and he returned her gaze with either approval or intimidation, I couldn't tell. But something in that transaction allowed her to continue.

"They're planning a kidnapping. Of the American ambassador."

"The American consulate?" Carlos echoed, jolted back into the scene.

"Yes. They said something about wanting to exchange him for some of their men being held here," said my mother, and as soon as she said it, two people clapped and howled, independently of each other. Octopus was nodding vigorously. Her use of real bits and pieces of information in her otherwise made-up story seemed to delight, rather than unnerve the revolutionaries.

"How are they going to get to the consulate? Did you hear any mention of security detail, leaked itineraries?"

"I heard them talk about homemade bombs, Molotov cocktails," said my mother, consulting the sheets again. "They plan on blowing up the consulate."

"I find that hard to believe. That is too bold, even for those micks," said Carlos, who was greeted by some hissing. Carlos broke character and shrugged.

"I heard very clearly, sir. The walls are very thin."

Carlos hesitated for a moment, and reached for his sheets, but my mother came to his rescue.

"They usually meet right now. They'll probably still be there for the next couple of hours," said my mother, allowing for a melodramatic flourish of her head. I wondered which American actress she was mimicking. If she wanted him to follow her on a wild-goose chase, she would have to reject in a flash of a second a tactic that wasn't working and choose another one, on the spot. She would have to create, out of thin air and words, a bond between herself and the Police Chief.

Carlos leaned forward in his chair. "What is the address?"

"Sir, you know very well we don't have addresses in the favela. No street names, no numbers posted, and all the units look the same. I'd have to show you myself."

Someone near me called out, "Pigs." Someone else sneered, but then stopped right away, silenced by a look from Octopus. I was surprised that there wasn't more heckling, more interruptions. I was surprised that they let the scene go on for as long as it did. I felt proud of my mother as she stood there, posture rigid, a look of determination on her face. But so much seemed to fall on her shoulders, I suppose I wasn't the only one who wanted her to succeed.

Then, all of a sudden, Pacifier got up. He'd been sitting in the audience, watching her. Both Carlos and my mother looked at him, confused.

"Aren't you Ana?" Pacifier called out, adding himself unexpectedly into the scene. My mother looked visibly shocked to hear her own name, as though she'd been unmasked. "Don't you live in Selma's building? What're you doing here? Do you still work doing voices on TV?"

Pacifier was acting as though he was trying to help with the preparation, so they'd know what to do if an unexpected wrench got thrown into the proceedings. But there was something aggressive in his tone.

A succession of emotions registered on my mother's face: confusion, fear, anger. But she settled finally on an unexpected choice: warmth. She smiled at Pacifier as though he was her long-lost brother.

"Yes, yes, it's me, Lana! From Telma's building!" she said effusively. "You're Luis, right? I'm so glad to see you working as a cop. It's so much better than being a shoeshiner. How's your mom? Does she still have the gout?"

Pacifier looked taken aback, as though he'd expected her to get flustered, and the fact that she wasn't flustered made himself so. "No, I'm not Luis, you're confusing me with someone else."

"Oh, I'm sorry," said my mother, putting her hands over her mouth. "My mistake. You have the kind of face that makes you think we've met before. My mistake."

Stunned, the oversized Pacifier now seemed disadvantaged by having too much height and width. He sat back down a little awkwardly.

Carlos turned to my mother, still in character. "You know that young man?"

"I don't, but who wouldn't want to know a man as handsome as that?" said my mother, smiling her charming smile. "A lot of handsome men in this precinct. But I suppose you have to be fit to work at a job like this. Anyway, I just played along because I didn't want to embarrass him."

I turned to Octopus, and saw that he was smiling at my mother with a mixture of delight and amusement, while Pacifier seemed a bit disgruntled.

As the day went on, the rehearsal continued. They'd start from the top, Carlos throwing at her different variations of what might happen. But my mother never hesitated, never contradicted her own claims. By the time the end of the afternoon crept in, the observers left one by one, until it was just she, Carlos, and Octopus. After taking it so many times from the top, my mother sneaking a quick smile my way each time, as if to say *I'm okay, we're okay*, I left to use the bathroom.

Instead of returning to the rehearsal room, I wandered off into the hallway to peek at what the rest of the house looked like. All the doors were left open, and some of the rooms were doorless.

In one empty room I saw a sewing machine, with a pedal. To me, the machine resembled a horse, with a distinguishable head, and a saddleback. There was thread of all colors, and large scissors next to them. On a basket, I saw policemen's uniforms. They looked pristine, unwrinkled and unworn, and reminded me of my school uniforms on the first day of school. They looked like they were made of the same fabric, polyester, though these seemed thicker, more fitted. I'd never seen a fake police uniform before, and it seemed odd to me that a policeman and a policeman's uniform were two separate things, independent of each other. In my head, their uniforms were glued to their bodies, a second skin. I wondered which of the men I'd seen in the house would fill out these uniforms. I wondered who would make those decisions, assign those parts. Octopus, no doubt.

I noticed, on the far side of the wall, a beautiful treasure chest. With a rich-looking cherrywood top and thick brass-covered borders, it looked out of place in that sparsely furnished house. It was the first beautiful thing I'd seen there, the first thing that made this seem like a home rather than a group's gathering place. After checking if anyone was nearby, I walked to the chest and touched it. I could sense its heaviness without even lifting it. I could tell by the fine engravings its considerable age, its heirloom status to someone who lived in that house. It was not locked.

Inside, there were guns. Small, large. Handguns, rifles. I'd

never seen a gun outside of my TV screen before. I swallowed dry.
I felt a rush of fear that I was transgressing on someone's property. Though I could see no thumbprints, I sensed that each gun
belonged to a particular person, by their shape, their coloring.
Each of these had been chosen. Each of these was taken care of
by someone.

Suddenly, I heard the sound of someone's voice out in the hallway and I let go of the top, which fell thunderously and startled
me. I turned around and saw no one. For a moment, I couldn't
focus on anything but my heart, racing, beating, and the guns staring up at me from behind the heavy lid.

At dinner, my mother and I sat squeezed at the end of a picnic
bench outside in the backyard. The group carried themselves in
the manner of a very large, familiar family—twenty or so shout-
speaking, waving their arms, talking over one another, getting up to
reach for things on the table instead of asking politely for someone
to pass it to them. They didn't seem to be related by blood, but the
outside world's rules of kinship, of family, seemed to apply here.

All the food was served in the pans and pots that they were
cooked in. There were fried chicken drumsticks, cheese bread
balls, tomato-sauce spaghetti with meat and potatoes, rice and
feijoada bean and sausage stew. My mother ate ravenously, alternating bites from the crispy chicken and the spaghetti, effectively
mixing them both in her mouth. I had a bellyful of cheese bread
balls, and was happy when the cook brought a second warm batch
from the oven. My mother was, as far as I could tell, the only adult
not drinking alcohol. Everyone else had a *caipirinha*, lemons

drowning in their cups. I wondered if their meals were like this every night—a party. They seemed content. Happy in their isolation. It would be hard to give this up and live with only one or two other people, back in the city.

I could tell by their words, their cadences, that they were well-educated. The teasing, almost always directed at Octopus, was tribute to his power. The camaraderie had an intoxicating quality that washed over my mother and me, relaxing us. Their bond didn't seem like the kind to have grown slowly and quietly over a period of years, trickling into the jar of friendship a little at a time. Their bond was the kind that was cauterized from spending many hours of many consecutive days together, building not friendships but extensions of the self. My mother would later explain that they'd all met at the same college, been radicalized by the same professors, held the same dog-eared copies of Marx and Che Guevara's autobiography in front of their noses.

Throughout the dinner, there was constant, raucous laughter. There were flies, of course, though no mosquitoes. Across from my mother, a woman who'd already finished her meal lit up a cigarette.

"You did very well today," she said, exhaling some smoke. The woman was younger than my mother, with chin-length hair and prominent cheekbones.

"Thank you," my mother replied, putting a hand over her mouth to cover her chewing. "And who do I have the honor of pleasing?"

"I'm Claudia, but the cops call me Brigitte, or La Bardot, because they think I look like Brigitte Bardot."

"I don't see it," said my mother, and I wanted to kick her for being too honest.

The woman smiled. "It's okay. It's because I'm not wearing my blond wig. I like to wear a wig and sunglasses for our missions."

My mother took this in and nodded. She swallowed. "If you're so comfortable with disguises, maybe you should be the one playing this part."

"Oh, don't worry. There's no competition. Octopus gave me that role originally, but when we rehearsed, I couldn't pull it off," she said, smiling, rolling her eyes at the memory. "I can distract someone for five minutes, lie about who I am. But a whole hour? That takes a trained actress. I saw what you did today. I couldn't do it."

Concern streaked across my mother's face, perhaps wondering if she'd done the wrong thing by taking someone else's job. The woman added, in a friendly manner, "Don't worry. I'm the one who told him to find someone else, a professional. And it's a good thing he found you."

I hadn't had a chance to tell my mother about the guns I'd found. Seeing the woman being friendly to us, I couldn't help but blurt out, "But isn't it dangerous? What he's asking my mother to do?"

The smile on the woman's face vanished, and she took a long drag of her cigarette. I wondered if she was going to tailor her answer to someone my age and I wanted to tell her that that wasn't necessary. I knew about drugs and guns and women of the night. I lived in Copacabana, after all. Like all other eight-year-olds in my grade, I knew all the bad words and I knew about sex, but I pretended not to, always, so as not to upset my mother. It was one of the things that I learned to do from early on—to pretend to know less than I actually did. But I needed to protect my mother, who couldn't fathom how alert I was. How could she possibly function, if she knew how deeply her child was capable of pain, how intensely I felt her fears, how ravenously I loved, to the point that my small body might shake, my tear ducts the junction of a river that started in my heart. I didn't cry because I was weak, or spoiled, or ignorant. It wasn't that I didn't understand what was happening, but quite the opposite.

"Ana will be long gone before they realize what happened," said La Bardot. She then turned her eyes back to my mother. "Your daughter is smart. I like her. But if I were you, I wouldn't have gotten her involved; it could be dangerous. Although we're recruiting students younger and younger these days, so maybe it's a good thing . . ." My mother tensed beside me and shot La Bardot a silencing look. "Anyway, the genius of the plan is that you'll show up there to warn them. You'll be there as a rat for the police, not as one of us. If, for some reason, you're ever questioned later, you can plausibly deny your actual role. You can say, 'I went there to warn the Police Chief. It's too bad we arrived there too late to catch them.'" She exhaled smoke and gave us a wry, superior smile.

It seemed La Bardot hadn't sat across from us by accident. She'd been placed there to reassure us, to field questions. She played some kind of important role in this group. I could tell by the self-assurance of her poise, her purposeful glances. La Bardot smiled and laughed a lot, as if she had enough of everything, and didn't mind sharing. She was the prototypical Copacabana girl, in the suntanned, careless way my mother wasn't, and I already knew I would never be. She seemed both out of place and completely at home in that crowd of activists, these actors.

My mother nodded. "I guess that's a better answer than 'I was there to distract you while they snuck the prisoners out.'"

"You were smart to figure that out. Yes, our friends who are in the prison are scheduled to be transferred. But the deputy doesn't know what the men in charge of it look like. Instead of the real police, it'll be us. Like a Trojan horse, no?"

I realized the people around us had stopped talking. My mother suddenly pushed her plate—still half full of spaghetti—away.

"But what if," my mother asked, "they see right through me? What if I get nervous and come across like an idiot?"

"Too many ifs," said La Bardot, shaking her head and blowing smoke. She changed positions, placing her left hand under her right elbow, and leaning back a little. "And you're not, and you won't be, on their list. There are too many bigger fish than you to fry."

I glanced over at my mother, who seemed to be taking this in. She nodded slightly, quietly. She glanced over at me, and returned my gaze. I wanted to tell her, don't do this. We can figure out some other way to live. Life was so expensive, but we could find some other way to pay for it.

"You need to have more confidence in yourself," said La Bardot. "You're a very good actress. They're going to believe you. And you're going to be saving the lives of seven very good men."

"How successful have you been in the past?" asked my mother.

"Very," said La Bardot, an unexpected smile brightening her face. "Just last month, we pulled off a very impressive bank robbery."

"Banks? You rob banks?" my mother spat out.

I thought of the guns and felt tingling, electric, as if my insides were filled with wires instead of ligaments.

"We need money like some people need medicine," said La

Bardot matter-of-factly. "Fast, lots of it. We need money to buy
guns, which are expensive, especially with the marked-up prices
of the black market." She put a hand to her temple, as though
it helped her think. "Only a few dealers are willing to supply us,
the ones who aren't happy with the rates offered by regular retail.
We need money to buy cars, which often require servicing, fake
plates, taking out bullet holes. Mechanics hate servicing us; we
have a history of stiffing them on payments." La Bardot let out a
girlish laugh, and then continued, in a hushed tone so I couldn't
hear, though I could, "And none of us girls will deign to barter
parts for sex. We also need money to pay for expertise. Chemists
who can explain how to make bombs and find us the necessary
substances. Former and current bodyguards who can outline the
flaws and loopholes in the security details. Ex–military personnel
with insight into the interrogations. So, as you can see, this isn't the
first time we've carried out a plan of this size. You have nothing to
worry about."

"Really? And yet I don't know anyone's real names," said my
mother.

"You know mine," said La Bardot, blowing out some smoke.
"But the code names are fun, no? Octopus is called that because
he's got his hands in everything. Pacifier, he doesn't pacify anything, but sometimes when he gets angry, we need to soothe him,
like you'd put a pacifier in a baby's mouth."

The conversation was interrupted when a large plate of bon
bons, chocolate batter covered in chocolate sprinkles, was passed
to us. They were wonderful—moist and chewy and soft—sticking
to all the right corners of my mouth. When I looked up again, I
noticed that my mother was staring at me, fiddling with her fingers

as she sometimes did. I must've had some chocolate stains around my lips, my chin. Eating the *brigadeiros* was a messy affair. She didn't wipe my face, though, she just kept staring at me, and I thought how silly it was for a mother to make the mistake of falling in love with her own child.

In the morning of our third day at the farm, Octopus led my mother into an alcove. He called it a "Bible room," because it was small and shaped like the Holy Book. Over the bed, someone, certainly not Octopus, had laid out a change of clothes for my mother: a sleeveless yellow shirt with an oversized collar, and a worn-out pair of brown polyester pants. My mother stared at the outfit, resisted it. There was even a pair of sandals with fake leather straps and rubber soles. Clothes someone else had already worn for a long time.

"I'm fine wearing my own clothes," said my mother. It was the first time the three of us were alone, and I noticed how short Octopus was, almost as short as my mother. He was really young, too. Whatever gravitas he had, he'd earned it solely through his deeds, his intellect.

"This is for the day of. You're going to have to dress like a janitor. A janitor on her day off, but still a janitor."

My mother reached for the shirt and touched its fabric, noticing its roughness.

"How did you know the right size?"

Octopus shrugged. "The first time we met, in your apartment."

"You want me to wear this?"

"I want you to be convincing."

"Should I try it on?" she asked, pretending to be seductive. "So you can see how I look in it?"

My mother and Octopus stood on opposite sides of the bed, the costume laid out between them like a hint of my mother's future self.

"That's not necessary," he said. "Just take it with you. Pacifier's going to take you and your daughter home now."

My mother looked relieved to hear this. She'd made it through her entire stay at the farm, and I could sense her entire body un-clench. "And next time I see you?"

"The day of the plan. You'll go to the police station at the time we discussed. You'll see La Bardot outside the station, making out with one of our men. If she drops her purse on the ground when she sees you, it means the plan is on and you go in. If she hangs on to her purse, you are to turn around and go home. It means the plan had to be aborted."

He started moving toward the door when I saw my mother extend her arm toward him.

"Wait!" she called out. "My fee . . . we never discussed my fee," said my mother. "When do I—when do I get paid?"

Octopus looked at her as though she'd spoken in Greek.

"Nobody here gets paid. We're all doing this to help our friends who are in jail."

"Yes, but those men are not my friends," my mother said, firmly.

"They're being tortured," Octopus said, "and when they're done being tortured, they're going to be killed. Unless we get them out."

My mother did not blink. "I understand that. But Raul told me I was going to be paid."

"We fed you, didn't we? You ate our food."

My mother looked at him incredulously. She then did something I did not expect. She lunged at him and hit him in the chest, in the arm, with her never-used fists.

"I have a little girl to take care of!" she yelled.

Octopus backed away from the rain of punches, none of which seemed to bother him very much. He had something akin to a smile on his face—a smile on the verge of being born, and I understood that he admired the fact that my mother had used violence. He was in the business of collecting information. *A little girl to take care of.* He stared down at me. Flashed his teeth.

"It was a joke," he said. "Of course you'll be paid."

"Some people don't like jokes about religion. I don't like jokes about my money," said my mother, still fuming, combing her hair back into place with her fingers.

"You enjoyed hitting me, didn't you?" teased Octopus. "I can tell you did."

"I didn't," my mother protested.

"It's because I'm small," said Octopus, who oddly didn't have a single hair or piece of fabric out of place. "If I were bigger, it wouldn't be as much fun."

"How much am I going to get?" my mother repeated.

"It's only a day's work," said Octopus, dismissively.

My mother shook her head. "You're not going to pay me based on time. You're going to pay me based on risk. I'm well aware of what happens to folks who get caught."

Octopus held her gaze. "Really? So you know that after he's done with his 'interrogations,' Police Chief Lima always lets them go." Octopus paused for effect. "I'm free, the person thinks, and starts running. And then Lima shoots him in the back."

My mother closed her eyes for a moment, and took a deep breath.

"Pacifier has your money. He'll give it to you today after he drops you off. The first installment now and the second half you'll get after the plan is over."

"How much?" my mother asked.

"Five thousand before. Five thousand after."

My mother seemed pleased by the sum. Octopus smiled, as though glad he'd met her expectations. "You know, I hesitated at first when Raul told me about you," he said.

"Why?" my mother asked, looking stricken.

"He said you were desperate. Desperation isn't a good quality in this business."

chapter four

THE SOUND THAT WOKE ME, I WAS SURE, WAS SOMETHING innocuous, like the wind rustling, or a finch taking flight outside our window. I opened my eyes slowly, adjusting to the blazing morning light. It was strangely tranquil—no buses roaring, no construction workers drilling, as though everyone had agreed to sleep in after Carnaval.

Rolling over, I remembered sounds I'd heard the previous night, sounds that I had assigned to either a dream or to one of our neighbors. Female voices—sharp and intense—followed by the sound of a woman grunting. Banging. On a neighbor's door, I was sure. I knew it must've happened to my neighbor, because who could possibly want to break in our home? Their lives could contain all kinds of terrors, but surely ours couldn't.

Or it had been a dream, surely, a dream with made-up sounds and made-up grunts, and no real consequences of any kind.

When my drowsiness finally left me, I got up and I could tell that my mother wasn't at home.

My mother always slept in, and I was the one to awaken her. I glanced toward the bathroom, the only other logical place she might be, but it was empty. Was I still dreaming, still asleep? I immediately stepped into the living room, where there was no sign of my mother. She wasn't in the kitchen, either. I could not remember ever waking up and not finding my mother in bed, much less not finding her in the apartment.

Panic rising, I continued to ping-pong from room to room, rushing from the bedroom to the kitchen to the living room to the bathroom, waiting for a different result each time. I patted my mother's mattress, over and over again, as though my eyes were tricking me. I'd been alone in the apartment numerous times while my mother was at work, but I'd never been alone when my mother was supposed to be there. A crucial difference. Calm down, I told myself. She had just stepped out to get some fresh bread, or she was at a neighbor's, or some other explanation that sounded utterly implausible. Because she never got bread for us, and she'd never go to a neighbor's that early in the day. I tossed my mother's pillow on the ground and pulled at her mosquito netting until it fell off the ceiling and lay splayed on her bed, creating no protuberance where her body should be.

I decided that my mother was coming back, she was coming right back, and I just had to find a way to pass the time. I rushed to the heavy window blinds and undid the locks that kept them open, shutting them rapidly, keeping out the sun and the breeze.

I walked back to the living room and I spotted the front door, with its three locks—a night latch, a deadbolt, and a chain lock. I set them closed, in rapid succession. If my mother had gone out to run errands, she would have locked the door behind her. She hadn't. I suddenly had too much energy and couldn't stand still. I unlocked the door and stepped out. I had not planned on what to say when I knocked on Janete's door.

Janete did not answer. The hallway was completely empty, which was not unusual but it was also completely silent, which was. I could typically hear the radio from my neighbors across the way, always tuned to the sermons on the religious stations. Or the sound of the couple down the hall having fights, throwing things at each other. I couldn't even hear the mice today.

I knocked again and the sound echoed through the bare hallway, ricocheting from wall to wall. I felt like ants were crawling over my back. My legs wouldn't stop shaking.

"Janete!" I called out. There was desperation in my voice. "It's Mara."

Janete did not open the door. My panic grew, pulsing outward from my stomach.

I knocked again, my knuckles announcing my persistence. Janete finally opened the door. She was not wearing her wig, but her scalp was covered by some kind of sheer fabric, and she still had full makeup on. She wore a bathrobe that was too small for her frame and that had visible holes near her armpits. She looked almost too tired to be irritated, and looked at me as though I was and wasn't really there. She did not invite me in, and it became clear our conversation would take place right there at her door.

"My mom's gone," I said. I could hear my voice crack, the tears that were about to well up. "I don't know where."

"What do you mean she's gone? What happened?" asked Janete, adjusting the belt of her bathrobe through its loop.

"Can you find her? Can you go and find her?"

"She's still not home? What time is it?"

I thought of Octopus and his men. "I think she's somewhere she shouldn't be. Somewhere dangerous . . ." I felt like I couldn't tell Janete any more.

"I think you're overreacting a little, don't you think?"

"I'm scared. I think something happened to her."

"What could possibly happen to a woman as kind and prudent as your mother?" she asked with benign sarcasm.

My shoulders sank as I openly cried.

Janete sighed and lowered herself so she was sitting on her ankles and could look at me eye to eye. She put a hand comfortingly over my shoulder.

"Listen, I have a friend with me right now, but as soon as I can, I'm going to come check on you, okay? Now go back in, turn on the TV, and watch some cartoons."

I refused to budge, and shook my head harder.

"Do you know where she is? Did my mother say anything to you?"

Janete waved her arms helplessly. "She didn't say where she was going, but she said she'd only be gone for an hour. Now, there's nothing you can do except go back to your apartment and wait."

I could tell she didn't understand the severity of the situation. I leaned closer to her so that my body almost fell on top of hers. Something inside me told me to make myself feel solid to her. "Can I stay here with you? Can I stay here until she comes back?"

Right then, as if on cue, I was startled by a sound from inside her apartment. It was the growl of a man's voice calling out for Janete. The way he said her name, not asking for her, but demanding her, made me dislike him right away.

"No, you can't, I'm sorry," said Janete. She shifted her position so that one knee was on the floor and the other knee became a stool where she could delicately rest her hands.

"Why not?" I pleaded.

Janete thought for a moment, but couldn't think of anything to say. Tears continued to fall down my cheeks. Janete turned her face away, but I could see a hint of sadness in her eyes. The man inside called for her again, his voice even more impatient than before. Janete got up.

"You are such a brave little girl," said Janete, wiping her nose with the back of her hand, and closing the door.

As soon as she was gone, I ran back to the apartment, shut the door behind me, and locked all the bolts. Because that wasn't enough, I hid inside the closet, not my section, but my mother's. I could barely fit there, my back pushing against the panel of wood, and wrapped my arms around my legs. I made sure to close the closet door, though it was hard to do it from the inside, without a hinge to pull. It was completely dark, with only bits of light peeking through the corners. I had pushed all my mother's hung shirts to the side to make room for me, but one of them kept sticking out toward my face. The top was one of her nicest—light blue, made out of silk, with a giant collar and sleeve cuffs. It smelled just like her. I reached for the sleeve and held it, my fingers wrapped tightly around the fabric. I stayed like that, wrapped in her scent, in the darkness, for hours.

There was a knock. I sprang out of my container and flew to the front door. It was just Janete. She came as a boy, which meant without her magical powers. She could see the deep disappointment on my face and, as if to compensate, she held me tightly against her arms.

"Your mom's not back yet?" she asked me, leading me to the sofa. "Already half the day's gone. What could be taking so long?"

What was taking her so long, or who? We sat down. I buried my face against her arm, wetting it with tears. Time and space were the enemy: accomplices, villains.

In between hiccups, I said, "I want my mom. I want her back."

But as the day dragged on, I realized I knew exactly where my mother had gone. She should never have agreed to help those odd, awful men.

"Come on," said Janete. "Come wait for your mother in my apartment. I'll fix you some food. No one took your mother. She's fine and will be home soon."

I hesitated. I did not follow Janete. Leaving the door open, I sat down on the floor right by the line that separated our carpeted apartment from the concrete hallway. Janete, on the outside, tried to lure me, but I stayed inside, inside where I belonged. Where my mother would find me.

"Mara!" Janete insisted, but in vain.

I stayed like that, sitting on my butt, with my arms wrapped around my legs, my head staring at the imperfections on the floor. Lived-in scratches, resilient dots, nicks and cuts that no one ever noticed. Janete stood by me exasperated, but her patience eventually ran out and she dragged herself back to her apartment.

I did not budge; neither hunger nor thirst could stir me. If I remained on that spot, performing the act of waiting, the universe would have no choice but to produce my mother.

Over the course of the afternoon, neighbors stared as they passed by. Two kids younger than me, who I'd seen but never spoken to, stood and stared, curious, as though I were putting on a show for them. They pointed a few times, before going off on their adventures. Their mother, a plump, short woman in a housedress, looked over at me and beyond, into the empty apartment, and asked if my mother had left me there as punishment. I did not answer.

Another neighbor, a man holding a toolbox, his shoes grimy and torn, muttered something to himself, as though I had personally offended him. I looked like a problem he wouldn't be able to solve.

A few minutes later, a neighbor with a gleamingly bald head who didn't know me or my mother told me, very authoritatively, to go back inside and shut the door.

I ignored him. I refused to speak to anyone. They had nothing to do with this. This was between me and my mother.

And I was good at waiting.

I had waited for my mother through the long, long grocery store lines that sometimes took up to an hour. I had waited for my mother at the bank while she paid our gas, water, and electricity bills. I had waited for my mother to finish haggling with salesgirls, to charm bus drivers into making unscheduled stops, to read her favorite magazines at the newsstands instead of buying them. I had waited for my mother to cook for me, before I swallowed my own tongue out of hunger. I had waited for my mother to get up in the morning after getting through the seven mystical stages of awakening—enchantment, disbelief, stupor, denial, bargaining, anger, and acceptance.

          ✿   ✿   ✿

My mother finally arrived shortly after twilight. She found me on
the floor, the door open, and immediately whisked me away and
rushed in, like a kangaroo mother tossing me back in the pouch.

She looked disheveled, her hair stringy. I could sense the molecules in the room changing color, changing shape, into something
entirely new and dark. I looked at her face for signs of where she'd
been—a haleness, or a hollowness—and found none. All that mattered was that she was back.

"What were you doing with the door open like that?" asked my
mother, as we got inside and she closed the door behind her. She
was nearly whispering, a hiss.

"I was waiting for you," I whimpered.

"Where's Janete?"

"Back in her apartment," I mumbled.

"She didn't stay here with you? What a *puta*. I've had such a
day. I've had such a terrible day," she said, and I noticed how she
could barely stand still. Her eyes were bloodshot, as though she'd
rubbed them after crying.

"Where were you, Mommy? Where were you all day?"

My mother shook her head, as though I'd asked an impertinent
question. She sat on the sofa and lit a cigarette. She looked at me
with cold eyes, like I wasn't her daughter but instead some hood-
lum she'd run across in her living room.

"I was afraid to come home in case anyone was following me.
So I rode in buses all day. All the way to Madureira, then back."

"Why would someone follow you?"

"Because I'm so goddamn beautiful. Why do you *think*?" she

snapped, raising and lowering her arm in frustration. She was as prickly as a pinecone. "Don't ask me these questions. You're like an interrogator. Did you join the police force while I was gone?" My mother put out the cigarette she had just lit—she'd normally smoke each all the way to the tiniest stub, nearly burning the tips of her fingers.

Now I could practically see where she'd been all day. I could see her leaning over me in the still dark morning, watching me sleep, right before she left, and heading to Janete to drop off her key and ask her to watch me. I could see Janete—sleepily, tired from sex and booze—agreeing without agreeing, and shutting the door, and heading back to her man, making a calculation in her head that eight-year-olds are old enough to be alone at home. After all, hadn't Janete assumed even greater responsibility and risk at that age? My mother then heads out, nervous but determined, following Octopus's instruction to take a cab to the police station in case the bus drivers went on strike, as they threatened to. My mother rides the cab, uncomfortable in her janitor's clothes, hoping the driver doesn't notice her or comment on her, as that might break her concentration, or slow her momentum. She arrives at the police station a few minutes before expected, and sees La Bardot in the corner, vamping, her legs wrapped expertly around the fortunate man cast as her boyfriend. She has a blond wig on, and giant sunglasses that she removes at the sight of my mother. My mother makes eye contact with her, and she sees La Bardot reach for her purse and drop it on the ground. I can practically feel my mother's heart threatening to jump out of her throat, like a nervous frog that she has swallowed. She walks into the station; asks, and then demands, to see the Police Chief, who initially refuses to see her, I'm sure, but then agrees once she promises information about the student terrorists. As she enters his office, something clicks inside my mother, I'm certain, something I've seen happen in the recording booth. The actress in her, awakening—*she* comes alive—then shifting into another person entirely. A concerned janitor. A humble citizen reporting a threat. Her performance to the Police Chief is convincing, engaging—I know it is—not doing too much, not doing too little. Police Chief Lima listens, and it is both easier and harder to perform in front of him, in his actual office, with his actual physical body in front of her—he is a large, hulking man with salt-and-pepper hair and a suspiciously well-trimmed mustache, a mustache that, my mother will later say, hinted at power and ambitions far greater than the 13th Precinct of Ipanema. Easier because her acting is fed by the reality of the office and of the desk in front of her, with its contents—the small globe, the maps of the city, the anonymous folders and binders, the portrait frames whose backs face her so she can catch no glimpse of his family. Harder because the stakes are so, so high, and there are gaps that she must force herself to be comfortable with, gaps that, as a novice actress, she used to feel the need to fill, awkwardly and uncomfortably. But she doesn't, and she allows the Police Chief to take in her information, as she offers it piecemeal. As she pretends to forget, or misremember. Then suddenly another load of information, to keep him interested. He has drive, she can tell. Ambition. This information can be useful to him, to the locked desires of torture, of punishment, that she can glimpse in his glasslike, dark eyes. He wants to destroy the terrorist groups. For fame and for opportunities. For the power it will deliver. She wonders how much a public employee, even at his exalted level, gets paid. But this is when my knowledge of my mother, however well-married to my imagination, gets stuck. Because something failed, clearly, something did not go according to plan, but I do not know what it is. And I realize that my access to my mother is not omniscient, and that though I've observed her intently and loved her intensely, there are parts of her personality I am not privy to. I can see it in the new way her brow furrows, the way smoke lingers in the air around her half-smoked cigarette. It pains me to realize the truth: that she is ultimately as unknowable to me as I am to her.

"Why're you so upset, Mommy? Did something go wrong today?" I asked, softly.

She took a deep breath and buried her face in her hands.

"He didn't believe me," she muttered into her palms. I wasn't sure if she was talking to me or to herself. "He didn't believe me at all. He was so dismissive. He said I was just a troublemaker making things up. I am *not* a bad actress. I'm really not."

I leaned my head against her shoulder, trying to comfort her. "I know, Mommy, I know."

"He kicked me out of his office as if I was *nobody*. I've never been more humiliated in my life." She moved her hand away from her face, and I could see that she was crying. "I've never met anyone so cold. Like he didn't think I deserved to breathe the same air as him. He made me feel so small."

I hated this man that I'd never met. I kept trying in vain to comfort my mother, running my fingers along her bare arm.

"Do we have any passion fruit juice left?" she asked, wiping the tears from her face. She gave me a weak smile.

I rose to check. We took turns being each other's caregiver.

In the kitchen, I did not turn on the light. We couldn't separate the light from the hotness, and we didn't need any more hotness in Rio. In the dark, I opened the refrigerator door, revealing a lonely, single potato, and a half-sliced onion. The jar of juice sat empty, just some seeds at the bottom. I was about to return empty-handed when I heard the sound of aggressive knocking. I heard her open the door, heard the unmistakable voices of the rebels.

I sat down backward on one of the metal dining chairs, doing a bad job of hiding. I was convinced they couldn't see me, as though being in the dark and being invisible were the same thing.

"What happened today?" someone demanded gruffly. Pacifier.

My mother ignored him, and directed her anger toward the others. "What're you doing in my apartment? I never said you could turn my home into a meeting place for troublemakers!"

"He didn't believe you, did he? That's why he wouldn't leave his post." Octopus. He seemed strangely, unexpectedly calm. As though he didn't believe in wasting emotions as powerful as rage.

Her silence contained her answer. One of Octopus's men walked to the window and closed the shutters, acknowledging me in the kitchen with a sharp glance and nothing more. While he did so, another man turned off the overheard fluorescent, leaving only the small bulb by my mother's face.

"Why would he believe me? I'm a stranger off the street. Your plan was a piece of shit," said my mother. She never cursed around me.

Pacifier started pacing around the room. "What did you say to him? Repeat, word for word."

"Like we rehearsed," said my mother, shrugging. "But he

wouldn't come with me. He said he'd send an officer with me, and I said, no, I didn't trust anyone but the Police Chief. I said it clearly, if he wanted me to lead him to the group, he had to come with me."

I peeked out from behind the darkness of the kitchen. Everyone stood around my mother—Octopus, Pacifier, La Bardot, and a few men I maybe recognized from the compound. My mother sat on the sofa by herself, her hands on her lap, her fingers interlaced. I saw her glance toward the kitchen, as though looking for my unnoticed self. What did she want me to do? Run out the back door? Or stay where I was? Take note of what they were saying?

"It's very difficult to know what to do next when all we have is Ana's account," said Octopus, somberly. "We weren't there, so we don't know exactly what he said, or what shades of meaning Ana missed." Octopus turned to my mother, apologetically. "I'm not saying you're holding anything back, only that it's hard to rely on a single account. The bottom line is, we were too optimistic. We're going to have to give him some proof that Ana's information is reliable."

"I'm not returning to that station. I gave it my best shot," she said.

"Really? Then give us back the portion of the money we already gave you," barked Pacifier.

My mother scowled.

Octopus shook his head. "Regardless of what happens, that money is hers to keep. For her work so far. We're not taking anything back."

Pacifier rolled his eyes skyward, shaking his head. "You are part of our group now. That means if they find out about you and catch you, you're going to be in a lot of trouble." He walked away from my mother, only to walk back to her with more urgency, even pointing a finger at her. "You're going to need us to protect you. You want to stay on our good side."

"I'm not part of your group," my mother replied, gazing at each and every one of them. "I don't care if this country's governed by saints or sons of bitches! I'm not an idealist spoiled brat like all of you. I'm a pragmatist. If I don't put food on the table for my daughter, who will?"

Pacifier crossed his arms and scoffed. "Has it ever occurred to you that maybe the government should put food on the table? And not just feed your daughter when times are hard, but give her a good education as well? I'm amazed at how apolitical you are." He threw his arms in the air, in frustration.

My mother recoiled. I could tell she did not like Pacifier at all at that moment.

"No one else is going to help us," Pacifier continued, his hands shaking a little. "Not the church, not the bourgeoisie. Certainly not the Americans. Who got us in this trouble in the first place, when they let those pigs remove our president."

The mention of Americans seemed to make La Bardot's blood boil. "Don't get me started on them. They had ships waiting in Santos to invade in case we resisted the coup. The Americans said Goulart was a communist. He was not a communist! He was a man of the people, the only one who could start land reform. Their President Johnson was so afraid of any hint of communism that he gave our country to the wolves."

"And you, Ana, you go through life with your eyes closed," said Pacifier.

"Do I? Or maybe I'm just not an extremist," my mother spat back.

"No one questions the diligence of an ambitious person who'll do anything for money. Or for sex," Pacifier protested. "But devote yourself to the good of the country and you're some kind of extremist." He turned to the others expecting their agreement. "Sometimes I wonder if the problem with this country is not the people on either side. It's the ones sitting on the sidelines." He turned back to my mother, nearly fuming.

Octopus rested a hand on his shoulder. He sat down next to my mother. I feared he might admonish her, too, but instead he said, gently, "Our friends need you."

"Your friends in jail? Are you sure they don't belong there?" asked my mother. "I'd like to know what they did to get arrested."

La Bardot sat on my mother's other side, almost a mirror image of Octopus. Her long legs were covered with yellow Lurex socks, and she wore high-heeled sandals. I watched as she laid a hand on my mother's arm. "Do you know what the Police Chief is doing to them? The techniques he uses? He strips them naked and hangs them upside down on a stick, their wrists tied to their ankles. Or he ties them down in the dragon's chair, a metal chair with a strip of wood holding their feet back. He gives them electric shocks that make one half of the body go in one direction, the other half in the opposite one."

My mother looked away. La Bardot's words hung heavy in the air, as if Lima and his victims were right there in the room, gazing, listening.

"Police Chief Lima is the worst kind of devil," La Bardot continued. "He will torture even a pregnant woman, and treat it like it's all in a day's work. 'I'll be home soon, honey,'" La Bardot mimicked him, adopting the voice of a tenor. "'I just have one more to go. And oh, did you get the blood off my shirts like I asked?'"

My mother shook her head and put her hand up between La Bardot and her. "It's not my fault. It's not my responsibility."

Octopus picked up where La Bardot had left off. "You're going to go back tomorrow. This time, you'll share a piece of information with Lima that will check out. That will earn his trust. That will turn you into a valuable source."

And then: "We will pay you more," Octopus said simply. "Because it'll take up more of your time, we will pay you more."

"My time," she muttered. My mother shook her head, then suddenly got up. I could tell she'd changed her mind the instant he mentioned more money, but she paced for a few seconds, making it look as though she were struggling with her decision. Finally, she said, adopting the exaggerated resignation of a martyr, "I'll go back to Chief Lima and finish this job. But let me make it clear. I'm not doing this to help your fantasy that you're changing the world for the better. That's arrogance. Delusion."

Octopus took her hand into his, and stared straight into her eyes, as though about to tell her that he loved her. "You go and warn him of the explosion. Once it actually happens, he won't think of you as just some woman off the street. He'll think of you as a valuable person."

And like that, suddenly, they were gone, and when I blinked, I felt like it was the first time I'd blinked since their arrival.

After my mother shut the door on them, she reopened the window and our apartment was once again filled with the noise of the traffic outside, the heat of Rio at the height of the summer. She then came to the kitchen and walked past me. I remembered she had asked for passion fruit juice, and now she would see for herself that we didn't have any.

My mother left the fridge door open, after seeing that no juice had miraculously appeared, and we could feel its last remaining breaths of coolness. The bulb inside went off, but she did not turn on the kitchen fluorescent, so all we had was a bit of light from the living room lamp. When it got too hot, we often avoided turning on lights, remaining in the dark.

My mother wrapped her damp arms around me, and kissed the top of my head. "You did very well, remaining so quiet."

I felt like she'd given me permission to acknowledge what had just happened with those invaders. If she hadn't, I probably wouldn't have had the courage to tell her what was knocking about in my heart. "You don't need to help them."

"It's all right. This will be over soon," she said, playing with my hair, digging her finger deep into the clumps and strands along the curvature of my head. "With the money we make, I'm going to be able to buy you some chocolate yogurt and flan. Rice pudding. I'm going to get myself a perm done by a professional, and a dress made out of silk. Maybe we'll go on a trip, even. Somewhere nice and cool."

"Mom," I said forcefully, to break her out of her reverie. "You can't do this. If something happens to you, who's going to take care of me?"

"Nothing bad is going to happen to me," said my mother, growing irritable. "I wouldn't take the risk if I thought something might.

I know how important I am. I'm your mother *and* your father. I am all your aunts and uncles, your grandmas and grandpas."

I pressed my head against her chest, letting her envelop me. I put my arms around her waist. I stared at the empty, darkened refrigerator, looking so unfamiliar without its usual hum, its usual might.

"You think I don't know my responsibility to you?" she clucked. "I'm the one who made it clear to your dad that he was to stay away from us. I made sure he'll never come back south. I made you just one parent away from being an orphan."

"Was that my dad? On the bus?" I asked my mother. Not being able to see her, only feel her, made it easier to ask such a question. Sometimes it helps when a person is not a person, and just a presence.

"What? When?" my mother asked, startled, letting go of me.

"On the bus. During Carnaval. When we were with Janete. You made us leave."

She was silent, and when I turned to her my mother twisted her face in a way I hardly ever saw, her face replaced by a stranger's.

"That wasn't your father," my mother said, but the way she had transformed so wholly told me she was lying. "That was the butcher. I owe him for my tab. I wasn't going to let him confront me in public. And that's a lesson to you. You never, ever let someone humiliate you in public. There's no shame in being short on cash, especially if you're an honest person."

That *had* been my father. Now he knew my mother wanted nothing to do with him, and he'd board a bus back to wherever he came from, probably the Northeast where she met him. Her action, taken out of impulse, had permanent consequences. Intentionally or not, my mother had made it so it was just the two of us. I felt her irreplaceability fill me, overwhelm me.

How could I convince her to stay home the next few days?

Even if I could think of a way to convince her, it wouldn't have mattered. It wouldn't have stopped her. She was a river, and I was just the boat careening from side to side.

chapter five

I'D NEVER BEEN INSIDE A POLICE STATION BEFORE. IT
was packed with people fidgeting. No one could stay still, not the
criminals, not the officers. The chairs were made of the flimsiest,
cheapest black plastic, as though the plan was to throw everything into the trash at the end of the day. There were rows and
rows of binders, and giant typewriters that made weird staccato
music.

The main room, where we were, had an open layout, so you
could see everyone from every corner. Against the wall there were
private offices, with windows, some with the blinds drawn. A hallway led into a group of cells filled with prisoners from wall to wall.
Then there was a door that read Selected Personnel Only, and
occasionally a sweaty, tired-looking officer came out. I noticed the
door had the same kind of soundproofing I'd seen in my mother's
dubbing booth.

My mother was waiting for Police Chief Lima to see her, and
I was waiting for her to be done. I wanted to be on a playground,

not in a police station. "It could be some time," my mother said. "He's a very busy man."

Indeed, Lima was one of the most powerful men in Rio de Janeiro. He had been nicknamed Panopticon, due to his ability to keep tabs on everything and everyone. He was credited with coming up with one particularly creepy mode of modern surveillance: He enlisted retired public sector workers to stand by the windows of their apartments with binoculars and watch their neighbors across the street. He figured why not, since they stayed home most of the day anyway, and in Rio, it was too hot to keep the windows closed. The spies were supposed to report any suspicious activities, and the Department of Political and Social Order was able to get many helpful leads that way. It was rumored that torture was their preferred method of investigation.

Finally, an hour later, as a man emerged from an office, I saw my mother jump out of her seat.

"Chief Lima," I heard her call for him, grabbing his attention.

He gestured for her to sit back down. We were lodged at a bench against the wall, and he sat down next to us. Chief Lima was the biggest man I'd ever seen—a tall giant, really. He must've weighed over two hundred pounds, and his body crowded the bench. He didn't wear a uniform, like the others. Just a suit and a tie. He looked old enough to be a grandfather, but lacked the kind eyes those men always had on television. He scared me, right away.

"Don't you have anything better to do than buzz around me, like a fly?" was the first thing he said to her.

My mother remained undaunted. "I'm trying to help you do your job, sir. I have information about the student terrorists."

"You have nothing but delusions of grandeur, ma'am," said Chief Lima dismissively.

My mother seemed offended by what he said and I could see her frustration ballooning inside her. It made me wonder if he was right—if my mother was there to make herself feel important.

"They're going to cause an explosion in front of the American consulate this afternoon," my mother said, with urgency.

"That makes no sense. There are a gazillion red-skinned agents guarding that place."

"I'm telling you. I heard it with my own ears. My neighbor is a member of the guerrilla group. I told you before, they gather there in the afternoons."

Chief Lima glanced toward the cells in the back, distracted. I couldn't see the prisoners being held there, but I could occasionally hear a yell, the clanking of metal bars.

"I already told you, next time you see them congregate, you give me a ring here, and I'll send an officer to check it out."

"No," said my mother as she'd rehearsed, standing her ground. "I don't trust your men. I only trust you."

Chief Lima gave my mother a long, appraising look. "You know what I think?"

"What?" my mother asked, cautiously, fearing what he might say next.

"I think there's something fishy about you." He looked at me directly with those steely eyes, almost appealing to me to agree with him.

My mother feigned offense. It was better than to show how she actually felt. "Me? You're wrong."

"Say I agree to go with you. Then when I arrive, it's some kind of trap. A rain of bullets waiting for me. Whatever this place is you're trying to lead me to, it better be teeming with unsuspecting terrorists."

My mother swallowed nervously. The Chief got up. He was done with my mother. He'd given her her five minutes and he'd fulfilled his patriotic duty to the common people. I felt a nervous vibration run along her arm as she said to his retreating back, "I'm trying to help you. I'm here because I want the same as you."

Within twenty-four hours, her prediction came true. There *was* an explosion—a car bomb that went off a block from President Wilson Avenue, where the American consulate was. It killed one person and wounded five others. And with that, in Lima's eyes, my mother went from a crazy person off the street to a potential spy for the antiterrorism police force.

La Bardot came by herself, bearing gifts. She pulled the cheap polyester pants from the plastic bag, and my mother shook her head. More janitor's clothes.

"You shouldn't wear the same outfit again," said La Bardot. She came in character, in her platinum blond wig and giant red hoop earrings. She wore a spaghetti-strapped shirt that left her shoulders and arms mostly bare, and a pair of shorts that showed off her strong, athletic legs.

My mother wouldn't budge. They stood in the living room, too restless to sit down. I slumped in a chair next to the TV, pretending to watch a cartoon. The two of them paid no mind to me. My mother had wanted me to stay at Janete's, but I refused to be abandoned again.

"I want to be comfortable and wear my own clothes," my mother said. "I don't need Octopus directing me."

La Bardot did not want to argue—she stuffed the clothes back in her bag and asked with a sigh, "Do you still have the map he gave you, with the directions to Barra?"

"Yes. So the plan is the same?"

La Bardot nodded. "Except this time it has to work," she said, reproachfully.

"It will," said my mother, flashing a glance at La Bardot, and then returning to her small compact mirror as she put on her lipstick. "Have you ever met Chief Lima?"

La Bardot shook her head and frowned disgustedly, expressing her opinion of him.

"I've now only seen him twice, briefly, but we're establishing a rapport, a connection," said my mother, smacking on her lips. "He is an important man, and important people, for some reason, are really drawn to me."

"He is a torturer," said La Bardot, enunciating precisely.

My mother began applying her mascara.

"Judgment serves no use when it comes to acting. It's better to think about objectives," she said, opening her eyes wide, her eyelashes growing darker. "I have mine, he has his."

"Lima is not a person. He's a monster," said La Bardot, reaching into her bag for a cigarette.

"Acting is more about observation and noticing how people actually behave," my mother replied. "What people are really like, instead of the assumption in your head."

"Then I'd be a terrible actress because I would play everyone as bored and disenchanted, because I think that's what everyone really is," said La Bardot.

"Including yourself?" my mother asked, with a smirk.

La Bardot shrugged. "Maybe." She paused for a second, then said, "I have a confession to make. When I turned down the role, it's not just because I had such little faith in my acting." La Bardot exhaled smoke slowly. "I was afraid to be in a room with Lima."

My mother put the mascara away. "He'd probably recognize you."

"No, he wouldn't. But the mere thought of sitting face-to-face with him, I couldn't do it." La Bardot looked away, embarrassed. "The way you're going about this. You're not the least bit afraid?"

"I am, but I'm really trying to just think of it as an acting job." My mother paused, absentmindedly tapping a makeup brush on her hand. "Can I ask you a question?" she said, taking advantage of this newfound honesty. "Have you ever been . . . intimate with Octopus?"

La Bardot laughed. "Why? You want to know what he's like?"

"No," said my mother, a bit taken aback. She glanced my way. Then she added, "I just feel like he's been studying me, figuring out who I am, and that can go both ways, you know?"

"Octopus likes to say that in order to belong to everyone in the group, he can't belong to any one person, so no, he keeps his hands off the women."

"Interesting," said my mother, nodding.

"You'll have to be very careful today." La Bardot took another drag, straightening up abruptly. "Are you almost ready?"

My mother walked toward me and kneeled on the wood floor. She put her arms around my head and I could smell her sweet perfume. I wanted her to hold me and let me spend the rest of the day nestled in her warmth.

"Don't go," I said. I reached for her, and wrapped my arms around her waist.

"I have to go," she replied.

I was mad that she would disobey me. She tried to pry herself away, looking at me as though my warnings of danger were a mere irritation, but she didn't listen to me, as though Fate wasn't a thing to avert, but rather a thing to hurry along.

La Bardot, watching us, moved toward the door, foolishly believing that she had the power to commandeer my mother. She said, "We don't usually work with people who have kids. One of Octopus's rules that he is breaking for you." To me, she added, "Don't worry, sweetie, your mother will be safe."

I didn't believe her. "Stay with me, please!" She'd been spared disaster once, but she wouldn't be spared twice.

My mother pulled my arms away from her, being careful not to hurt me. I began to sob and hiccup. I stretched her shirt to the point that I almost tore it. When she got me off her waist, I reached for her legs, and when she got me off her legs, I reached for her ankles.

I cried loudly, helplessly. I kept repeating, "No, no," as my mother got farther away from me. Though her progress was slow, she was getting closer and closer to the door.

At one point Janete must've heard me through the wall. She came into our apartment, took one look at La Bardot and my mother trying to escape, and instead of preventing them from doing so, immediately and absurdly began to abet them. Grown-ups colluded, their minds poisoned by the same fallacies.

La Bardot didn't seem to mind Janete's imposing presence. Janete grabbed me from behind and held my arms back, so that I lost my hold over my mother and was left with just the air to punch. I frantically tried to free myself from her, but Janete used her weight against me. My crying became as loud as screams, interrupted only by my throat gulping for air.

I was in such a state I could no longer form thoughts or sentences, and just kept crying out, "Mom! Mom!"

I no longer had any physical pull over my mother, but still she remained on the same spot. Maybe she hoped that I would stop crying. Or maybe my cries had punctured some of her conviction. I could see the hesitation on her face, and La Bardot could see it, too, because she reached for my mother's elbow, prompting her. But still she lingered—a child's cry belongs to her mother and her mother alone.

"Go," said Janete, who didn't understand how anything worked. "I've got her."

I could barely see my mother through the blur of tears. But I could make out her image following La Bardot out. Even after she closed the door and left my sight, I kept crying and screaming for her. As she walked down the stairs, as she reached the main door, as she exchanged the claustrophobia of our apartment with the openness of the sidewalk, she could still hear me crying and fighting for her until I had not an ounce of energy left in my body.

chapter six

OF ALL THE THINGS MY MOTHER TAUGHT ME OVER THE
years, and there were many nuggets of wisdom that she dispensed,
one was to think of older women as potential mothers. Second
mothers. Proxy mothers. Mothers for a moment, for a minute. This
meant I had to respect and love my teachers. If I got lost, and
needed bus fare to get home, I shouldn't hesitate to present my
lost self to an older woman. If I went out alone to buy milk, I was to
stay close to a woman with children. Because even when a mother
is not your mother, she is *a* mother, and therefore can be trusted.

This didn't apply to men. But even still: When I saw the post-
man, I hugged him for no reason other than he was old enough
to be a dad. Same with the pharmacist, who patted me on the
head and gave me free packets of Pop Rocks popping candy. I
suppose their uniforms made them seem paternal. Men were bad
and mean and nasty, my mother said, which is why I was surprised
when she still smiled at them in conversation and didn't hiss at
their backs. They wouldn't necessarily think of a girl like me as a

daughter, she said, but as a toy, and they'd break me so badly, I'd never be able to be put back together again. I pictured one of my legs where my arm should be, or my feet facing backward, forever doomed to walk away from what I really wanted.

Which brought me to Janete, who was both masculine and feminine. When she was dressed like a man, like she was now, she was gentle and sweet and quiet. When she was dressed as a woman, she was loud and silly and energetic. For a while, she'd kept her arms of steel around me, making herself into a cage that held me until I could fight no more. I lay with my head against her chest, wetting her shirt with my tears and drool. She never pushed me away, and kept patting the back of my head with her soft hand. I could always tell who loved me and who didn't.

Though my body was drained, the urgency never left. In fact, with each minute that passed, it only increased.

"We have to help my mom. We're the only ones who can," I said, my voice tremulous, my mouth trying to remember what it was like to make words instead of sobs.

Janete squinted her eyes, serious. "Your mother will be back any minute now."

Shaking my head, I said, "She should've been home by now. It's been hours."

Janete reached for me and moved a strand of hair out of my wet face.

"La Bardot said something about the Barra neighborhood," I considered.

"La Bardot? What a pretentious name," scoffed Janete. "I'm a dead ringer for Donna Summer, but I don't go around calling myself that."

"Can we go to the 13-DP?"

"The police station? Why would your mother go to that awful place?" asked Janete. With our bodies no longer entangled, I could feel a shift in the room. Janete was no longer a jailer but rather my accomplice.

"That's where La Bardot took her. Her new friends are not good people. They're using her. She's going to get hurt."

"You don't know that, Mara."

"Please, please? Can we go? See if she's there?"

I could see her thawing. She cared about my mother and wouldn't forgive herself if she failed to rescue her. I could tell she would help me, and without waiting another second, I flew out of the room, fast, fast, like a kite released to a breeze. "Mara!" Janete called out after me, and I turned back briefly to see her hand on her hip, a look of resigned frustration on her face. She was pretending she was against it, but I could tell her goal wasn't to stop me, but to slow me down. Because though my feet were tiny, maybe half the size of hers, they donned magic sandals that made me glide through concrete. I didn't look back again, just assumed Janete was behind me, as I ran, ran, ran toward my mother.

I had to save her. Who else would?

We ran most of the way, Janete trying to catch me, until we both tired and walked the remaining distance hand in hand. I imagined all sorts of scenarios over the twenty blocks we ran, with flashing lights and guns drawn. Instead, arriving across the street from the police station, we saw La Bardot pacing nervously back and forth. The man who was with her sat on a stoop, his hands squeezing his temples. I didn't think I'd seen him before. His shirt had a giant collar and was unbuttoned enough to reveal half his chest.

He had a red scarf around his neck. He kept his eyes lowered, so no one could see his face. As I approached, I could see La Bardot was wearing oversized aviator sunglasses and a yellow rubber belt with a giant round metal buckle. Her blond wig looked uneven, too clearly fake. If I could tell La Bardot was a fraud, wouldn't the Police Chief see through the entire plan?

"What're you doing here? You have to go home immediately," La Bardot hissed, swatting the air in front of me as though it would push me back the way we'd came. I noticed a trail of cigarette butts at her feet.

"Have you seen my mother?" I asked, without preamble.

La Bardot pointed to the police station. "She's still in there," she said tersely.

I looked over in that direction. A bus had stopped nearby, and a group of passengers came out of it and dispersed.

"She hasn't come out?" I asked.

La Bardot shook her head. She glanced at Janete, who stood behind me with her hands on my shoulders. To Janete, she said, "Take her back to her apartment. Now."

But I wasn't going to leave. "No. I want my mom."

La Bardot looked at me with a hint of fear on her face, as though she'd never been on the receiving end of a child's anger, and didn't know how upsetting it could be.

"She's fine," said La Bardot, tightening her shoulders. She turned to her accomplice, lowering her voice. "I don't know what's taking her so long. She was supposed to just leave if she wasn't able to convince him, and we'd regroup and come up with a new plan." She turned to the station. "They must be keeping her waiting or she's trying harder than she should, I don't know."

Janete sighed, and held me closer to her. She looked more worried than ever. But there was nothing we could do except wait.

Half an hour later, when it felt like the four of us could no longer contain ourselves, I saw Chief Lima finally emerge from the station, followed by my mother. This was momentous. Mom looked grim-faced, nothing less than devastated, her head down, her shoulders curved inward.

I immediately called out, "Mom!" but there were four lanes of traffic between us, my voice the buzz of an insect flying by. I watched as Lima opened the door of a police sedan and my mother got inside obediently. He got in after her, and another police officer got in from the other side, so that my mother was flanked by them in the back passenger seats. I couldn't see her very well, only the side of her face, the back of her head, and neither told me much. I wanted to see the expression in her eyes.

They drove, flickering away as fast as a mirage. I hoped they were on their way to Barra, that the plan had worked. But I felt no relief, and wouldn't until my mother came back, until I felt the soft creases of her palm in mine. But this was what she wanted, wasn't it? My mother who knew what she was doing. I just prayed that Lima wouldn't do anything rash once they arrived at their destination and he saw there were no rebels to catch. I thought about how large a man he was, and cringed at the idea of his explosive temper.

La Bardot watched their departure with as much nervousness and anticipation as myself. Without saying a word, she strode to the nearby pay phone.

She dialed. I didn't hear her say "Hello," only the words: "He's gone. It's all clear."

She strode back to us with an unconvincing grin and I felt Janete's grip on my shoulder tighten.

Moments later, a van turned the corner and noisily, its tires screeching, double-parked a couple of yards to the left of the police station. It was the van from the country safe house, but they had finished painting it, and it actually did look like a real police van, down to the smallest specifications, even "13th Precinct" stenciled on the side. Pacifier came out of the driver's side, wearing a brown, double-pocketed police uniform. I recognized his gait, the blunt way he slammed the door shut. Octopus came out on the other side. He had shaved his beard and cut off his hair, and looked almost unrecognizable in the police cap, uniform, and boots. Pacifier opened the back of the van and two more familiar men came out. They left the back doors open and, after exchanging a final set of looks, charged confidently into the station, Octopus leading them inside.

Then, something really strange happened. Lima's sedan reappeared.

He should've been heading toward the highway. But it looked like he had just circled the block. The police sedan double-parked a few meters behind the fake police van. I glanced at Janete, confused, but then saw La Bardot—ashen, her chin dropping.

"*Foda*," she muttered again and again.

No one came out of the police sedan. I could make out Lima's head through the window. My mother was blocked by the driver's body, and I wanted to call out for her again, but I knew she couldn't hear me.

Suddenly, traffic broke and La Bardot charged toward the station. Her legs cut like scissors through paper, and the soles of her shoes slapped the asphalt with impunity. I watched her go, then turned my attention to Lima and my mother still in the car, both not making a move. What were they doing there? Why were they back so soon?

La Bardot disappeared into the station. My heart raced, Janete pulling me closer. La Bardot's partner discreetly began to walk toward the van. I kept waiting for the police sedan to drive away, go where it was supposed to go, but it remained parked, with no one getting in and no one getting out.

Then, in a matter of seconds, I saw Octopus and his men emerge from the station, not in the confident manner they'd gone in, but rather, scattered, a hurriedness in their gait.

Bullets began to rain down on them.

Lima's massive arm stuck out of his passenger window, holding a gun. The same was true on the driver's side, as Lima's men fired shot after shot, far louder noises than I'd thought possible, hitting metal, concrete, flesh, and bone. I moved behind Janete, clutching her leg.

Octopus and his men tried to run for cover, but they were out in the open street exactly where Lima wanted them, stark easy targets in the daylight. A shot reached Pacifier, who immediately clutched his arm and then fell to the ground, as he tried to open the driver's door. I saw Octopus point his gun at Lima. A second later the glass in the windshield of the police sedan shattered. Another second later Octopus fell backward in a thud. La Bardot fired her gun at the police while running for cover, strangely graceful. I was dimly aware of pedestrians shrieking and running. Janete pulled me to the ground and dragged me behind a green Fiat.

"Stay with me," said Janete, her mouth right above my ear. "We are coming out of this with all the same body parts. I'm not going to let you get hurt, you understand?" She was panting.

There were no shots coming in our direction, but we could

hear them loudly, and it felt as though they were. I saw a woman a few meters away running, holding a child in her arms. She'd been pushing a stroller and left it behind, and for a moment I couldn't take my eyes off the stroller. It simply sat there right in the middle of traffic, waiting to be hit. Cars in the lanes next to us sped away from the scene, no rubberneckers here. A man walking toward us had been holding a sack and he dropped it on the ground as he also ducked behind a car. Oranges—heavy and plump—flew out of the sack and rolled on the ground, seeming to gain momentum.

Janete hissed a prayer: "Our Lady of Aparecida, protect us!"

The gunfire continued, and Janete eventually looked out through the window of the car we were hiding behind. She covered me with her body, keeping her hands and her arms over my head, a human shield. I carefully broke free and peered out the same window. I glanced in the direction of Lima's car, but I could not see my mother. I prayed she was crouched, keeping herself hidden from view, from the bullets. I saw Octopus on the ground, a bright red line on the road, pointing toward La Bardot, who lay only a meter or so away.

Lima and his men emerged from the car. The doors to the station burst open as a bunch of police officers joined him. To my shock, they kept shooting the bloody corpses in the streets, even though Octopus and La Bardot and the others were long past dead.

I saw my mother emerge slowly, tentative. I found myself gasping in relief, my heart beating fiercely in my throat. She looked changed—disheveled and confused with her hair different, too big. She stood, orienting herself. As Lima and the police officers trampled over the bodies to investigate the van, my mother wandered in the opposite direction. She didn't run, as though all she was capable of doing was taking one step after another, her body guiding her on instinct and reflex. I wished to scream for her, let her know I was here, let her pet my hair, let her tell me everything will be okay, hushing me with whispers. But there were too many officers, too many guns, and Janete's tight grip. She just kept walking, as though she could not see the horrible scene behind her. I followed her every step with my eyes, praying she'd move quicker, praying an officer wouldn't see her, gun her down. I was grateful for each step she took. On and on she went, as people around her screamed and ran, until she finally disappeared into the chaos of bodies on the horizon. I stumbled and fell, my gaze steadily focused on my mother, and Janete hurriedly pulled me upright. I screamed, "Mom!" but only half the word escaped my mouth before Janete clapped a hand over it, a grim, determined look on her face. She took my arm firmly in hers and pulled me forward on the sidewalk.

It was as though our legs carried us home without me realizing. All I could think of was my mother, the bodies in the street, how one could have been her. In the bus, in the streets, we must've bumped into people without apologizing, stumbled enough to worry the homeless. Did we talk? Did we say anything to each other? I just remembered Janete holding my hand, stroking my palm like my mother would.

We opened the door.

My mother was already there, sitting on the sofa, cupping her forehead with her hands. Crumpled-up tissue paper all around her. She looked up when she saw me, threw her arms akimbo, and I ran to her. I buried my head on her lap and cried, and she cried with me. She ran her fingers through my hair, caressed my wet cheeks with the back of her hand. Janete watched from the door.

"Where were you, Mara? Why weren't you here when I got back?"

"I've never seen something so awful in my life," said Janete. "Those young people. They were babies."

My mother turned sharply to her. "You took her there? Mara was there?" Janete backed away, shaking, and closed the door behind her.

A few feet away from the couch, I spotted a dead beetle on the floor. It didn't look like my mother had killed it; it just lay there, as if it had given up on its own. My mother didn't like insects and was especially merciless about killing flies, chasing them around with a plastic swatter, her shoulders moving up and down rhythmically like an ape. But my mother had a weakness for beetles, especially ladybugs, and when I once asked her why, she said it was because they were beautiful. When I was starting first grade, a ladybug once sat between the pages of a book I was reading. Surprised, I was about to slam the book shut on impulse, when my mother stopped me. She put her hand next to the red-carapaced insect and we both watched as it hopped onto her indicator finger. My mother then walked swiftly to the backyard as I ran behind her and she led her passenger to a leaf.

My mother lifted me so she could see me.

"We need to clean you up," she said. She was far dirtier than me, but I didn't question her. She brushed my tangled hair, wiped the tears off my face. I was covered in dust and soot, and dried sweat and panic.

My mother ran a bath for me, and she washed me in a way she hadn't since I'd been a baby. She took a scooper that I used to dig through sand at the beach and used it to pour water over my arms, my legs. She cleaned the back of my ears, the parts of my neck hidden by my hair, in between my fingers. She soaped and shampooed me last, and we watched as the water turned bubbly.

She dried me off and then led me to bed, though it was not evening yet. I did not protest bringing the day to an end. Then, she left to take her own bath. I was so scared of being alone, though, that I slipped out of bed in my pajamas and stood by the bathroom door, waited for her to be done.

What happened today? I wanted to ask her. What went wrong? Did Lima come back to the station for reasons she couldn't control? Did the Police Chief say something that made my mother go back on her word to Octopus? Did he see through her act? And why was she in the station for two and a half hours? And why had they let her go? Did he mean to?

As we lay in bed that night, my front glued to her back, I broke our unspoken pact to ignore the events of the day. "What happened?" I asked.

She did not turn to me. Staring out toward the window, she said, "He didn't believe me at all. The Police Chief. He didn't buy my performance. He saw through it right away." Her voice cracked. Nearly whispering, she said, "He beat me and tortured me until I told him the truth. I told him everything. I gave away their plans. I told him everything I wasn't supposed to. I resisted as long as I could, but eventually, he broke me."

I could feel her heaving back against my belly. I tried to breathe, the shock from her body rippling into mine. I closed my eyes, not sure how I would ever open them again. All those people who died, had died because of my mother.

Bel Air, California

The early 1990s

Mara, age twenty-six

chapter seven

BENEATH THE SOLID LAYERS OF ROUTINE LAY ANOTHER
one, rife with risk, hurt, and loss. It turned everyone into actuaries.
There weren't a lot of good reasons to be up at four in the morning. When Kathryn got in the car well before dawn to head to the
hospital for her surgery, I had the engine already running. Like a
getaway car. On the way, Kathryn swore that her heart had relo-
cated to her stomach. Said she could hear the thump thumping
from her abdomen, sadness, fear, and frustration welling up from
that landmass behind her belly button. She'd never noticed before
the way her belly rose and fell with each breath. She'd never noticed how her hand instinctively cradled her belly against shock or
disappointment.

Now, in its diseased condition, the belly, the preferred target
for the world's punches, took center stage. The fists of the world
liked a soft landing. Her new heart didn't want to be cut out
and disposed of—where would it go, her organ, once they separated it from her? Kathryn wondered aloud. But what choice was

there other than surgery, given the rapidly multiplying cancer cells breaking through the walls of the mucosa?

It was inside of her, the cancer, right in her belly, and the obvious symbolism didn't escape her. She'd given birth to it—the cancer had come out of *her*, her own cells, not some airborne virus or poison pushed down her throat. It was growing, growing, over the many months it took to move from its first battle in the stomach on to spread to the lymph nodes; unnoticed, giving no hints of its existence, silent even as it tirelessly colonized more territory.

I felt revulsion at the creature growing inside of her. In a few hours, the surgeon would remove it from her, but there was no true way to separate the victim from its killer—locked in an embrace— the good would have to be rid of with the bad.

When we reached the labyrinth of small roads abutting the complex, it was eerily quiet, no cars or people anywhere, the sky that odd hue of ascendant blue overpowered by traffic lights and lampposts. Moments like these made me think of that entire catalogue of incidents outside regular, planned life.

We valet-parked at the hospital, the massive gem financed by Ronald Reagan open and empty, miles of marble on the floor. The giant lobby echoed our footsteps, and there were no signs of human life until we arrived at the check-in room, and found twosomes everywhere—a few married couples, a father-and-daughter duo, sisters. A kind of Noah's Ark. One by one they were swallowed into curtained prep bays.

As Kathryn lay on the hospital bed, I sat on the chair next to her. Doctor after doctor stood at the foot of the railing introducing themselves. She shook some of their hands. She was told by the anesthesiologist fellow that she'd be getting an epidural—news that probably made her feel even more the parallels with child-birth, given the look of anguished irony on her face. The surgery chief resident reviewed her case—a partial gastrectomy, a D2 re-section due to gastric cancer. They were going to cut into her; take her stomach out and put only the clean part back. But even with surgery, her odds of survival were not good.

Watching Kathryn suffer made me wonder what was worse, being tortured or having cancer. Both changed the meaning of the body. No longer the purveyor of pleasure, but instead a battle-ground. Both dulled the spirit, and were the means to break down the afflicted. Both led to death, and when they didn't, their effects were long-lasting, leading to continued hardship. Both entailed prodigious amounts of pain, though they differed in the forms of dispensation. Both rendered the victim completely vulnerable, stopped her in her tracks, demanded and gained total submission. Both involved a clear enemy.

The torturers laughed at any private fantasies of autonomy. They chuckled in unison at the concept of self-reliance. As I waited next to Kathryn, I thought of all the men and women who'd been murdered by Chief Lima. They were all around us, surrounding us in the hospital bay—Octopus, La Bardot, even Pacifier—all of them regarding Kathryn with the same mix of pity and sorrow, accepting her as one of their own.

The ICU had the texture and consistency of a bad dream. We were in the tiny, curtained room for what felt like hours. There was loud and constant coughing, chatter, beeping. So much neediness clumped in such proximity.

Kathryn was a lump. Something a construction worker might've complained about carrying. She was the sum total of her weight, her self measured in pounds. In her loose hospital gown, with the buttons on the back, there were only faint traces of her normal self—her gestures, her book tented on her chest as she rested.

When dawn came, a tired-looking Filipino orderly came to transfer Kathryn to a private room on the sixth floor. He pulled her body toward the gurney like a slab of meat. The orderly struggled to roll her onto the gurney without breaking her free of her tubes and IV. He pushed her—as slowly and painstakingly like a janitor—down the empty hall and toward the bank of elevators.

"I wish things had turned out differently," said Kathryn, when she finally woke. She tried to slide up on the bed, but couldn't. She looked like the chalk police outline of her own body.

"You're up. How do you feel?" I asked, getting up from my chair.

She lay back again, closed her eyes. "Did Mr. Weatherly call?"

"No," I said.

Her eyes remained tightly shut, as though she were willfully trying to remain elsewhere. "I don't wish that he'd love me again, but that he had never stopped loving me in the first place," she continued, in her reverie.

The sunlight behind her made her look like overexposed film.

"I don't wish that we'd fix our relationship, but that it had never been broken in the first place," she repeated, slurring her words a bit, adjusting from the anesthesia. "So I could wake up in this hospital bed with my marriage still intact and the divorce was just a bad dream."

I couldn't imagine fighting cancer *and* a divorce. She remained calm, resolute even, as though she finally realized that this—compounding catastrophe—this was the reason you had to keep your life in order.

"I'm sure he'll come to visit you soon," I said, offering her some useless, rote optimism.

Kathryn looked at me unhappily.

Outside the window, we could see Bel Air from a distance. From that angle, it resembled a large arboretum. The stately houses looked tiny, swallowed up by the miles and miles of magnolia, eucalyptus, and sycamore trees.

"I wonder if . . . it's feeling like you threw away a flashlight just before the lights went out?"

"Yes," Kathryn nodded. "You phrased it so perfectly. That's something I admire, when someone knows what to say to make you feel understood."

"I have a lot of experience with that," I said, sitting back down and crossing my arms.

"Do you? When you're so young?"

"My mother . . . she had a lot of issues when I was growing up."

Kathryn reached for the plastic cup on the movable tray in front of her and took a sip of water. "So you had to take care of her?"

"Yes. You remind me of her, actually."

Kathryn set the cup down and batted her eyelashes. "Oh, so she's talented and beautiful and fun?"

"She's a little crazy."

"I see," said Kathryn. She didn't look offended. "So out of all your clients, I'm the one who inspires the most devotion, yes? Because I remind you of your nutty mother."

"Yes."

"Is she—is she in America, too?" asked Kathryn.

I shook my head and got up.

"She's in Brazil," I said, standing, gathering some trash that had accumulated on Kathryn's tray. "I had to leave her behind."

Kathryn furrowed her brows, but she didn't press.

"I'm sorry that . . ." she began, tentatively, "you're estranged. I'll bet it's been a while since you two talked on the phone." I knew she meant this kindly. She had a lot of painkillers in her body. "If you want, you can think of *me* as your mom. Even though I'm too young to be your mother." I looked down at her, withering away on the bed. She was and she wasn't. She was eighteen years older than me. "Actually, if I think of you as my daughter, it'd make it easier for me to leave you my house."

I shook my head, not wanting to indulge that strange kind of talk again. "You're very kind," I said. I slung my satchel over my arm and prepared to leave. "I'm going to take my break now that you're awake. You know you're supposed to press the red button for the nurse, right?"

Kathryn held up her palm as though to stop me. "I have a favor to ask. A mission of sorts. Cloak-and-dagger."

I didn't like the sound of this, but I let her go on. "I need you to go to Nelson's condo and get him to come visit me. Maybe convey the depths of my suffering. Try to appeal to his sense of compassion." I knew her better than that. What she really wanted was to confront him, to demand satisfaction, to find out why he hadn't come to visit her yet.

I mulled over her request as I stood by the curtain next to the door. "I'm just your caregiver. Don't you think this is something you ask a friend to do?"

"Yes, I agree. As a matter of fact, this is the sort of thing that I'd ask a daughter to do, if I had one," said Kathryn.

I pulled my car out of the parking spot as it started to rain. I waited for a couple of UCLA students whose backpacks looked like giant cancerous lumps. I turned onto the road and felt a slight bump against the back of my car. The bump, however, was so slight that I ignored it and kept driving. Much to my surprise, the car that bumped me was suddenly by my side, the driver gesturing wildly at me as though I was running away from the scene of a crime. I wasn't sure what he wanted me to do. I slowed down a little as I tried to figure it out. The car got in front of me and stopped, in the middle of the road. I braked as hard as I could, and I almost hit him from behind, missing his bumper by an inch. The man got out of his car, leaving his lights on, and within seconds was banging on my windshield.

My window was closed, but I could hear him yelling, "Don't you have eyes? You almost caused an accident back there."

"I'm sorry," I mouthed out of politeness. The doors were locked, but I tentatively cracked the window. Had I really almost caused an accident?

"Show me your insurance papers," he demanded, his eyes peeking through the slit of open window. He had a beard, his shirt stretched over his bulging belly, and he looked to be middle-aged but had none of the warmth and kindness I associated with American men. I could hear in his voice the cheap amusement of someone used to having power over powerless people. And I pictured him using it in a DMV, Social Security office, or airport Customs.

I didn't have insurance and there hadn't been an accident. Hadn't he been the one to hit *me*? I glanced at the rearview mirror and saw cars piling up in my lane, then some of them abruptly turning to the lane next to mine, their tires screeching in annoyance as they passed me.

"I don't have it with me," I said, rolling the window down just an inch more, a concession to his upper hand. Flecks of rain beat against my warming cheeks.

The man stood there not seeming to mind the rain, his outrage a fuel that made him insensate to the elements. I almost felt like he was enjoying himself.

"You don't have insurance, do you?" he asked in a manner somewhere between self-satisfaction and exasperation. "You're all the fucking same."

I felt a shiver of fear. The man looked at me like I didn't deserve the benefit of the doubt. I did not budge, did not speak.

He pounded my windshield a couple of times to accentuate his points. "I almost hit you. I would've if I didn't have excellent hand-eye coordination. And if I hit you, my insurance would've gone up and that is why people like you should not be on the roads. A woman, to boot."

The cars behind us were now honking loudly, and the few pedestrians out in the rain glanced curiously in our direction. The sky darkened as if controlled by this man's mood, our faces illuminated by the harsh beam of headlights from cars.

"Or you're taking this a bit far. Your car is fine," I heard myself saying. I wondered if I could get around his car and leave. Would he follow me? How much anger could one person contain?

"What's your name?" he asked, pressing his finger against the window. I wondered which part of my face his finger floated over from his vantage point.

"My name?" I echoed.

"I want your name," he demanded. His request dripped with ill will.

"Why?" I repeated.

He didn't answer, as though the reasons were obvious. But then he said angrily, as though he might enjoy the redundancy, "So I can report you to Immigration. So I can have you deported."

What did he consider a fair punishment for me cutting him off on the road?

I knew what he meant. An "illegal" couldn't apply for a driver's license, and technically, couldn't drive. But we did. We all did.

"My name is Lucille," I replied. "Lucille Ball." I closed my window all the way, taking back the inch I'd given him. I thought he might hit the windshield again with his fist, but he didn't. The rain started falling harder, and he no longer seemed immune to it. He shook his arms at motorists that honked at us.

"You will," he finally bellowed. "Starting tomorrow, you will have to give me your fucking name." I wasn't planning on ever seeing him again, until I realized that to him I wasn't an individual, wasn't Mara. I was a class of people, a second-class type of person, and he was going to run into me over and over again. With this promise of future retaliation enough to satisfy his present anger, he got back in his car and mercifully drove away. I made a U-turn and drove in the opposite direction, taking the long way back to Hollywood just to avoid finding myself on the road with the man again.

Tomorrow. With everything going on with Kathryn I had for-

gotten the election. He was probably one of the crazies just sali-
vating to vote yes on Prop. 187. He was just eager to do his civic
duty, to screen any brown person he deemed unworthy of sharing
his home.

I kept the radio off. I was too shaken to listen to music, my
heartbeat in rapid sync with the rain falling down around me.

Prolonged rain in Los Angeles was an anomaly, a hiccup. It was still
drizzling when I reached Nelson's new condo in Westwood across
from the federal cemetery. As I walked by, I wondered what it must
be like to look out onto the perfectly spaced crosses every day.

Shortly after letting me in, Mr. Weatherly asked me to call him
Nelson and handed me a tissue box. I dried my face. I suspected it
looked like I'd been crying. As I walked in, I realized I had made a
puddle with my things in his perfect home.

But to me the home was strange. The living room didn't have
much furniture, just a heavy leather club sofa facing a circular
glass coffee table. The space in front of it was empty, as if the
chairs had either left of their own accord, or never been invited
in. In the dining room, a long wooden table sat in isolation, with
no candelabras or tablecloths to spoil its barrenness. The wall behind it practically begged for a painting, empty and starkly white.
Further in, I could peek at a den, where it was clear Nelson was
spending most of his time.

"Are you still unpacking?" I asked.

"Yeah, a lot of my stuff is in those boxes," said Nelson, pointing
toward the stairway. Three large Public Storage boxes blocked the
landing. "So how is Kathryn?"

"The surgery was a successful one. She's wondering why you haven't come to see her," I said, suddenly feeling very agitated. As the rain worsened, I realized I was going to get really wet on the way back to my car. "Do you by any chance have an umbrella?"

"It's in one of the boxes," said Nelson. He was wearing sweatpants and a T-shirt with a hole on the shoulder instead of his usual white coat.

There was a crash of thunder and lightning.

"And of course I'm coming to visit her," he added quickly, saying it as though it were all one word. "I just don't want her to expect some kind of dramatic bedside reconciliation."

I twisted my face. "I don't think she expects that." I didn't mind lying for her. "She just wants you to cheer her up."

There was a pause and then Nelson said, with a mirth that seemed forced, "You should come in. Please come in." He led me into the living room. "At least until it stops raining. Do you want something to eat? I was just about to sit down for some pho."

I was about to say no, but he was already back in the kitchen and tending to a large pot. I'd been sitting all morning in Kathryn's room and hadn't had breakfast or lunch. This somehow felt unprofessional, but I pulled a chair at his dining table. He poured the soup into two bowls and dropped in some shiny, fragrant basil leaves. It looked very appetizing, the broth rich and aromatic.

While we ate, Nelson turned the conversation to Brazil. I didn't mind; it felt like comfortable ground, and at first, I liked talking about my country with him. As long as he didn't assume everyone did capoeira and sunbathed topless at the beach. To those people, I felt like retorting, Oh, you Americans with your musical theater and Thanksgiving turkey and Ben Franklin's *Almanack*! None of my friends or my mother's friends or anyone I knew thought much about the martial art of capoeira. No one practiced it, unless they had an interest in Afro-Brazilian traditions, and back in Brazil, I had been considered white. I'd only become Latina upon arriving in California, a fact that initially mystified me, as I'd never felt any kinship to the citizens of other Latin American countries, certainly no more than a German person shared an identity with a French or Italian national. In Brazil, I'd listened not to samba, but mostly to Debbie Harry and the Rolling Stones, and read books not by Paulo Coelho, but by Sidney Sheldon and Harold Robbins.

Nelson asked me, Why did you move to the U.S.? What was your childhood and adolescence like? I piled up the evasions and kept repeating, *The usual*. I didn't want to tell him about my experiences. What could I say to him? What would he like to hear? I kept my memories buried in the basement of my mind.

Nelson asked, "You weren't happy there? Did something bad happen?"

I replied, "Do you know anything about Brazil in the seventies and eighties?"

"You mean beyond Carnaval and favelas and the very colorful plumage of blue macaws? I do remember a Costa-Gavras movie," he said as he slurped some of his broth. "But I think it was set in Chile."

Most people stuck to the exotic, glossed over the dark history.

"There was also hyperinflation, and a military dictatorship put into place by your Lyndon Johnson and a man named Robert Mc-Namara," I said matter-of-factly. "There was a lot of violence."

"Hopefully your family was protected from all that?"

I shook my head no, without saying anything more. Nelson looked at me sidelong, seemingly reluctant to pursue that line of questioning further. "Isn't it incredible, how much you can fit into one life?" he mused.

"What I went through wasn't really that extraordinary," I said, finding his interest intrusive rather than flattering. "Considering where I come from."

"How old did you say you were when you came to the U.S.?" he asked, oblivious to my reticence.

"I didn't say. But I was sixteen." I could see his brow furrow as he gathered the puzzle pieces.

"Are your parents in California, also?"

"No. What about you? Are your parents in California?"

Nelson shook his head and took a sip of his water. "They're in Missouri. I went to a boys' prep school there. Studied Latin. Played lacrosse. That's what I was doing when I was sixteen, while you were fleeing heaven knows what atrocity."

The pho, once steaming, had grown cold. I stirred the lone bean sprout left with my spoon just so I had something to do with my hand.

"Are you worried about what kind of person is taking care of your ex-wife?"

"No, not at all," said Nelson, taken aback. "I think she's in great hands. But sometimes I think of all the things that can happen to a person and you multiply that by the number of people in the planet and it amazes me. How can the world fit so much?"

I broke eye contact. I put my spoon down on the table and noticed that the rain had stopped.

"Thank you for the soup. It was really good," I said.

"I'm glad you enjoyed it," Nelson said, smiling kindly. "This was a nice change from eating alone."

His smile lingered in me while I headed to my car, and I thought to myself that I should avoid seeing Nelson again.

When I got back home later that day, I again helped Bruno circumvent the laws of the land.

Since moving in together, I'd grown close to my roommates, and I even started enjoying Bruno's company. Some nights, Renata brought home leftover appetizers and side dishes from the restaurant, and we'd have an impromptu pig-out party, eating off the aluminum trays she'd packed the food in. We'd pass them back and forth as we sat on the sofa, watching Renata's soap operas. She had a cousin in São Paulo who recorded them and sent them to her assiduously, although her cousin had trouble remembering to set her VCR to NTSC, and the recordings trembled and shifted.

"Renata, you have to make sure to vote tomorrow," I said when the tape went to commercial.

"I don't know if I'll have time to vote," said Renata. "And it's not like my vote is gonna make a difference."

"What if the racist proposition passes?" I asked her, ready to deploy guilt as a tool. "What if one vote makes a difference?"

"Maybe it wouldn't be such a bad thing if Prop. 187 passes," said Bruno, toying with a video recorder. "We have too many illegals in California. You're gonna bankrupt the whole state."

I couldn't believe what I was hearing. "But Bruno, you're illegal, too."

"Hold your horses," said Bruno, joking around. "Illegal no, undocumented yes. I didn't come here riding through the desert on a coyote. I landed in LAX on a plane, and I was wearing Ray-Bans. Yes, I overstayed my guest visa, but when I came, I came legally."

"Makes no difference to the folks in Orange County," I said, shaking my head.

"Look, I don't go to the county hospital, I don't have kids at public schools. I'm not a drain," said Bruno, leaning forward on the sofa so he could speak directly to me. "I came here to find success. I didn't come here for the free stuff."

I thought of the Brazilian couple who had come to buy my old mattress a month ago when I was moving to Renata's apartment. After they hauled away the queen-sized mattress, they came back and started pointing at random objects, asking if they could have them as a sort of free gift with purchase. They pointed at an extension cord, a trash can, a set of dishes I'd just acquired from Goodwill, all with rapaciousness or fear.

I wanted to find a sharp pointed retort to Bruno's flawed thinking, but I was shocked to realize I had none. I was an immigrant. But how can a person be illegal?

"Your vote counts for sure, Renata," I said, but more quietly and less self-assuredly.

Bruno shrugged. "If Californians pass Prop. 187, I'll just move to New York."

"That's not how deportation works, Bruno."

Renata turned to me. "Worse comes to worst, you can always marry for a Green Card."

I wouldn't marry someone for a Green Card like she had, but I did spend much of my time thinking about ways of getting one. I applied to the diversity lottery every year, and I prayed that Brazil remained on a list of countries underrepresented in the U.S. During my first seven years in America, I'd paid a lawyer to apply for the lottery, until I found out that all I had to do was type up a form and send it to the right address, double-checking the zip code since each region went to a different one. The biggest disappointment in my life each year was receiving a Green Card diversity program denial notification.

"You all can feel however you want, but this proposition scares me," I said. "What happens if it passes? It would be horrible. Are they going to start by plucking Mexican kids out of the schools?" I thought about the earlier incident in the parking lot, of that driver's thick, crossed arms, of his rage. "Civilians will just start policing everyone."

Bruno grew more contemplative, and said, with doubt in his voice, "I should've gone to Portugal instead. At least I speak the language." This was one of Bruno's pet peeves, the fact that people often mistook his poor language ability for low intelligence. Of all three of us, his English was the weakest.

"I have an idea," said Renata, turning to me. "If the proposition passes you can go to Bel Air and seek asylum with your employer."

I smiled at Renata. "She's got bigger things to worry about than the legal status of her caregiver."

Renata reached into her purse. She produced an envelope from Pacific Bell with the plastic window prominently torn up. "Look at this phone bill." Renata turned to me accusingly. "I get that you love your mother, but do you really have to call that often? Can't she read? Can you send her letters instead once in a while?"

"I'll pay for my part," I said, grabbing the bill from her.

"Okay, Miss Rockefeller," Bruno said. "If you're so rich, maybe you should pay a higher share of the rent."

"I hate figuring out shares," said Renata. "Reminds me that I'm terrible at math."

"I'll figure it out for you," I said, glancing at the amount. It was indeed very high.

Renata had dated a string of Brazilian men who invariably went back and I wondered if she'd thought of going back with one of them. I found a telltale sign in her desire to give a Brazilian name to her future child.

I didn't regret immigrating to America. The last ten years had been lonely, but I'd gotten used to it. When I first arrived, I was so intoxicated by the promise of a new life that I didn't notice how unhappy I was. There were too many new things to take in, new people, new places. A visit to the beach felt like a trip to the moon.

"Everything is so expensive," I said. "I don't regret moving here. Although I don't know where I'd go if they start deporting us."

"Back home, to Brazil, of course," said Renata, switching her tray of caramelized plantains for my tray of French fries made of yucca. Bruno double-dipped so much into his tray of bean stew that we simply let him have it.

"No, not Brazil," I said quietly. I didn't add anymore. With everything that had happened to us in the years after Lima, I couldn't. Wouldn't.

"No I couldn't, either," Bruno said, uncharacteristically contemplative. "I like driving at night knowing I won't get held up by guys at the red light."

Renata ignored Bruno and glanced at me suspiciously. "Go

back to Brazil. You make it sound like it's not an option. You still have family there."

"You know going back isn't as easy as clicking your red slippers together, right?" I said. "Nothing would ever be the same after so much time away."

Renata handed Bruno her tray of yucca.

"Okay, Mara. I'm going to compromise," said Renata. "I won't vote for sure, but I'll try to."

I smiled at her, happy for a partial victory.

"I've never voted before. I don't think it's for me," she added. "I think it's for old white people. The right to vote."

"You might like it. You might like it so much you do it twice," I said jokingly.

During the days after the surgery, Kathryn liked to sleep in. I forgot she lived there as I cleaned her lonely house in the mornings. The house became the body whose well-being I was responsible for; the body I wiped, bathed, and rearranged; the body I had to return to a Platonic ideal, the version unspoiled by human touch. The house, I remembered even as I tried daily to push the thought from memory, that Kathryn had said would be mine.

I also began to notice little things that had escaped my attention before. Like all the lemon and avocado trees in the backyard. Or the fact that there were hornets' nests outside many of the windows. Once, a raccoon crossed my path and made me jumpy. There were wildflowers growing next to camellias and a single red rose I'd nicknamed Bloody Mary. Bees, beetles, spiders, fireflies, and ladybugs were abundant. All of them—they could all be mine.

Hear this silence, Kathryn liked to say, whenever I brought her breakfast or helped her walk to the backyard. No sounds of lawn-mowers, voices, music. Even the knives clopped in a muted manner. The water boiled while holding its breath.

I didn't like silence. Back home, I'd cook and hear Janete cack-ling on the phone, turning her conversations into performance art. There were mothers calling out to their children on the street; warnings needed to be given, heeded, ignored. When music came on, I could never tell where it came from. Even at night the symphony continued—sirens, couples arguing, the elaborate jingle announcing the start of the news shows. The noisy stretches and yawns my mother performed before going to bed.

Visitors came bearing flowers for Kathryn for many days. Being ill turned the sick person into a celebrity of sorts. Those around her wanted news, gave her attention. The sick inspire devotion, curiosity. She drew people's thoughts like a magnet, in a manner and a fashion she never could've while healthy. There was a dyad: the sick person awakened the healthy person's desire to care, in the same way that a famous person awakened a regular person's longing for fantasy. Something primal. They came for a few minutes, or sometimes they stayed for hours, and I listened as Kathryn received them all in her bedroom, drinking hibiscus tea with them, exchanging pleasantries, Kathryn subtly apologizing for reminding them of their own mortality.

In the downtime between making and serving meals, I sat by myself in the kitchen, or took a walk in the backyard. I had never known such stillness in my body. I felt as though the house had swallowed me in its vastness. Would she really be insane enough to leave it to me after she died? Yes, I took care of her and ran the

occasional errand for her and had grown fond of her, genuinely
concerned about her well-being. I had committed. But I was not a
relative, nor an old friend, nor a lover. When I wandered through
the house, my body didn't radiate possession the way Kathryn, or
even Nelson, did.

And why was it a given that I'd be happy in that house? Even
now, I thought I would enjoy being the de facto owner of a big
house in Bel Air, but instead I just felt the echoes of a giant vat
of loneliness. I didn't welcome it, this loneliness. I didn't want to
surrender to its potent oxidation. I wished I could bring Renata
and Bruno over. I wished I could hear familiar voices having muf-
fled conversations in the room next door, bells ringing far away,
squeals of soccer-playing children, gossipy neighbors exchanging
greetings across the street, the plaintive sounds of plumbing and
flooring that old houses made, that even my cheap rent-controlled
apartment in Hollywood made. But Kathryn. How could she stand
to live in such gated and guarded silence? Why were Americans
so accepting of aloneness, with its ever-tightening knots and vises?

Sometimes when I looked at her, I would see traces of my
mother's face. In the slant of her nose; in the way she half closed
her eyes when laughing.

If only I hadn't ruined things, hadn't gotten involved in the
mess. I wouldn't have had to flee, and I'd be next to Ana right at
that moment. She'd hug me and kiss me. Instead, I had Kathryn.

Kathryn wasn't dying; she was *most likely* dying, and therein
was the difference. Some days I looked at her with sorrow and
some days I wondered why all the fuss, she was going to be fine
after all. This liminality, this in-between-ness, sometimes made
me feel I was taking care of two Kathryns, one that was dying and

one that seemed well. Why am I in this house, awaiting an epiphany from her illness? I noticed how her sweaty hair lingered on her forehead just like my mother's, and felt a similar compassion for them.

Was life a train with tracks already built, or a bird that flew this way and that way into a friendly horizon?

Ana, too, had suffered, but I still felt an unwanted tinge of bitterness laced with poison in the love I felt for her.

I just couldn't forgive her for what she'd done to me.

Rio de Janeiro, Brazil

The early 1980s

Mara, age sixteen

chapter eight

PEOPLE ALWAYS WANT TO HEAR WHAT THEY BELIEVE TO be true. Whenever a tourist asked me what it was like to live in Copacabana, I knew they wanted to hear some exotic, accented tale, flavored with tropical colors. A map of the New World's spices, a star next to the treasures of the undiscovered land. They wanted to hear of beaches where the sand was so fine, it glistened like the shavings off diamonds. Of water so cool, the sun felt like a friend. Bubbly and brown, like an ocean of milkshake. A place where you could hear the squeals of children nearby, and you knew it was the happiest they'd ever been. Where couples traded intimacies, and everyone was in a good mood. Where everyone was kind to one another. No one wept. Where you plucked giant avocados and papayas the size of fists off the groves. Paradise. Where red-tailed carps swam in dark green ponds and dusky-legged guans sliced through the sky while slaty-breasted rails sang. Where the moss-covered hills sparkled with the sun's lazy peach-colored glow. Where the lake water shone brightly rippled, carved into perfectly symmetrical servings. Where the beaches turned the city into a dream, like a magic trick.

All that was really true. But also, on the sands I often found trash—empty coconuts and bottles of Brahma beer. Cigarette butts. Perforated blister packs. Foam clamshells with leftover food. An upside-down map of the world. All the vices of the citizenry, catalogued and tabulated.

On the streets of Copacabana: a free-for-all accommodating buses, pedestrians, and poorly parked vehicles jutting out onto the road. There was no space between anything or anyone—if a taxi driver reached his hand out, he could graze a side-view mirror, or the back of a cyclist squeezing by the cars. In one corner, at a construction site, a building stood half finished, surrounded by scaffolding on all sides, unable to stand on its own without it. Workers without helmets stood precariously on top of metal bars, taking equipment from harnessed colleagues in bosuns' chairs, a kind of baton relay. Everywhere, buildings that had been erected a century earlier, by wealthy coffee barons and governments with bellies full of coffee baron money. There were exquisite churches, cathedrals, and hotels, columned and buttressed and gargoyled, made of soapstone, marble, and crystals imported from Italy, Portugal, and Spain. Along the boulevards, large trees provided bountiful shade, canopied umbrellas relieving the street merchants and beggars from the otherwise unrelenting heat. Boys with surfboards and girls in roller skates whizzed past kiosk attendants, office workers, parents carrying children on their shoulders.

Shortly after my sixteenth birthday, my mother and I moved to Rua Vinícius de Moraes, number 502, a unit that seemed like a bargain at the time. We could walk to the beach or the Copacabana Palace, where the nightly charge for a suite cost the same as our rent for a year. The apartment seemed promising until we realized that the roof above us happened to be the favored escape route for thieves who'd just pillaged the drugstore on the first floor. We often woke to the sound of footsteps, followed by the back-and-forth of policemen caucusing.

Sometimes there was gunfire. Once, a perspiring police officer on the fire escape asked, through the bars of my mother's bedroom window, if he could come in and use our restroom. My mother said no. The police always lingered, and we began to resent them more than the thieves.

We debated moving, until, that is, my mother's health began to decline. She could not sleep, her unrelenting coughing jolting her awake. The cause of her disease, a doctor explained to us, was her smoking. A serious heart condition.

My mother had been a heavy smoker all her life, but the cause and effect did not follow. Everyone knew smoking was a benign activity. Not only that, but a glamorous, sophisticated activity. Everyone we knew smoked—neighbors, friends, strangers, characters on television. Every restaurant table and bar countertop included an ashtray. The streets were littered with the familiar sight of cigarette stubs. Smoking made me look forward to becoming an adult. We couldn't fathom that my mother's completely normal and unremarkable habit had led to this disease, but it confirmed, in a sad way, the inevitability of my mother's specialness. Everyone lit up with no consequences to their health, but she, she alone was chosen to suffer for it.

So every day I asked her, "Did you sleep last night?"

I asked this question the same way some daughters asked their mothers if they'd had coffee that morning. I asked this question hoping to hear, "Yes, I did," but that answer never came. She never slept for more than a few hours. She sat in the living room in the dark, with her unrelenting coughing. The forcible night watch of the sick. She told me that a mad clock sat lodged in her chest, going too fast or skipping beats, and all the things I took for granted—even breathing and lying down—were uncomfortable to her.

I'd always adored my mother, but since her illness, my heart grew with the strange love that fills one's heart when one gives, gives, and receives little in return. I reacted to every grunt or look or sound that came out of my sick charge, looking for signs of either pain or peace, the line so blurry. It was easy to love a person who depended on you for food and drink, a person who'd had all her normal prerogatives removed from her. I began to wonder if love was just a refined form of compassion, the heart's choice, for whatever reason, to devote itself to another being. There was nothing more pure than the love of a caregiver for a patient. She did not have to earn it, did not have to be charming or alluring. She just had to need. This was the irony, I decided, that though humans were wired toward selfishness in their everyday lives, given the opportunity, a person could give another everything, and that all of us were just waiting for the chance to do that. To love, to give, and to surrender the best parts of ourselves to someone else.

Our only respite from worry was the movies we watched together at night. My mother had once dubbed a drama directed by François Truffaut and become a fan. After she introduced me to his work, it turned out we both liked the same ones— *Jules et Jim*, *Day for Night*—and disliked the exact same ones— *La Peau Douce*, *Baisers Volés*. My mother impressed me by singing along with Jeanne Moreau the lyrics to "Le Tourbillon de la Vie." There was a time she wanted to be Jeanne Moreau. Most girls wanted to be Audrey Hepburn, I noted, or Marilyn Monroe.

"No." She shook her head. "Only anorexic girls wanted to be Audrey, and only overweight girls wanted to be Marilyn." I knew she wanted to specifically be the Jeanne Moreau of *Jules et Jim*, just like the Audrey Hepburn girls wanted to be her in *Breakfast at Tiffany's*.

"But," I replied, "they want to be her only in that scene—in the early morning when she's standing in front of the store wearing Givenchy and dark glasses. Not the scenes where she's talking to Mickey Rooney doing a yellowface impersonation of a Japanese man."

"If that is true, then," my mother retorted, "I want to be the Jeanne Moreau wearing a mustache and boys' clothes running across the bridge with Oskar Werner and Henri Serre chasing me."

I agreed. "I think women are at their most beautiful when they're running, don't you think?"

The only thing that would help my mother was a heart transplant, and since we couldn't pay up front, we were on the waiting lists of several hospitals. I called them every month, to check on the status of her application, but apparently there were a lot of other sick people ahead of her, and it felt like her turn would never come. Sometimes her chest pains grew so intense that she could barely stand. She seemed to shrink, and sometimes coming home from school, I'd have to look twice at the couch until I saw her form lying there, napping.

So we waited. We stayed put.

Because of my mother's condition, I did not believe her at first when she told me about the phone calls.

I thought perhaps her weak heart was affecting her sanity. Perhaps the pain in her body made her read too much into mere prank calls. She claimed they came during the day, when I was at school. By the time I got home, I'd find my mother shaken and enervated. She couldn't tell me who it was, or what the content of those calls was; only that she was being terrorized.

How so? I asked her, and she couldn't answer.

Was it a stranger or was it someone who knew her? She would not elaborate.

Unsure of what to do, I told my mother to stop answering the phone altogether. If the call was important, like a cardiologist or a friend, the person would call back during dinner, and I would be home then. But my mother claimed to be incapable of not picking up the phone.

"I didn't feel like I could," she said, in an agonized tone, her words shivery and tremulous. "I didn't feel like I had the right to."

I mulled over the words. I leaned over her and massaged her bare arms. Her long hair tangled, split ends and middles. My mother the actress, so talented and larger than life—I hated to see her like that.

"You sure you don't know who it is?" I asked.

"I don't know," she mumbled toward the window.

She was so hushed these days, a diluted version of my mother. It often felt as though I wasn't talking to my mother, but rather, to her disease.

"Was it a prank call?"

"I don't know," said the plaque in her coronary artery. "It was a man. He wouldn't say his name."

The way she wouldn't meet my eyes told me that my mother could guess who this man was.

"I swear I didn't ask for this," the ugly, waxy, yellow substance continued. "I am innocent." Panic gathered in her charred throat.

"He's not going to call again, and if he does, just hang up," I said.

My mother did not say anything. She had a "tell" when she lied or became evasive. Her lips opened slightly, as if she owed the other performer the next line, but couldn't recall it. The actor's nightmare. I looked into her eyes and found them oddly masked. She looked up to the ceiling as if there were a door there, waiting for her to open it. I wanted her to, and I wanted to follow her, walking upward.

At school, I couldn't concentrate. I ignored my teachers and friends, and responded only halfheartedly. I was a machine that shut itself off without warning. In line at the INPS office, to pick up my mother's disability check, I gave strangers vicious stares, as if the man next to me was the one calling my mother. I found laughter suspicious. Large gestures, too. Any expression of mirth registered as an affront.

I wished Janete were still around to help. She'd moved back to the Northeast a year ago to take care of her sick father. I was old enough to understand the rules of parents and children by then. If a person brings you into the world, the least you can do in return is help them when they're ready to leave this world. I knew Janete was leaving behind her dreams and desires and joys, but sometimes there are things even bigger than that.

My mother and Janete's goodbye was awkward and protracted, and took place over the course of several days. Janete gave my mother her phone number and address in the Northeast, but as far as I knew, my mother never called her. I suspected my mother put her in the same compartment as my father, someone who existed only in the iceberg of memory. One night, we were watching the news and heard of a new deadly disease called AIDS. The newscaster informed us that it could be transmitted through kissing and mosquitoes, and it had been developed in a lab in America as a weapon to attack their enemies. My mother said casually, "Janete needs to be careful," and left it at that.

At home I tried to extract information from my mother. She returned my inquiries with ellipses or monosyllables. If I didn't know any better, I would think she'd regressed to a stage prelanguage. Her eyes kept drilling a hole in the same space in the ceiling.

I'd ask her useless questions: What did he say to you? What did he sound like?

She continued to drill into the ceiling, with mounting sorrow.

After a few months of unrelenting phone calls, my mother finally thought she had unmasked the identity of the mysterious caller. She was half lying, half sitting on the sofa, her body sprawled, as if she'd fainted and had no time to rearrange her limbs. She wore only a bathrobe, and I could see her frail thighs peeking from under the cotton.

"Lima," she said. "I think it's Chief Lima," my mother said, her eyes full of red, her expression darkened and fragile.

Police Chief Lima. For a long time, he'd been the third member of our family. The one who haunted our dreams, colonized our silences.

"It's him. I know it's him," she said, shaking her head in disgust. "He doesn't say anything, and he doesn't say it's him, but I know it's him."

"Are you sure?" I couldn't believe that these many years later, almost a full decade, he'd dare contact my mother. His ilk no longer had power. Police Chief Lima himself had retired and disappeared from public life. It turned my insides to know that he might be directing his attention to my mother.

"I can't explain, I just know it." Agony wrenched her eyes shut. "I know this makes me sound crazy, but I recognize his breathing."

I shook my head, disturbed. "Why would he call you? And how did he get our phone number?" The question sounded stupid the second it came out of my mouth. Our number could be easily found in any phone directory. There were only so many Ana Alencars in Rio de Janeiro.

"I don't know," my mother said, shaking her head. "I don't want to know. But it's him. It's really him."

I didn't want to press any further as to how she could be so sure. "Don't answer the phone," I said, retying and straightening her bathrobe. "Starting tomorrow."

"If I thought it wasn't him, I could ignore it. But because I know it's him, I feel like I have to. I don't know how to explain."

I leaned closer and buried my head in her hair, pressing my lips against her scalp. I held her the way I'd hold a baby, soft and lovable. I always thought our lives were good. Hard, but good. We were happy, she and I. I marveled at how inaccurate our lives suddenly seemed. I was grateful that she couldn't see the tears budding in my eyes. Her ears felt cold against the back of my hand. I squeezed her harder; I wanted so much to protect her.

"Then get out of the house," I whispered, quickly wiping my own drops away. "Stay downstairs at the *lanchonete* while I'm at school, or go to a neighbor's house, have a cup of coffee with someone."

My mother sighed and shook her head. "I don't have the energy, Mara. I want to stay home. Please let me stay home and rest."

I pulled away and saw how completely spent she looked, her skin like a wafer about to crack.

"I'm not going to go to school tomorrow," I told her firmly. "I'm going to stay home. I want to hear these phone calls myself."

When the military took over, my mother was about my age, and everyone had been sure it was only for a few months. After that, the generals would leave, and we'd get to choose a president again. When we all went home that first day, to cook our dinners, water our plants, watch our soaps—no one thought, Oh boy, we are *screwed*; run for the hills. We slept peacefully at night; we picked fights with our lovers; we died of boredom. Some of us were even glad Goulart was gone—he was so weak, wasn't he? And wasn't he a socialist, deep down?

No one knew they were going to stick around for two decades and kill and torture more than a thousand citizens. Drowning, burning, suffocating, hanging.

When the dictatorship finally ended, my mother tasted a spoon-ful of fame. She was interviewed by the Catholic diocese of São Paulo for a book they were writing about what was now termed the "years of gunpowder." The book consisted mostly of firsthand accounts from victims and survivors. My mother's story, like the others, was told semi-anonymously, and she was identified only by her name, and her age at the time she was tortured: Ana, 24.

I'd heard over the years of the clashes between the student guer-rillas and the police. Violent protests with Molotov cocktails and cars set on fire. Metallurgical strikes organized by the students. But I wasn't really a revolutionary. I got involved by chance. I came into the police station on the morning of March 12 as part of an undercover action by the student activist group Revolutionary Popular Movement. Someone must've tipped off the chief of police because he told me that he knew who I really was and why I was really there. He demanded to know what the plan was. I refused to say anything. He took me to a soundproofed alcove in the back of the police station, and had me take my clothes off. From the ceiling, cold jets of air kept streaming in. My ears nearly bled from the sounds bursting from the speakers: an airplane turbine, a factory siren, bombs exploding. And then suddenly, silence. And then noise again. The walls started shaking, slammed by hammers and timber blocks. The air felt like sandpaper against my throat. The ventilation was turned off, and oxygen suddenly became scarce. The room remained bright at all times, like the inside of a lamp bulb. He put me in the dragon's chair, made of corrugated iron, cold and harsh. He held me down with straps covered in foam and inserted clasps on my breasts, fingers, thighs.

The chair had wooden slats that held my legs and feet back, and when he pressed a button, the shock made my body lurch violently forward while my legs spasmed, feeling like my body was splitting in half. I could tell he was enjoying this at a personal level. He wouldn't take his eyes off me and this went on and on. He was pure evil, no compassion whatsoever. At one point the phone rang, and it must've been his wife, because I heard him tell her what he wanted for dinner. Chicken with French fries. To this day, I throw up if I see someone eating that. My hands still sometimes shake for no reason. I have to turn around and leave instead of going into a room populated only by men. I can't stand ceiling fans, because there was one in that alcove. The memory still makes me scream at night.

Her story only took up half a page. This was how I learned the details of that day.

Around the time the book came out, eight years after the shootout at the police station, the government offered amnesty to both sides of the struggle—to the members of the military and police, and to the guerrilla groups and activists. My mother, along with other survivors, was invited to join a protest and walk in the front row alongside the TV actresses Lucélia Santos and Christiane Torloni. My mother reported that they were both really pretty in real life, though one of them sweated a bit too much. She was also invited to fancy lunches in ballrooms, where she told her story to rich ladies, and somber panels in front of journalists and politicians. At a party afterward, the singer Chico Buarque told her he'd write a song about her, though he never did. In front of those people, my mother smiled and put on a brave face, but when she got home, she invariably locked herself in the bathroom and cried while she bathed.

I suppose it had been traumatic to me, too, witnessing what I did when I was only eight, but I didn't spend much time thinking about it, being distracted by helping my mother. She never asked me how that day had affected me, and she never encouraged me to talk about it. It was as though what happened belonged only to her.

I sat by the phone and waited for it to ring. I stared at it for so long, I could see it with my eyes closed: the scratches on its round receiver, the rotary numbers printed in elaborate serif, its gray-blue color. Nerves hissed up and down my spine, as if a snake slithered underneath my clothes. My mother paced a few feet away.

Finally, the phone rang: an alarm warning us to leave the room, its trill persistent and shrill. Once, twice, the phone vibrated its brass sprockets. I rested my hand over the receiver, wrapping my fingers over its lustrous handle.

My mother also put her hand over the receiver, and then slowly brought it up. Our foreheads touching slightly, like those of Siamese twins. I directed the mouthpiece closer to her lips.

"Hello?" she asked.

Both of us grew tense with expectation. Her eyelids fluttered. The person on the other end of the line breathed heavily, in and out. We listened to his breathing and he listened to ours. We had agreed ahead of time that we had to make him talk.

"Hello?" she repeated, unable to hide the shakiness in her voice. "If you don't speak, I'm going to hang up." I gave her a nod of encouragement and she added, "I know who you are."

What a good actress my mother had been when I was a child, leaving no trace of our rehearsals.

Still, the person did not speak. We listened to his intakes of breath. It wasn't the heavy, masturbatory panting of an obscene caller. It was the wheeze of someone trapped.

"All right, then," my mother continued, adding to the bluff.

"Wait," he panted breathlessly now. "Don't hang up."

His voice startled both of us. This monster had human form.

"After all you've done, the least you could do was leave me alone," my mother said, her eyes widening. She put a hand to her mouth to silence a gasp. I could tell she recognized him for sure now. We were standing so close to each other I could practically feel the vibrations on her skin, the growing dampness on her forehead.

"I should, but . . ." He hesitated, as though it was as hard for him to speak as it was for us to listen. "I want to know if you still remember me." As I listened in, I tried to memorize his intonation, and listen for any distinct sounds in the background, like a train or traffic.

"I wish I didn't." She was looking at me when she spoke, and to an observer, it would look as though she were saying that to me.

"We didn't spend much time together, but it was very meaningful to me," he said, sounding sad.

My mother's fingers began to shake a little. "You have to stop calling me. I don't want to hear from you." She closed her eyes, and seemed to forget that I was there. "You should go back to the pits of hell where you belong."

I looked at her, saddened. It had been almost ten years, but it could've been yesterday. This man had suddenly cracked her open, and so much pain spilled out, without end, her face glistening.

"You don't have to feel the way others tell you to feel," he said. He sounded like an old man, but not infirm. I could picture him, sitting amidst luxury in a quiet study. "Don't pretend you weren't the most alive you'd ever felt. Don't pretend that it wasn't both awful *and* thrilling."

He spoke barely above a whisper without disguising his voice. I desperately tried to match his voice to my memory of Lima at the station when I was eight, but I couldn't really remember. When I thought of him, he was pure image, all muscular bulk, no sounds.

"I really don't understand what you think you're accomplishing by calling me. I don't understand what you want from me," said my mother, wiping her tears away.

"I felt like we spoke the same language. I felt a connection with you," he said. "It's led to a lifelong attachment." He said this as though he were admitting something vile.

"No!" she suddenly yelled, and immediately had to recover from the effort. "I'm going to tell the police."

"Tell them what? They worked under me for years; they venerate me." An admission. He sounded different when he said this; indignant or impugned.

"I'm not afraid of you. Do you hear me? There's nothing you can do to me."

"That's not entirely true, though, is it?" he asked, calmly.

My mother exhaled a breath of fire and yanked the phone away from me. "I'm going to call the papers tomorrow. I'm going to remind them what you've done to all of us!"

I stared at my mother, a bit taken aback by her bravery. I'd never expected her to confront him so directly. She moved the phone away so I could no longer hear. Whatever his reply was, it made my mother's face contort in anger. I worried for her heart; I wanted her to hang up. He continued talking, and my mother listened, still taking him in. I didn't understand why. She gritted her teeth, crying, nearing an explosion. I glanced at the lever I could press to end the call.

Finally, my mother took the receiver and slammed it on the base.

We stood still for a moment without exchanging any words. The relief was so big it had to find a place to land.

"Maybe he won't call again," my mother said, "now that he knows what I'm capable of doing." Our eyes met, and then she collapsed into a coughing fit.

She slumped on the couch behind her, utterly spent, and I tried to imagine the effort that it had taken to go through that conversation. As much as she tried to bury those memories, they probably came back every time she walked onto an unfamiliar street at night; every time a man bumped into her too aggressively; the shock of static; every time she sensed a presence behind her, just out of view.

"He won't stop unless we make him do so," I replied.

It wasn't very hard for me to find where he lived.

I had spent my share of hours after school handling foxed pages in basement archives. I'd held a part-time job at the municipal library, where I had often been the only person wandering through the ghost-filled aisles of obscure sections. At microfiche stands, I handled the levers and knobs like a seasoned machinist. I had a precocious gift for skimming. A librarian had once told me that any piece of information a scholar wanted had been written down somewhere: a census poll, a deed of purchase. It just took knowing where to look.

At the municipal records room, I told the clerk I was doing a report on real estate owned by the military police for my geography teacher. I asked for the indexed records of the state revenue collector's registry. After perusing for hours through the carbon copies he gave me, I eventually learned that Police Chief José Mello de Lima paid property taxes on a house on Avenue Marshal Mascarenhas de Moraes, right here in Copacabana.

The discovery of his proximity was both thrilling and unnerving.

That night, I lay in bed awake listening to my exacerbated mother hack and wheeze, trying to decide what to do with that piece of information. I knew where the disembodied voice on the phone was housed and gated.

I was unsure if I could control myself if I went to his house. Would I do something spectacularly stupid, something that might even land me in juvenile prison? Though I was always a rule-follower, obedient and polite, I could feel a piece of me—a shadow self, I might call it—arriving unannounced, taking possession. I could hear Lima's low whisper slithering into my ears with overwhelming heat.

I was struck by the feeling of otherworldly power, perhaps the same that, according to my mother, granted Desdemona and Queen Margaret their powers of prescience. A power that marionetted my actions with sticks of courage. It was a feeling of being myself and not being myself, surrendering to parts of my body not ruled by my brain. Where did such courage come from?

As I lay in bed, I knew what I would do the next day, and once the question was settled, I was able to fall asleep, washing away all the steps taken to come to the decision. By the time I woke the next morning, I would think the choice had been an unmarked gift, delivered surreptitiously in the night.

Instead of going to school, and without telling my mother, I took the bus to the west side of Copacabana. I found Lima's house a few minutes from the beach, less than a mile away from the local shantytown, in the middle of a quiet hillside street with cobblestone pavement. I had to walk up a long stairway to reach it, a steep vertical slope. From the outside, I could see only the imposing gate, next to two-story brick houses with more modest exteriors.

I pretended, a bit awkwardly, to be waiting for the bus. If someone noticed me, they wouldn't find anything odd about me being there for a long time; it could take hours sometimes for the buses to arrive.

I started to question what I was doing there. I didn't know if I was going to confront Lima in his driveway, or follow him to a public place. Things seemed slippery now, out in three-dimensional reality, than they had in the protection of my bed, my mother, weak as she was, lingering in the next room.

I waited and waited under the hot morning sun, lowering my eyes and looking away whenever one of the neighbors came out or drove by. Most of them looked wealthy, descendants of old latifundium families. From the street, I couldn't tell the real size of the houses. The houses weren't crowded together like the apartment buildings in my neighborhood, but rather had lush lawns and trees and carefully tended flower bushes. Behind Lima's gate, I guessed his driveway probably led to a big house with many rooms, maybe even a pool, and a view of the apex of the hills.

Finally, about an hour after my arrival, Lima's gate opened, and a green Monza emerged. It had tinted windows, and at first I couldn't see its passengers, only its slick, shiny exterior, which looked freshly washed and waxed. But as I brazenly craned my head toward the car and the driver turned onto the main road, the passenger in the back lowered his window slightly. I spotted his pale, wrinkled forehead, and caught a tiny glimpse of his eyes. He looked, to me, like a lizard.

I wanted to scream, but the sound died before it reached my lips. It struck me then, the futility of me being there, and I decided to walk away and not come back. There had to be a more normal way of dealing with this, like going to the police, moving to another house, or even changing phone numbers. It had taken months to get ours installed, and it'd take another few to get a new one, but in the meantime maybe Lima would find another hobby. Or die.

Lima's car had turned the corner and I adjusted my shoulder bag, preparing to leave. I followed the uneven cobblestones, expecting that at any moment a maid or butler would materialize behind the gate, asking who I was or what I was doing there. I was nervous like a shaking cattail trapped in the wind.

Suddenly, someone did appear, but it wasn't a maid. It was a teenage boy about my age, wearing a bright neon purple T-shirt and what looked like surfer shorts. His light brown hair was long overdue for a cut, and his skin looked deeply tanned. He smiled lopsidedly at me as if he knew me, as if he'd been waiting for me.

"What are you selling?" he asked, leaning down and pulling up the metal lever that kept the wooden gate in its place.

"Me? I—I'm not selling anything," I said, nervously.

"You look too young to be a journalist. And my dad doesn't give interviews," he drawled, sounding as if under the effect of narcotics. I was surprised that he was Lima's son, and not his grandson, unless he was referring to someone else. He closed and glided out from behind the gate, with a smile that suggested he didn't want to go back in, as if whatever waited inside wasn't as enjoyable as talking to this complete stranger in front of his house. I felt almost sorry for him, suddenly.

"No, I'm not a—a journalist, either," I said, wondering if the press was trying to get men like Lima to admit to the survivors' accusations. "I was just lost, and I saw the gate open, and thought there might be somebody here." My fingers were shaking slightly, and I hid them behind my back.

The young man had moved the gate almost all the way to the front, but instead of shutting it, he kept it open a crack so he could speak to me. "And what were you looking for?" he asked, still speaking in a relaxed drawl, still smiling.

"What?" I asked, confused. I had no idea what he meant.

"You want directions, I can give you directions. Just tell me where you were trying to get to."

"I was—I was looking for the beach," I said, trying to sound convincing. I hoped that this would be the end, and he would let me go.

The young man smiled again, scratching his long bare arms.

"That's great, then. I was just there, I only came back to grab a blanket. I can not only tell you, I can actually walk you there." He smiled. "What's your name?"

I turned to him, about to say that I'd changed my mind, and I'd decided not to go to the beach. But then I realized he might find that contradictory and odd—might find *me* odd—and tell his father about the stranger loitering outside their house.

"Betania," I found myself saying. "And yes, you can show me the way. Thank you," I replied, unable to stop looking at the set of keys in the boy's hands.

His name was Lazarus. He had chosen that day, of all days, to play hooky, and if I'd come a day earlier or a day later, I would've missed him. Was it luck or something more menacing?

It was about ten minutes walking from their house to the beach. Being midday, most of the people at Copacabana Beach— and there were plenty of people there—were either pickpockets who had dropped out of school, old retirees reading *Istoé* under large umbrellas, or prostitutes trying to get dates with the tourists in the nearby hotels. The sandwich sellers walked by with their straw baskets, holding up samples in the air. They were mostly effeminate men on this side of the beach, their swim trunks tiny, their eyes covered by cheap sunglasses. Copacabana's glorious, bohemian past had long been erased by constant violence and muggings. Copacabana seemed to me like a showgirl whose best days were behind her, who sparkled most vividly in people's nostalgic memories.

I didn't say much on the way there, trying to find excuses to disentangle myself. Lazarus, however, was a big talker, and he smiled and chatted at the same time. Even though he'd just met me, he acted as though we'd been friends for a long time, I suspected because he led a somewhat lonely existence. He talked easily about music and surfing and didn't seem to look for much conversational contribution on my part. Maybe the way I nodded and listened made him feel comfortable. He'd clearly mistaken my nervous silence for attentiveness.

When we got near the water, I expected Lazarus to go off on his own, having brought me safely to the beach, but he simply stood there, stretching a bit and staring at the hills in the distance and the low, foggy clouds around them. I wondered what it would be like to lead an existence like his, free to spend hours at the beach, without anyone to care if he missed school. Lazarus looked impossibly aimless.

Soon, I wasn't anxious around him anymore; I'd even forgot my earlier apprehension at being caught. Standing around like this, watching the waves roll toward us, I almost didn't think of him as the Police Chief's son.

Earlier, I'd thought, if he knew who I was, and why I'd gone to his house, he would think I was mad, and he would run away from me. But right now, I was just a pretty girl he'd met by chance, a small diversion to kill time before lunch.

I took a deep breath, trying for a moment to forget who we were, and what had brought me to Lazarus. I let the sun cover me, and I closed my eyes for a moment, wondering how such a thin coating of skin could protect me from the hottest star in the sky. I felt a tear roll down my warm cheek. When I opened my eyes, I found Lazarus staring at me.

"You're one of them, aren't you?" he asked quietly.

Lazarus was sitting next to me, his legs crossed, his hands

reaching in and out of the sand. He had a forlorn expression on his face.

"One of who?" I retorted, wiping my cheek.

"Daughters, or the women themselves. They show up sometimes. I watch them watching our gate. I never know what they're looking for, what they think they're going to get. I've never spoken to one of you before."

I swallowed, unsure if I should pretend to have no idea what he was referring to. The women his father had tortured. "What made you talk to me, then?"

"I don't know," he replied, and I could sense the honesty in his voice. "I think the way you came up to the gate. You just looked so sad."

"Do you know what your father did?"

Lazarus shook his head. "No," he said, staring at the water. "And also yes. I don't want to know." His lips twisted in an expression of distaste, then he added, "Did he do it to you?"

I could barely breathe now. "My mother," I whispered.

Lazarus nodded, his hands still sifting through the sand, a bit of sparkle here and there where the grains met the sun.

"So you want to hurt my father?" He suddenly stopped playing with the sand and lifted one of his legs up, resting his arms and face over it. I saw his elbow pointing at me, his face almost as anguished as mine.

I sighed, suddenly sure my answer. "I want him to stop. He's been calling my mother."

Lazarus's eyes did not change expression, as if he already knew about this hobby of his father's. I wondered if Lazarus had ever picked up the phone by accident, and heard one of the conversations. In the sun, I could see his deep wrinkles, how much time he must spend outside. Despite our mutual age, his gaze struck me as innocent. He did not seem to have any calculation in his bones.

"Maybe I can arrange for you two to meet," Lazarus suggested. My heart beat wildly as I tried to grasp this miraculous opportunity he had handed me, my face scrunching up involuntarily.

Lazarus saw the intensity of my reaction, and he recoiled slightly. His eyes looked on the verge of withdrawing the offer, and I wondered if he'd meant to only say it in his own head, trying it out to see if it made him feel better.

"You don't seem like the vindictive type," he observed carefully.

"No. I just want him to stop calling my mother."

Lazarus nodded. I noticed the sun disappear all of a sudden and I turned to see that a white ice cream stand had wheeled behind us, the word "Kibon" splattered across it. Its giant red umbrella covered us in its shade.

"Ice cream?" asked the vendor, a short, brown-skinned man with a mustache. He was reaching into the frozen box, as if we'd already agreed to it, but we shook our heads no, eager to return to our conversation. The ice cream seller went on his way. When the sun hit my face again, it felt oppressive instead of pleasant.

"You can come tomorrow tonight. I'm throwing a party. It's mostly my classmates, and my father won't know any of them, anyway."

I was surprised to receive his invitation. But of course a sociable boy like him, who'd spontaneously throw away an hour or two with a stranger, would have a lot of friends. I was tempted to ask him questions about his father, but I refrained, not wanting him to change his mind.

I didn't immediately say I would come. But we both knew that I would, that I could not stay away. I told him I would see if I could. I left soon after, and he waved a friendly goodbye over his shoulder as I trudged back over the beach, shoes in hand and sand burning my feet. I took the bus home wondering why he would invite me. I couldn't realize then that I'd made the mistake of seeing the world through the eyes of one of his father's victims, when I should've been seeing the world through Lazarus's own eyes—those of the executioner's son.

The next night, I lied to my mother, telling her I had to work on a school project with a friend. When I came into the Lima mansion and heard the song "Eu Sou Free" playing, I thought it might be a record player with big speakers, until I passed by the actual band in the backyard, singing the song. Sempre Livre was an old-fashioned all-girl group, an exception to all the all-male ones on the radio, and they'd cheekily taken their name from a popular menstrual pad.

I had never heard the song in its entirety before, and in the din of the party when they sang "Eu Sou Free"—"I Am Free"—it sounded a bit like "Eu Sofri," "I Suffered."

The Lima mansion was as enormous inside as the outside suggested, despite the small gate and unassuming driveway. I didn't have any trouble getting in, which surprised me a little, until I saw some of the guests, all students my age, and I blended in effortlessly. Deep down, though, I felt like a foreigner around those *mauricinhos* and *patricinhas*, spoiled rich kids who ignored the facts about Lima and the men of his generation. Their parents might know, but they wouldn't care; they belonged to the class that profited most from the repression. As long as the dictatorship kept the Left down, they also kept down the working class, who weren't allowed to strike, and had to labor for low wages. Rich folks turned a blind eye to the Limas of the world, happy to rationalize that if torture did happen, it happened to those they called "terrorists," the students who car-bombed politicians and kidnapped members of the military.

I looked for Lazarus, using that as an excuse to familiarize myself with the house. As I walked by the various groups—some sprawled on the sofas, smoking pot, others dancing in little circles near the band outside—I felt completely alienated from them. They didn't have a care in the world, a single worry or responsibility to their names. It amazed me that there were people in the world like this, living so nearby.

I found Lazarus in the backyard, by himself, moving his head up and down to the beat of the song. The song was long, about five minutes, but by the time I reached him, it was coming to an end. I heard it being followed by a gap, and I realized the group must be lip-syncing to a recording of themselves. Lazarus spotted me at once, and he gave me a smile that I thought was out of sync with how much or how well we knew each other. I realized, as he walked up to meet me in the middle, that he had chosen to favor me over a lot of the other people at his party.

"Are you enjoying yourself?" asked Lazarus, smiling. He wore an orange short-sleeved shirt and jeans, and he was playing with the white tie he'd loosely slipped around his collar. He was taller than I remembered, and with a jolt I saw that he was handsome.

Too nervous to smile back, I said simply, "You know that I'm

THE CAREGIVER

not here for the party. When can you introduce me to your father?"

Lazarus shook his head. "Listen, I thought about it some more, and I don't think you should talk to him. I don't want any problems." He paused, waiting for my reaction. "Besides, he's not home. Is that all right? But I'm glad you came, anyways."

I opened my mouth to protest, but instead, I just smiled weakly and nodded slightly, a vague gesture that could mean just about anything. Despite the noise, and the people, I was sure that Lima was in the house, thinking back to his sickly gaze the other morning. I knew I would not leave that house without confronting his father. I imagined Lima was somewhere on the second floor of the house, in a study I imagined filled with mahogany bookcases and the faces of stuffed deer and bears looking out from the walls. Something creepy, claustrophobic.

I left Lazarus by himself and returned to the house. The decorations were old-fashioned—antique glass curios in the dining room, a large horizontal mirror above the built-in shelves. I tried to think of a discreet way to get to the second floor, and did a little pantomime, in case anyone was watching me, of looking for an unoccupied bathroom.

I was immediately struck by how quiet it was upstairs, the band and the party below now only a faint echo. It was much darker, too: wood paneling covering the walls, portraits of Lima and his family posing in front of what looked like a sugar plantation. I vaguely remembered reading somewhere that after his successful defeat of the student guerrilla group, Lima had become a kind of minor celebrity and used his new status to divorce his first wife and marry the wealthy daughter of a senator. His now deceased second wife had helped him push for legislation in favor of environmentally friendly ethanol fuel. A popular stance after the 1970s oil crisis. It turned his sugar plantations into gold mines.

Along the corridor, I saw some pictures of plantation fields. Workers with huge knives whacking the sugarcane, clearing a path in the dense sea of shoots and stems. Sugarcane, machetes flying through the air, liable to hurt or maim if the cutter wasn't careful. In the hot sun, in the tropical monsoon, blade against stalk, a sharply angled *thwack*. The sugarcane as cargo loaded into powerful crushers, their teeth sharp and wide, breaking up the soup of stalks into unrecognizably small pieces, dirt-brown powdered versions of their previous selves. Rollers and diffusers compressing the cane into residue and fiber, red boilers darting like the last moments of a fireworks show. A hot, bubbly liquid dashing down slats like a fermented river. Lima's own oilfield, gushing as long as the earth would give him bagasse.

As I traversed the hallway, I moved in quiet steps, as if passing by a room full of napping children. I was glad for the thick carpeting that kept my steps from being heard. I tried to guess which room was his study, praying he'd be inside. All of the doors were closed. In my own home, we never closed the door to the bathroom unless it was occupied; same with the bedrooms. I felt a film of sweat on my back making the fabric of my shirt stick to my body. Near the end of the hallway, I chanced upon a small area with a console table and some flowers and a lamp on top of it. It was the kind of thing one might see in a hotel, in the lobby, next to the elevator. There was a phone. I put my hand over the receiver, and glanced back, toward the lit part of the other end of the hallway, to see if anyone was coming. If I were Lima, I thought, how would I pass the hours while everyone else remained distracted by the party, when everyone else had completely forgotten about me?

I picked up the phone, being careful to slide my fingers over the switch hook in case the phone was, as I hoped, in use. Before I even put the handset against my ear, I could hear the voices on the line, and they made me close my eyes. As I listened, I heard the same voice that had called my mother, though this time he was not speaking softly, and he seemed to be talking to a man. But it was the same person, I knew, with the same slightly European accent—an affectation of the upper classes. It wasn't just the voice that I recognized; it was the slight thread of melancholia running through the words. I put the handset back on the cradle, once again careful to make sure the switch hook stayed down; I didn't want the person on the phone to know someone had been listening in.

I looked around, trying to guess which of these rooms hid Lima. Then, through the crack below the door, I saw some light in one of the rooms. I decided to try it; if I ran into a family member, I could say I'd been looking for a bathroom. But as I opened the door, and the room shone dimly in front of me, I recognized the aura of a man I had met before. Though he no longer looked like the man I'd once met, or even like the recent pictures I'd seen in the microfiche newspaper articles in the library, I knew at once that this was Lima.

"Who's there?" he called out, hanging up the phone. He looked in my direction, but his eyes did not rest on my body. It made me wonder if there was somebody else next to me. Without waiting for me to reply, he added, "The party's downstairs. There's no reason for anyone to be up here."

I stepped quietly into the room. The lights were off, and the only source of illumination came from the TV. Still, I could see yellow-tinted photos of people hung in frames, some dressed in 1930s and 1940s garb. In the corner, there was a statue that looked as though it had been transported intact from the early days of the Republic. And in a giant armchair, made to look small by his tremendous stature, was the Police Chief. He'd gained a remarkable amount of weight. He was the fattest man I'd ever seen, a giant mass of dough parked on a chair, a woolen throw over his lap.

"If you don't leave now, I'm going to chase you off with my cane," he barked, waving a long wooden backscratcher in front of him. The reflection of the TV caused him to flicker in front of me like candle.

I gathered all the courage I had in my body. "I came to talk to you."

This silenced him for a few seconds. He still would not make eye contact, would not look at me directly, only in my vicinity. He rarely blinked, staring continuously at the same spot. His eyes had no life in them.

"Who are you?" he asked, suspiciously. "Aren't you one of my son's friends?"

I shook my head, but my movement prompted no reaction from him. "I'm not," I replied.

I saw his hand shake slightly as he gripped the head of the backscratcher. "I knew this party was a bad idea. Did you come here to try to rob me?"

"I'm not a thief," I said, offended. "I'm not the person in the room who is a criminal."

I didn't intend to come on so strong, but I was melting away into my shadow self.

I expected him to react with force, but instead his face curled into a smile.

"Ah, a fan," he said, in a sarcastic tone. "You know my work? You came to pay your respects?"

"I came to ask you to leave my mother alone."

"Who's your mother?" he asked, furrowing his eyebrows.

I hesitated. No turning back now. "Ana Alencar."

The Police Chief's mouth opened slightly, as if to let out an exclamation, but he made no sounds. He started nodding. "And you are her . . ."

"I'm her daughter."

His eyes suddenly showed some signs of life. He sat a bit more upright, one hand gripping the arm of the chair and the other the backscratcher he used as a cane. He looked like an emperor in his throne, though not one at his peak, one in his declining years.

"Lazarus brings too many people to this house. He shouldn't have such a big mouth."

"I found your address at the municipal records," I said.

The Police Chief cracked an unexpected grin. It unnerved me much more than his earlier coldness. "You're very resourceful. Clever. Ana was like that."

"So you don't deny that you're the one who's been calling her? The one who hurt her?" The words jumped rapid-fire out of me, unable to contain my anger. I thought of how nice it'd be to charge him, maybe head-butt him, slam him against the wall. Somehow find a way to use his weight against him.

"I don't know what she told you, but I never hurt your mother," he said quietly, calmly. "I helped her."

I shook my head. "I know who you are. You hurt a lot of people. You tortured them."

The Police Chief did not react to this, as if I were talking about a person he had heard of, but did not know very well. He had turned his past into an acquaintance. If everything my mother told me was true I could see why the Police Chief would want to distance himself from his horrendous deeds.

"By the sound of your voice, you must be in high school," he said.

"I'm not here to talk about me."

"And probably very beautiful, if you take after your mother."

"If you keep talking about my mother like that, I'm going to hurt you."

I reached for a sharp letter opener sitting on the console table next to me. I took it instinctively. I could see its blade glowing, suddenly alive.

He smiled slyly again. His voice grew silky, almost plangent. "You want to try? Why don't you get closer to me?"

"All I want is for you to leave my mother alone. Don't contact her, don't call her, forget she exists." I didn't expect the wave of emotions that suddenly flooded me. "Why did you call her after all these years? Why?"

"I felt like it."

That didn't satisfy me.

"You're old—maybe you're dying," I accused.

"No," he scoffed. "I am and I am not. Everyone is. You are dying right now."

"But you must have some disease?"

"That's a funny thing to ask a fat, old, mostly blind man."

I waved my hands in front of me but he did not react. I stepped a few feet closer, and still he did not react. If he was faking it, and I couldn't imagine why he would, he was doing a terrific job.

"If you're sick, maybe you'll be able to relate to my mother's condition."

"What's wrong with her?" he asked, sounding concerned. That surprised me.

"I don't expect a man like you to have compassion, but my mother has a heart condition. Your phone calls upset her."

I heard a sudden noise burst from outside, like a guitar being tuned too loudly, but right away the silence returned. I noticed for the first time how every piece of furniture and every object seemed anchored to its place, as if they hadn't been moved in years. That way the Police Chief could navigate the room, know where everything was, without bumping or breaking anything. There was a clear path between the chairs, the tables, and nothing on the floor that Lima might trip on. I had not, in a million years, expected this. What caused him to go blind? And when?

"Is she going to die?" he finally asked.

"No," I blurted out, horrified.

"Is it something that can be cured through surgery? A heart bypass can be a real lifesaver, though it's expensive."

"You know enough. You don't need to know any more." I glanced toward the door. My time in that room, I sensed, was up. Lazarus might come looking for me, and if he found me in that room, he'd be very upset. I didn't want that, for whatever reason, for this kind, lonely boy.

I'd done what I'd come to do. I'd said what I had to say. I had gone much further than I had ever dared to hope.

I reached for the door and opened it farther, making a creaking noise.

"Wait," the Police Chief called out, with urgency in his voice. "Wait a minute. I want you to take something to your mother."

"Excuse me?" I halted, squinting, confused. I knew, I knew with all the sureness of my soul, that this was the man who had tortured my mother. So why was he acting as though he were an old friend? I began to wonder if he was calling my mother for a specific reason. Had their conversations always been as volatile as the one I witnessed? I thought suddenly of my mother's sly smile in the dubbing booth. He got up from his chair heavily, with difficulty, sending his sour aroma of medication and soiled sheets into the air. I could see brown spots everywhere on his hands. As he walked, I held the door open, one foot in the hallway. But he did not walk in my direction, and instead moved toward a wall on the other side of the room, where he revealed a hidden built-in safe. No one in the Brazilian upper class kept their money in the unreliable banks. They exchanged their cash for dollars and kept them in their homes. He lumbered over to me, tossing a bag in my direction. It fell thunderously on the ground in front of me. When I reached for it, curious, and opened the bag, I saw that it was filled with cash. A few thousand American dollars. More money than I'd ever seen before. I looked up to see the Police Chief leaning on his desk for support.

"Take it to her," he ordered me, pointing his backscratcher in my overall direction with authority.

I could not believe what had just happened. "I'm not here to—"

"Take the money," he said, shaking his head. "You're only a child, but you're old enough to know what to do."

"Is this restitution?"

"I didn't hurt your mother," said the Police Chief. "Like I said, I helped her. And she helped *me*. Take the money. She earned it. It's all hers."

"What do you mean, she earned it?" Did he really think he could make it up for torturing her by giving her that money?

"This money belongs to her. Fair is fair."

I didn't know what to do. I didn't want to accept a gift from that monster, but those bills in front of me were not abstract— they were health and relief from pain. What would be worse in my mother's eyes: accepting charity from *that* man or turning it down?

"I will never call her again," said Lima. "She will never hear from me again. That, I promise. Now go!" he roared suddenly.

I rushed down the stairs. I rushed down the halls. I rushed past drunk teenagers swaying their bodies to the latest track by some American band. I kept my face down, and all I could see was a broken succession of feet, until I made my way outside. There, I was greeted by the sight of the gate in the distance being opened by a maid, with help from a butler.

Then, the sound of sirens promised the arrival of police cars.

It dawned on me, what had just happened. Lima had tricked me, made it so the police would find me with his money, made it look like a robbery had taken place. I was in trouble. Serious trouble. Within seconds, I saw the red lights flashing, their tires crunching over the gravel.

I immediately ran toward the back of the house instead. The heavy bag slowed me down, but I clung to it like the lifeline it was.

I could barely see in the dark, trees leading toward a woodsy area. There was no walking trail, and I had to crouch and slide my way through spiky thickets and matted branches. I was about to enter a grove of almond trees, following a rich carpet of leaves on the ground, when suddenly a hand reached for me and I screamed.

"Hey, hey! It's okay."

It was Lazarus. I felt my heart push against my throat. The sirens raced into the front driveway of the house. He looked at my face, registering my panic, and then looked down at the bag I held stealthily in my arms. I knew then that I would have to fight for my escape. Lazarus would try to drag me back, hold me down until the police arrived. But his smoky breath hovered over me for a second, then moved past me like a cloud drifting.

"What's wrong?" he asked. "Are you all right?"

"The police! The police are here!" I panicked.

"Yes, my asshole neighbor called them because of the noise. Looks like the party's over."

I stood with my mouth open. "They're not here because of—"

"Doesn't matter," he said, practically rolling his eyes. "It was a boring party anyway. Let's split."

To my surprise, instead of pulling me back toward the house, he pulled me forward, as if to show me the right way out. His hand still on my arm, his skin against mine almost a caress. He led us, pushing through foliage, our heads lowered underneath ficus branches, as he carved a pathway through the scrubland.

We climbed up a hill, above the neighbors' backyards, the faint trace of crooked television antennas, and clotheslines. Laundered shirts and pants hung upside down, flattened and longing for bodies to fill them; sheets shivered in the wind, like oversized banners.

When we finally reached the top of the wooded area, Lazarus and I came upon a gate with bars shaped like fleurs-de-lis. Lazarus opened this back gate and led us out.

Out on the street, there was a road leading to a favela. I saw in the distance the tiny makeshift homes plopped down in diagonal lines, some made of concrete, some made of wood—the materials probably stolen from city garbage. It was as if someone had taken all the trash in the Dumpsters, and built houses out of it. The pungent smell of urine filled my nostrils as we walked, and I found myself crossing my arms, so as to hide the bag against my chest, underneath a denim jacket Lazarus had taken off and placed over my shoulders.

We were walking completely in the dark, as there were no streetlamps here, and no electricity in the shantytown. I felt the tension in my body grow with every step, scared that a drug dealer, or robber, or even worse, a policeman, would stop us at some point. We didn't speak. Finally, after turning a corner, I saw a cab come in our direction and I practically jumped in front of it to hail it. Its stopped headlights illuminated all the particles in the air twirling, all the dust that was normally invisible. As I walked toward the cab, I felt again a filmy, viscous layer coating my skin, and I couldn't wait to wash it off. Lazarus, meanwhile, remained in his spot, and when I looked back at him, I saw something akin to regret in his eyes.

"Are you going to be okay?" he asked, concerned.

"Yes," I said, swallowing. "You should go home."

I realized he didn't want me to leave. As the cab door stood open, I hesitated, the headlights still shining upon his dusty confused face, abandonment tinting his eyes. The innocence of that look tore me in half. I took his hand and I led him inside the cab. I didn't know what I was doing, only that I didn't want to be alone, and I couldn't go home just yet. Not until I figured out what story I would tell my mother.

Lazarus pulled down the chain, and the yellow lamp bulb hanging from the ceiling illuminated the motel room: the circle-shaped cot, the dresser with broken laminate, the bars on the window blocking the view of the highway. He was my getaway partner, but also my hostage.

I perched myself on the tip of the cot, almost like I didn't deserve the comforts it promised. I'd been holding the bag of money against my chest, hiding it under my jacket, and I finally let it slip from between my legs. Lazarus had never remarked on the bag, never asked what was inside.

I wondered how much he already knew.

Lima said that he'd helped my mother; he said that she'd helped *him*. Willingly? As though they'd been amicable? I didn't know this woman he described. This woman was not the same woman I loved and lived with all my life. This woman was not the one who had taken care of me for as long as I could remember. That woman did not keep things from me. The possibility was crushing.

Lazarus sat down beside me, gently, as if aware of the turmoil blazing through my head.

"You went to talk to my father, didn't you?" he asked me, quietly, his eyes avoiding mine.

"He's not what I expected." The words sounded off, as if I'd said them underwater.

"He's changed since the diagnosis," Lazarus said. I could feel the vibrations passing between our bodies.

"What diagnosis?"

"What did he say to you?"

"He said so many things. I don't know if any of it was true," I said.

I looked at him. Lazarus. I wanted to feel safe with him, this stranger, desperately, but for all I knew, at any moment he could push my body against the bed and crush my neck with his hands.

Instead, Lazarus remained where he was, his face as opaque as milk glass. He looked serious, but not sad. Caring, but not worried. The space between us felt too big, and I reached over to him, my fingers on the stubble on his chin. To my relief, he did not push me away. I began to graze his jaw more and more, feeling the hard but pliable texture of his skin. I explored his face gently, tapping his lips, my palms a bit shaky. I felt his nose in the space between my thumb and my indicator, his breathing a kind of touch. I could feel his lashes tremble in my palm, and then close.

What had happened between my mother and Lima all those years ago? Those hours they'd spent together in the police station, she had always made them sound torturous, but how exactly had they been filled? I glanced away from Lazarus to the bag. The thought that Lima could be her abuser and her savior was overwhelming.

I sniffled, unable to control my breathing all of a sudden. To my surprise, Lazarus reached over to me and placed his lips over mine, as if to make me stop. I felt his tongue inside me, filling me up, and for a moment, it made the throbbing pain disappear. I liked that, wanted more. We held each other at a perfect angle, breathing into each other. As I tasted his lips, I felt in touch with the chemical parts of him—the combination of molecules that produced his scent, the way it combined with my tongue to create our sense of each other. I put my hands over his face, and though I didn't know why, I kept patting his cheeks, ears, temples, as if to reassure myself, at every second, that the body in front of me was really there.

I let Lazarus wrap his arms around my waist, liking how he comforted me, and I buried my fingers in his hair, making fists again and again. Both our bodies shook slightly, and we grabbed at each other as if we were vanishing. With him, it felt right to mix sex and fear. I'd never made love before, but the night felt ripe for firsts.

Hungry, he pressed his face against my neck, his lips on my clavicle. As my eyelids relaxed and fell, I lifted my arms and re-moved my shirt and bra. Lazarus started kissing my shoulders, my nipples, his lips smooth and humid against my breasts. Then he moved downward, as if following a trail. I felt his tongue flutter restlessly around my belly button.

"Hang on," I said.

I got up, and, still shirtless, matter-of-factly walked to the door and bolted it. The nakedness felt like a clothing of sorts, a thing out of context. After I locked the door, I didn't return to Lazarus right away. Instead, I walked past him to the window. Trying to stay out of view, I looked around to check if anyone could see us. In the backyard, I caught a glimpse of a chambermaid in uniform marching hurriedly from the garage back to the motel. The maid looked up and locked gazes with me. She was a girl only slightly older than me, barely out of her teens, probably from the countryside. I wished her no harm, but the maid gave me a frightful look. I pulled the window closed, sealing the room as if behind a zipper.

When I turned back around, Lazarus was sitting on the bed. He had taken his shirt off, and I could see the freckles on his shoulders, a large mole by his belly button. I walked to him and made him lie on his back. I pulled his pants and underwear down, and then my own. I straddled him. I guided him inside me, occasionally lowering myself to kiss him. I had no idea where I'd figured out how to do this. The room grew hotter with the window shut. At one point Lazarus lifted himself up, and I put my arms around his drenched back. Our eyes stayed open, never blinking, staring at each other. He held my head with both hands, clinging.

I tasted him the way an epicurean would. No selfish thoughts clouded my mind as shivers coursed through my body. Our hands and knees mirrored each other's perfectly, like two halves of a dyad. In the dark, like this, we would spend the entire night.

There was stillness in the morning. Grayness, wetness. A damp, dewy chill. I sat on the bed, putting my bra back on, my hair disheveled on my shoulders. I opened the curtains and I spied concrete highways leading to Búzios, Petrópolis, and São Paulo, a city with a mouth big enough to swallow you whole. As cars piled upon cars, this was not a postcard-pretty view of Rio de Janeiro, but it was the land I'd woken up to. It looked lovelier to me than any of the Seven Wonders of the World.

Lazarus was still asleep, his head beside a pillow, clutching the sheets. I ran my hand over his hair, like the tips of wheat fields.

His eyes slowly fluttered open. Without moving, he watched

me as I put on my blouse and my skirt. I moved the comforter so it'd cover the blood on the sheets. He looked at me as if he knew everything, all of me. I lingered, unsure if I really had anything left to do, or if I was just delaying my departure. I kept looking out the window, and then back at him, finding bits and parts of me I feared accidentally leaving behind.

"What's your real name?" he finally asked.

I knew I looked nothing like a Betania. If I lied again, chances were we'd never hear or see each other again, and this strange night could finally be over, erased.

Neither of us said anything to the other for some time, the line between us so fragile, it could crack with a single syllable. Finally, I spoke the five words my young self was unaware would create waves, ripples for years to come.

"My name is Mara Alencar."

When I got to our apartment, I turned the key and pushed the door open. The curtains were still drawn, but some hazy light grazed through the gaps in the wooden shutters. I quickly closed the door behind me and raced in, my heart beating madly. Right in the living room, under the jaundiced glow of a lamp left on from the previous night, my mother lay half asleep on the sofa, cradling herself small, boxed in between the two armrests. She looked crinkled, like dried fruit. She had been up all night, worrying.

If not for the bulging bag of cash tucked below the waistline of my pants I would have wondered if the entire night really happened at all. I sat down next to my mother on the couch, not waking her, and placed the bag with the money on the space between us. I pulled the notes out of the bag, covering the sofa. Pretty soon I could no longer see its furry brown fabric. My mother stirred, reaching for my hand, squeezing it harder than I expected. I wondered what it was that my mother was dreaming about. We turn blind, deaf, and mute in our sleep. I could say to her whatever I had stuck in my throat and she would never know.

I felt all my tiredness hit me all at once, as if my body had been too polite to bother me before, but now gave up any pretense of chivalry. I stared out into nothingness and the nothingness suddenly became filled with the Police Chief's blind eyes. I thought of his heaviness—how incredibly heavy, the weight of a thousand stones. I then noticed, for the first time, the specks of blood in my hands, under my fingernails, and I had to toss my head back, to hold back a desperate need to vomit. I forgot that the blood had come from me.

"Mara," my mother called out as she awoke. Her eyes opened. "Good God. You crazy girl, you tore my heart in half!" She unfolded herself, sitting up. "Are you okay? I was so worried about you. Where were you last night?" Still a bit drowsy, she moved her legs to clear a bigger spot for me on the sofa. As she did so, some of the money fell on the floor and she finally noticed the packets on the sofa. "What is this? Where did this come from?"

"Promise you won't be mad if I tell you what I did."

"Where did you get this?" my mother asked, fear etched in her brows. "Where did you spend the night?"

"I still don't know what happened. It was so confusing."

My mother held the notes in her hand, her mouth agape. "This is a lot of money, Mara."

I hesitated. "Police Chief Lima. I went to see him yesterday."

She began shaking. The mere mention of his name was enough to unsettle her, but to know that her daughter had met him, and that she had taken this from him—the intimacy of the gift— seemed to undo every part of her being. My mother looked at me with the frozen eyes of Lot's wife. I told her of every choice of mine, from the moment I discovered Lima's address, to the moment I left his house, omitting Lazarus . . . the motel outside the city. I thought suddenly of my mother's weak heart.

"You shouldn't have gone. You should've asked me first, so I could say no and keep you chained here," my mother said.

"I'm sorry, but I had to make him stop calling you," I replied, with lowered eyes.

She shook her head. "I can't believe what you did. This doesn't feel real." She reached for a handkerchief and tapped it against her brow. She rested her left arm on the sofa's armrest with her palm up, as if awaiting an injection. "I need—I need to breathe."

"It's fine, I'm here. I'm not harmed in any way."

"You in the same room, with him, I can't—I just can't . . ." My mother kept shaking her head and then suddenly froze, as if something had clicked. "Did he say anything to you?"

"About?"

"You should not have gone there."

"Was it wrong for me to accept the money?"

My mother looked at the bills. "He should've given you *all* his money."

"There's a lot here. Why did he— Why did he give me this money?"

"How should I know? This money. This money is nothing.

What matters is that you're safe and sound and here. I worried like a dog all night."

We embraced. I reached for the nape of her neck, careful not to leave marks. Her skin was so sensitive that if I pressed too hard, her epidermis would often break, turn raw, and take days to heal. I rested my hand there for a while, looking at my mother, our faces mirroring each other's like two halves of a mariposa's wings.

"He swore he wouldn't call again. Isn't that incredible?" I asked, freeing my mother from the weights in her ankles. I felt something powerful wash over me with this knowledge, a further shift in our precarious balance of power. "He will never, ever call again."

chapter nine

A WEEK LATER, MY MOTHER AND I RODE IN THE CAB heading to the Hospital of the Americas, each of us looking out our respective windows, lost in thought. Down the slopes of Rebouças, I stared at the bread loaf–shaped, moss-covered quartz hills. In the horizon, halos of sun created concentric circles. I couldn't help but look at the view proudly, as if by virtue of being born there, I'd had some part in producing this beautiful land. As if to love something is to own at least a part of it.

My ears plugged up and I opened my mouth wide to pop them. Traffic lights were intermittent and red ones rare, the drive a nearly vertical drop. The city glimmered in the lake, a carpet of lambent dots, a candlelit feast. We kept sliding downward endlessly. It was like diving into an ocean, each fall revealing a new one just underneath.

The driver kept chattering about the hundreds of thousands of dollars the president had been pouring into renovations on his mansion in Lago Norte. He had put motorized waterfalls in the gardens, importing oxygenated and filtered water from Lake Paranoá for his Japanese carp. The president was building himself a garden worthy of a maharaja, a sumptuous Babylonian fantasy home. Normally, I would've echoed the cab driver's outrage—our favorite national sport being bashing corrupt politicians. But I had enough on my mind. The money for the operation sat inside a straw bag with the top covered with wildflowers; I held the straps shut with my knees.

At the Catholic hospital, a long line skated around almost the entire building, patients numbering in the hundreds. Sick bodies leaned against stone pillars; concrete floors echoed with sniffling and coughing. Old and middle-aged faces flashed a mixture of bitterness and resignation. As a clerk led my mother and me toward the second floor, it felt odd to walk past people who'd clearly been waiting forever.

"The end of the line's back there," I heard someone behind me snicker, a malicious tinge in his voice, followed by laughter. I turned around, but couldn't tell who'd said that. A dozen other people seemed to feel the same way, staring with resentment.

At the director's office, his secretary received us with strained politeness, like something she'd put on that morning along with her lipstick and mascara. She put the cash through a counting machine; the bills made a whooshing noise. They took pretty much everything I had received from the Police Chief, save for a thousand dollars that my mother had set aside. She had decided that after the surgery we'd go to America on a nice vacation. Miami, where all the Brazilians went, and everyone spoke our language. Or Los Angeles, where she would seek not the young stars, but the ones of yesteryear, whose voices she had once dubbed. I had never been outside the country before, and it sounded like we were planning a trip to Mars.

Once the payment was processed, a nurse walked with my mother down the hallway, and I caught the inside of a room here and there: white walls with pictures of Jesus, twin cots with quilted blankets at the bottom. Sick folks, mostly old, lay on their beds, some praying, some talking to family members. The rooms were almost completely bare, with no medical equipment of any kind. The walls had clearly not been repainted in a long time. All the windows had bars on them.

When we reached Ana's room, I saw that the number—205, was that of our apartment backward, which I took as a good omen. We put our things down and got her settled, a process that took much less time than I thought it would. I waited for the nurse to leave.

"I'll wait here until the surgery's done," I told my mother.

"In that filthy waiting room? By yourself? No, absolutely not. I don't want some man trying to cop a feel, some middle-aged creep chatting you up." She coughed violently, a regular occurrence that now peppered every conversation. "You go home, where you'll be safe. Eat a sandwich, take a nap. Knowing you're home will help me relax for the surgery. Otherwise, I'm going to be anxious."

"All right, then. I'll go once they take you into the operating room," I said, hugging my mother. "I love you."

"I love you, too, my pearl," she replied. I turned as I exited the room, and my mother looked almost regal in the crisp hospital bed, opening a magazine as though she had all day to be waited upon.

On the way back home, I stopped at a *mercearia* to buy some

sterile bandages, as instructed by the sheet of postoperative directions, and some Merthiolate for a cut in my hand I hadn't noticed.
When it was my turn in line, the cashier did not acknowledge me.
I hadn't looked at the price stickers, and when he asked me for
ninety cruzeiros, I did a slight double take. The amount seemed
much higher than it should be, and while I hadn't done a survey of
recent bandage and Merthiolate prices in the local *mercearias*, I
could sense something amiss. The cashier repeated the amount, as
if I were either slow or hard of hearing.

"That doesn't sound right," I said. I had imagined that one
small benefit of the president's recent plan to freeze prices would
be an end to the rampant inflation. But the *mercearia* had clearly
raised prices on its goods.

"Look at this list," said the cashier, pulling out a sheet listing the
names of different products and cruzeiro amounts next to them.
"These are the prices of every item in the store. That's what they
were before the freeze."

I glanced at the sheet, a Xeroxed page hastily put together, with
false prices, much higher than they were supposed to be. The cashier pointed at it self-righteously, with the fury of an overcompen-
sating cheater, daring me to argue with print and paper. I could see
how a poor, uneducated person, like so many in my neighborhood,
might see that official-looking sheet and be intimidated by it.

I pulled out some cruzeiros from my pocket and paid for the
items. We both knew I wasn't going to denounce the store to the
hotlines set up by the government. How useless they were, as busy
as those phone lines for contests on radio shows. I pictured indignant customers complaining of culprits in every corner, every
store. Most businesses would find a more sophisticated way to get

over the price freeze than the owner of this *mercearia*, but either way, prices would keep rising. I felt a little funny as I left, knowing I'd just been lied to, but part of me felt like there was nothing I could do. The president had saddled the merchant with a crazy law, and now he tried to pass on the loss to his customers. The clerk was just following orders.

Without even waiting to get home, I leaned against a wall outside the store and opened the Merthiolate. I pressed the small net attached to the cap against my cut, watching as its red liquid bubbled over, a burning sensation. The edge of it had already scarred, and I knew I should've disinfected it much sooner. I kept pressing, as if it could heal me, save me from further harm. Its sting made me grit my teeth.

I decided to pass the time and distract myself by sitting at a *lanchonete* near the hospital. In the glass counters, finger foods beamed. I was starving. Neat rows of *empada* pies filled with hearts of palm, shrimp, and cheese; dark and crunchy *kibes* filled with ground beef; and *bolinhos*—little cakes made with yucca and codfish and meat. A single waiter, on the other side of the counter, strolled up and down unhurriedly, serving some and ignoring others.

Once I got my coffee and the plate of *coxinha* I'd ordered, I went outside to take a seat. From my plastic chair in the open air I could spy the denizens of the morning about to crash into one another like bowling balls on the sidewalk. I distracted myself by watching a suntanned man in his seventies wearing only a watch above his waist. A pearled and blazered woman around the same age rode behind him in a scooter, her face unmoving and wrinkle-free.

I cut open the *coxinha*, releasing its heat into the air. I took sips from the tiny cup of coffee, trying not to worry about my mother. I played with the large plastic ashtray resting on the laminated tablecloth; it had a row of indentations for cigarettes to rest, and from the side it looked like a mouth's gum line with half the teeth hammered out.

Across the street, the farmer's market had found its rhythm, and I watched as the farmers hawked fruits as fresh as if they'd just fallen off trees. Huge papayas turned counters into seas of gold and aquamarine. Peaches preened so juicy red, they looked as if about to burst. Their sweet aroma tickled my nostrils. I watched a woman hold up an avocado, admiring it like a trophy. I knew she would grind it into a puree, mix it with sugar, and serve it as a dessert.

The sun shone with no variation—the same brutal, intense morning one. From my chair—a seat at the edge of the ocean—I could see a doorman washing the street in front of his high-rise building. With a mop and a bucket, he soaped the asphalt, turning bubbly white the cobblestonelike quartz pavement, the pungent smell of Pine-Sol replacing the fragrant smells of fruits.

On the table next to me, two men dipping their small baguettes into their café con leche were discussing which streets to avoid that day—the students from PUC and Federal were planning another protest against the president. Their talk, the same talk about inflation and elections over and over again, made me feel sleepy.

Loud groans came from another group of men at the other end of the bar-restaurant shaking their heads in despair at a TV mounted against the wall. Apparently our soccer team had just lost a game to the Argentinians. Fickle and uncooperative static crowded the top and bottom of the frame. The camera panned as the Argentinians ran across the field, hugging one another, the announcer bellowing their names. I watched as the Argentinians celebrated, one of them reaching across the barricades and putting on his opponent's uniform over his own.

"This country's shit," I overheard a man at the counter say, wiping his thumbs on his sleeveless undershirt. He held a boiled egg in his hand as if using it to prove a point. "I am *tired* of this *merda*."

Back at the hospital, I noticed for the first time how it resembled a church, with high ceilings and glass mosaics as some of the skylights. Statues of saints weeping and praying stood at the windows. I watched through the open balustrade the quiet, near wordless movement below of the nurses pushing sick people in wheelchairs and orderlies delivering patients in gurneys, as if they were on the platform of a subway where all the commuters had suddenly lost power over their bodies.

I had a bag with some books and a teddy bear for my mother, as well as some dahlia piñatas I'd hastily picked up on the way out of the subway station. As I walked through the hospital, I thought about the long week my mother still had ahead of her at the hospital. I hoped that it would go by fast, and that I'd be able to bring her home soon.

When I opened the door to her room, I saw that my mother hadn't been brought back yet. I set my flowers down on the small counter. On the floor, I saw the plastic shopping bag from Casas Havana that my mother had used to bring her change of clothes. Its creases and tears appeared familiar to me, as well as its size.

I reached down under the bed. I turned the bag upside down but nothing fell out, no piece of lint, no line of thread. It didn't smell like my mother, only of plastic. I put it back where I'd found it. It looked like a thing left behind on purpose.

I walked back toward the door, searching for a nurse. As I peered out, I noticed a black woman holding a drenched compress against her bleeding head. She stood right outside, in the hallway. She had an angry but resigned expression, as the blood slipped past the space between her fingers and dripped onto the floor. Next to her, a Middle Eastern man looked at her helplessly, his hand gently cupping the back of her head. I couldn't tell if they were lovers or coworkers or what. I kept looking for a nurse, occasionally glancing back at the couple. Finally, the bleeding woman blinked at me and said, "Car accident." Then, the man looked at her apologetically.

A few seconds later, I flagged down a nurse in a nun's habit walking by. The woman gave me a friendly look, and for a second I thought it was the same nurse who'd helped me that morning, but she wasn't; she just wore the uniform the same way, the cap slightly angled. She had a clipboard in her hand.

"Can I help you?" she asked.

"Yes. I'm looking for my mother. She just had heart surgery. Are they bringing her back to her room or is she somewhere else?"

"They usually do, yes. We bring the patients back to their rooms. What is her name?"

"Ana Alencar," I replied.

"Let me see, Ana Alencar." She squinted her eyes slightly and consulted her clipboard. "Yes, she was in operating room B6. Dr. Nanini. She should've been brought back by now. Let me go check."

I nodded. "Thank you."

I returned to her room while I waited. I walked to the far wall. Through the glass window, I could see the streets of Copacabana. This felt like a luxury to me, the ability to look out at the world waiting for us outside.

A few minutes later, the nurse returned, now joined by a doctor.

"Are you Ana Alencar's daughter?" the tall, curly-haired doctor asked. He offered me his hand, which I took limply. "Is your father here, too?"

I shook my head nervously. "No. Where is my mother? How is she?"

The nurse gave me a once-over, and avoided my eyes.

The doctor guided me to the bed, made me sit down. Beads of sweat glowed on his forehead. He kept his hands inside the pockets of his white smock.

"I'm very sorry to inform you that there were complications. Per standard procedure, the surgeon made an incision down the center of the patient's sternum, took a blood vessel from her chest, and redirected it around a coronary artery. During the procedure, we literally stopped her heart for an hour, which is normal in these cases, but when it came time to revive her . . ."

I couldn't hear him anymore. I felt like a pillow was smothering me. I couldn't breathe. And then dizziness struck me. Lightheadedness. My heart smashing against its cage. My body being drained of blood.

". . . passed away at ten o'clock, from postsurgery complications, after several attempts to . . ."

The doctor's lips moved, but the words were garbled, distorted. The room suddenly felt arctic.

". . . so sorry to tell you that . . ."

As his words sank in fully, I felt a pit in my stomach and almost doubled over. A sudden black cloud lodged itself in my brain.

". . . cannot imagine the grief and sorrow that . . ."

I closed my eyes and began to cry openly. That very morning I'd been lifted by the knowledge that the tide had changed for the better. Knowing that our lives would be easier, different. After the surgery, I thought my mother would go back to her normal self again. I wouldn't have to take care of her so much. *We're going to be free*, I had repeated the words in my head over and over again, *We're going to be free. We're going to be happy.*

Suddenly, I thought of Lima. Handing me the cash. Encouraging my mother to have the operation. Knowing the risks. Trying to silence her. It hadn't been enough that he had almost destroyed her life eight years ago. He had to come back. Why had he come back? Had he come back for *this*?

"He did it," I said sharply, interrupting the doctor while he droned on.

The doctor and the nurse looked up, confused.

"Excuse me?" asked the doctor.

"It was the Police Chief," I said, between hiccups, tears streaming down my face.

"Who's—"

"He's the one who caused it. He gave me the money. And then this happened."

The doctor and the nurse exchanged looks. He asked her to bring me some chamomile tea, but I shook my head. I wanted both of them to hear this, to know this.

"This never would've happened if I hadn't gone to him." I could barely get the words out and the doctor and the nurse strained to understand me. "So you see, it's my fault, too. I made this happen. It's both of our faults."

The doctor and the nurse remained silent, watching me, unsure of what to say. The doctor started nodding sympathetically. The dejected babblings of the bereaved. He'd probably seen worse. I heard him say something about my "state of shock."

Not wanting to be in that room a second longer, without saying a word, I grabbed the empty plastic bag that had once carried my mother's clothes. I left the books, teddy bear, and flowers behind. As I walked out of the room, I could feel the two pairs of eyes following me, puzzled by my exit.

Then, something odd happened. Looking down, onto the first floor, I had the vague but persistent feeling that I recognized my mother's back.

I was sure it was my mother—her hair, her particular walk, her height. Ana. My eyes were so sure, so convinced, that I found myself rushing down the soapstone stairs, toward that apparition.

As I started losing sight of her, I walked faster, pushing past some of the people blocking my way. Finally, I called out, "Mom! *Dona* Ana!"

The woman either did not hear me in the crowded lobby or did not recognize my voice, and I saw the woman grow smaller in the distance.

I practically tumbled down the wide steps, my heart pushing against my throat, the shafts of light through the glass mosaics teasing me. I ran faster than I knew I could, bumping against patients slogging their way through. My loud steps echoed through the main lobby, and the guard in front, seeing me running like a wild gazelle, yelled at me to stop. I sidestepped him by charging toward a different exit, and pushed past the heavy stone door, the explosion of hot air nearly suffocating me.

Out of the hospital, I looked desperately in every direction. "Mom! Mom! *Dona* Ana!" I screamed, hoping I'd be rewarded by a face in the crowd turning toward me. But she was already gone. I scanned the backs and faces of everyone in the streets. No one matched my mother. I sobbed, clutching the plastic bag with my hands.

It can't be. It can't be. You cannot be gone.

I staggered forward as if I'd just been grazed with a bullet. Pedestrians bumped into me, people stared and pointed, but nothing could jolt me out of my despair. From all sides I could hear the bustle of Rio de Janeiro that beat on, unfazed by my suffering—street preachers perched on broken boxes offering salvation; salesmen announcing two-for-one sales of T-shirts with the image of Christ Redeemer. Then a well-dressed woman who suddenly turned to me and asked for change, undaunted by my wet, haunted face. When I said nothing she wandered away, toward the sea of stores, with their heavy metal gates they'd lower at night, at closing, the extra protection that turned every commercial street in the neighborhood into a citadel.

"Mom . . ." I cried out, to no one in particular.

I couldn't go home, not when my mother wasn't there, so I wandered aimlessly along the boardwalk, crying. Finally, as if by instinct, I found myself outside Lima's house. Would there be solace inside? When I thought about the Police Chief, and how much I hated him, the pain subsided.

I stood next to a cannonball tree across the street from his house. Its trunk resembled the insides of a sick patient—the bulbous fruits in the shape of tumors, the vines as tight around the bark as clogged vessels. All over the ground, fallen cannonball fruits sat with their skin broken, flies and maggots scavenging them.

It began to rain, a light drizzle. Trapped pedestrians started to seek shelter under store awnings. Men and women ran, ran with no concern for grace. A block away, a newsstand owner and a shoeshiner were packing up.

And then it began to rain so hard that I could feel it inside my ears. This was God's fury and torment—a sign that he mourned our loss. The downpour had broken through the polluted and crowded skyline in a matter of seconds. A reminder of my exact size relative to the cosmos, the futility of nudging the future. Gutters turned into rivers, trash cans toppled in violent gusts of wind, and all the locals scrambled to evade the wrath of the black sky as it dropped heaven's burdens onto the souls below. The cannonball tree shook with fury but I did not leave my post for what felt like hours.

I saw the side gate open.

Lazarus emerged, like a specter from the fog.

The house, unencumbered by the guests from the night of the party, looked even larger than I remembered. A crystal chandelier I hadn't noticed before hung from the ceiling, as grand as the kind in an opera house. It looked recently dusted, polished. There wasn't any hint of menace and doom. Not that I worried about my safety. Not that I cared enough about that.

I followed Lazarus wordlessly through the house, as we passed by a couple of giant mirrors, in which I caught my own reflection and hardly recognized this new girl. On days like this, in the top-floor apartment I shared with my mother, I would have to collect pots and bowls from the cupboards and place them on the ground to catch drips.

I heard a loud conversation coming from the dining room as Lazarus led me in, the interruptions and eruptions like the criss-crossing of telephone wires. I could hear the bonhomie, the ca-dences of gladness, of the good life, of confident souls. I could hear the complacent, walled-off snorts of the old, which had a dif-ferent timbre from the indulgent, permeable clucks of the young.

Here I was, in that hole in the world where I'd fallen in once before, in the dark warm quicksand of the night. Outside, the rain continued its concerto.

The Police Chief sat at the head of the table, eating. An ele-gant meal had been laid out, salad Niçoise and some cuts of beef. There were six or seven other people, all around the same age as the Police Chief, wearing formal clothes. I had interrupted some kind of luncheon. The entire table glowed with reflections. Off the silverware. The chandelier. The Rolexes on the men's wrists. One woman sporting a white diamond glistening like tinfoil. The shiny necklace rising from a woman's chest like a pregnant moon.

I imagined the moments preceding my entrance: a maid in-forming Lima and his guests of the presence of a strange girl standing outside, across from the house, apparently lost, her eyes red with tears, her stare fierce and unrelenting; Lima asking his son if that was me, and, upon Lazarus's visual confirmation, finally, telling him to invite me in.

"Is it you, Ana's daughter?" asked Lima, remaining seated, his hands still holding a fork and a knife. "Were you going to ring the doorbell at some point or just stand outside in the rain all day?"

"I think she's been crying," said Lazarus, taking his seat.

The other guests grew silent, staring at me, the grief so evident on my face. They were confused. I wasn't dressed or perfumed like themselves. My kind of intensity didn't belong at that party.

The Police Chief's expression, too, grew somber. "Sit down. Have some lunch. Is everything all right with your mother?"

"It is your fault what happened. It wouldn't have happened if you'd left us alone." I choked on my words, the rare beef on his plate making me feel nauseated. "My mother's dead."

The Police Chief closed his eyes, and pressed his fingers against his temples. To my surprise, he began to whimper, a quick tear racing down his face. A couple of his guests, at the far end of the table, started whispering.

Lima opened his heavy-lidded eyes again and turned his head in the direction of my voice. "When? When did this— How did this—"

"Today. It happened today," I said.

He paused as if considering the weight of the statement, or perhaps its truth. "I'm sorry for your loss," said Lima.

Lazarus stared at him, looking a bit helpless.

"This is your fault," I said, the words racing out of my mouth like flying razors. "You tortured her."

"I never hurt her."

"Eight years ago, you—"

"That is not true."

"You put her on a dragon's chair; you tied her upside down—"

"It's becoming apparent to me," he said, standing now, "that in spite of your love for her, you actually know very little about your mother's life." He pointed a fork generally toward me. "And you're not the least bit afraid? I mean, if I really *am* this monster you describe."

Some of the guests laughed. I noticed now that the woman to the Police Chief's left stared at me quizzically. She had an elaborately coiffed hairdo, the tresses curled like knotted ropes. The man to her right looked at me with pity. They all did.

Every great act was a matter of timing. I pictured the next few seconds: If I had a gun, holding it in the air and pointing it at the Police Chief, a loud series of gasps spreading across the table. Screams. Panic. Cocking the hammer, pulling the trigger. Firing the gun, a single shot in the Police Chief's chest. *Click*. A fatal wound. A stampede. Guests leaving without their jackets. Some trying to get ahead of others. The maid crying. The deafening noise of sirens. A red rotating light. The police taking me away, handcuffed. The mournful remnants of the party—empty plates, broken glasses, chairs turned in every direction. Shards and slivers. Dirty silverware. Half-filled jars of water and containers of coffee. Crumbs and leftovers and peels.

But no, I had no gun. I didn't kill him. The last thing I saw was the bright glow of a chandelier, the rain beating against the window, a fever peaking through me, and everything went black.

I woke to the sound of my own startled breath. My eyes looked onto the dark ceiling, my heart pounding. I couldn't believe I had allowed myself to be unconscious in that house. I knew the Police Chief was a dangerous man despite his blindness, his fatness, his incapacitated state. They had locked me away in some room in the house. But I marveled at the normalcy of the room. This was no interrogation room like the one in which Lima had once locked up my mother. There was no dragon's chair here, no corrugated steel, no binding straps, no electroshock machine.

There was: a bed covered in doily-shaped cotton linens that I was lying in. It smelled powdery, dusty. A nightstand made of unvarnished oak. A half dozen hardcover books. A large closet that included a built-in vanity mirror and table. Its hinges and knobs were upside down, inside out, as if it had been assembled in a hurry.

Rubbing my eyes, I reached for the lamp next to me, but the bulb did not come on. It was easier to stagger to the window than to the light switch on the wall, and I pushed open the wood blinds. It was still light outside, though the rain had ceased. How long had I been asleep?

The door was unlocked. Evidently I wasn't a prisoner.

As I walked down the hallway, there were no signs of anyone until I heard Lazarus's voice from behind a door. He was singing. Playing the guitar. I touched the painted wood with the tip of my fingers, as if this door were the second layer of skin covering him. I believed, as deeply as I believed anything, that my exit from that house depended on the same person who'd shepherded me in. If I wanted to get out, I needed Lazarus to help me.

The room was dark, though more gray than black, making the furniture seem out of focus. Even from where I stood, I could feel the heaviness of the velvet curtains blocking the window. The adjacent wall was covered completely, from floor to ceiling, by a giant rosewood closet. There was a large bed, and lying there, with a guitar on his lap, was Lazarus. The floor was littered with clothes—shirts inside out, pants with each leg pointing in a different direction, a towel or two. A tray sat next to Lazarus, filled with half-eaten food—the spine of an apple, the flaccid skin of a fig, a plate browned with the fatty juice of beef and bedecked with chicken legs and vinegar. The room smelled musty, medicinal.

I came into his room so quietly, so like a feather, that he did not notice me at first. He had his back to me, facing the window, but I could see part of his face. I listened to him sing the chorus to a sad old Roberto Carlos song. Some loves, the lyrics went, were too big to take home with you, and so you had to settle for a postcard. *A burn, a sadness, an ache.* Some loves you left and promised to go back to, but you knew it wasn't possible. *A burn, a sadness, an ache.* Some loves you could only have for the briefest of moments.

For a few seconds, I didn't betray my presence, watching him. I didn't want to break the spell. A sadness lingered over him— almost a physical thing I could touch. I hadn't seen it in him before—not quite like this—and the irony struck me, that in order to truly see someone, the person could not know you were in the same room with them.

"Lazarus . . ." I said, stepping forward.

Lazarus looked up and his look of sadness turned instantly into a smile, but instead of making me happy, the smile just reinforced the sadness I'd seen in him. I could see the air around him shift, the room changing the way one changes in front of a camera. He put away the guitar, as if it belonged only to the private part of himself.

"Are you feeling better?" he asked. "We thought we might have to call a doctor."

"I'm fine. But I want to leave. Can you walk me out?" I asked, my legs feeling like melting Popsicles.

"You're leaving?" he asked, looking disappointed.

"I can't stay a minute longer under the same roof as your dad."

"He's not going to hurt you. Even if he wanted to," said Lazarus.

"Were you the one who brought me upstairs?" I asked.

"Me and the driver. Don't worry, my dad didn't come anywhere near you."

A shiver ran down my spine. "How can you—how can you live with him?"

"I know. He's a strange man," said Lazarus, getting up. He looked around the floor and found a pair of socks, a pair of shoes that he put on. "You know we own every appliance known to man, but he makes the maids do the dishes by hand. The laundry, too. He thinks the washing machine uses too much water. 'People who live in apartments have no idea how high the water bill can be!' is his favorite refrain." When he was done lacing his shoes, he reached for a joint from the nightstand and offered it to me, while lighting another one for himself. "Sometimes he has the maids save the water from doing the dishes and pour it into the plants in the backyard. That water's full of soap, the poor plants."

I shook my head, turned down the joint. "I was actually thinking of the people he hurt, back then."

"Ah!" Lazarus smiled ruefully, inhaling and exhaling. "The folks who throw watermelons over the gate."

"Watermelons?"

"Yeah, they break in an explosive way." The joint between his fingers was so small I could barely see it. "Those folks know what they're doing. Eggs, too. And crucifixes." Lazarus sat his still un-finished joint carefully on top of a paper cup, not wanting to waste it. "You ready to go?"

"Yeah," I nodded.

Lazarus led the way out of the room. "You don't need to be afraid of him. He has diabetes. The doctor says he's only got a few months left."

I didn't feel sorry for Lima. Let death come for him; let it offer him its final and elegant period. I felt sorry for Lazarus, though. He, too, would soon lose his only parent.

Outside, there were no bugs, no animals. The front yard almost felt like the floating deck of a ship. A long clothesline stretched from one end to another, hanging low, slicing the sky in half. Leaving the house I felt as though my senses had changed. The once familiar sky now a vastly different shade of blue. Along the pathway, some pots of geraniums and lilies had been knocked over, lying on the concrete with the elegance of drunken sailors.

I stopped, almost involuntarily. As luck would have it, the Police Chief sat under a gazebo, alone in his wheelchair, only a few yards or so away. I left Lazarus's side even as he reached out to pull me back and walked over to the Police Chief. I stood in front of him. Him, whose face looked like it had been broken and then put back together in the dark. In his wheelchair, his posture was hunched and tired-looking. Without speaking, I stood by the table in front of him. Lazarus looked at me with a confused expression on his face. I didn't know what I was doing, either.

"I shouldn't have come here," I finally said, with rancor in my voice. "But since I'm here, and before I leave, I have to ask you a question."

"Go ahead," said Lima.

I gathered the courage to say the words. "Why did you give my mother all that money?"

He sat there with his pale and spotted skin. The figure sitting there didn't match the Police Chief of my mother's stories, or even the Police Chief of the other night, and I wondered how much had been bluster all along. His mouth gaped open, as if wanting to be fed, or to suckle. I felt instant revulsion, but also a strange familiarity—this wordless begging to be cared for. He appeared almost worthy. Underneath his damaged spirit lay a body as miraculous as any other person's.

"Your mother would not want me to tell you," he said.

"But I want to know."

He couldn't see them, but I fought back tears as well as I could.

"All right, I will tell you."

As the Police Chief began to tell me my mother's story, I focused closely on his voice. It was easier to listen to him than to look at him.

"I gave her the money because I owed it to her."

"How?" I knew Lima was sick, but had he lost his mind?

"Eight years ago, on the day of the failed raid, your mother came to me and asked me for a hundred thousand cruzeiros in exchange for information that would lead to the capture of key members of the Revolutionary Popular Movement." He said it matter-of-factly. "I took the information, but gave her no money. I believe the situation has now been rectified."

It was as though he'd said this all in a secret code I had to decipher.

"I don't—I don't understand." Terror tightened around my

neck. Like water in a rushing stream, only one direction possible, no turning back.

"She led the student activists to believe she was working for them, but she wasn't, she was working for herself," he said, as though speaking of an admired peer. "And she had a healthy respect for the power of money." He squinted his eyes at me. "What don't you understand? She came in to make a deal with me. Let me repeat, so we're very clear: She offered the students on a plate in exchange for cash."

"No, she didn't offer, she said you tortured her, and that's how you found out—"

"No, I didn't lay a finger on her. I didn't need to. She was very eager to find some way to profit from her information. And I was eager to put the information to use." A shadow fell over my face. "Your mother . . . if she hadn't helped me, the loss of the prisoners would've been a huge embarrassment. Instead, I destroyed them. I got promoted. She made my career." His fixed stare made him look as if he could see all this unfolding in front of him, as if he had box seats for a screening of his life. "I was able to buy this house because of her."

He spoke so plainly, as if talking about an office job, which perhaps, to him, was what it had been. A job that someone else would do if he didn't want to. That this house, this life, was a hard-earned promotion.

I couldn't stop shaking my head. "You're a liar. I don't believe you. You're pretending you were not a torturer—"

"I *was* a torturer!" exclaimed Lima, widening his cloudy eyes. "And I would've tortured your mother, make no mistake. But I didn't need to. She did my job for me!" Lima let out a small chuckle. "And at the time, I didn't feel bad about stiffing her, but a man can change. And I was glad I was able to settle that old account. She deserved every penny."

I shook my head. "But why would she lie? Why would she make those claims?"

"I don't know. Because I'm an easy target?"

"Why would she pretend that she was tortured when she wasn't?"

Lima shrugged. "I don't know. Maybe to get attention? Maybe to throw the rebels off the scent, so they wouldn't suspect what she did? If the survivors had found out what she did, they would probably have killed her." He kept unpeeling my mother's story, down to the innermost pith. "But she didn't need to worry. Those leftist groups, they would all have been captured anyway. They were always taking too many risks."

"My mother would never have sent those men to their deaths."

"No, she thought we were just going to arrest them. And we would have, if they hadn't tried to escape."

"That's not my mother. The woman you're describing, that's not my mother," I said, searching for a lie somewhere on Lima's face. "She wasn't an activist. She was an actress."

"That's how they recruited her, I remember," he said, almost fondly. "They wanted her to play the part of a janitor who had overheard sensitive information. They wanted her to recite a little play with neither head nor toes. They didn't count on your mother having her own goals. She did not want to be a part of their mission. She didn't think prisoners should be able to escape just like that. Ana was on the side of the police. On the side of the dictatorship. On the right side."

"Stop. Please stop," I begged. "You have no credibility. You're a known torturer." I considered these facts, as if for the first time, and simply said, "I don't believe you."

"I am," he said, nodding vigorously, "a torturer. That was my job and is now my reputation. But I didn't torture your mother. She helped me, and I helped her. She collaborated with me. She was a collaborator."

"You're lying!" I screamed.

I ran, leaving Lima in the shade of his gazebo, Lazarus lingering by the gate. The driveway once struck me as a mile long, but I saw now it wasn't much more than a few steps, the pebbles shifting under my feet. I could hear Lazarus calling out for me, but I ignored him, careening out on to the street. The rain puddles reflected a blinding sun, a blur of white blinding me as I raced away to the bear of my throbbing heart. I couldn't slow all the feelings coursing through the city inside of me—the alleys, the avenues, the geography of my past. I joined the throngs of men and women marching along the busy boardwalk, my steps mingling with theirs, my body only one of so many in the late afternoon crowd—this crowd that absorbed me and made me both anonymous and whole. The ficus groves. The carpet of almond leaves. The heart-shaped leaves of a low hibiscus bough shimmying to some song whispered by the wind.

Before I knew it, I was at the beach, and I took my shoes off so I could walk on the white sand, the grains gluing like talcum to my callused feet. Dusk folded the last vestiges of sunlight in a neat peach-colored blanket. The air dry, electric, ripe for brushfires. I kept walking among the seaweed, the algae fronds manacling my ankles, my toes.

The high-rises of Rio de Janeiro loomed behind me, lit and fueled, born out of the dreams of people like my mother, and I wept for my loss.

Ahead of me, the sands stretched out for miles, undulating dunes, speckles of gold everywhere. The ocean water glistened in shades of emerald green, shiny as Mylar, the sun setting dramatically—an explosion of red and orange, the whole sky a dream, an abstract painting. In a short while, everyone at the beach would stop what they were doing to gather and clap for the sun as it dove into the water.

A torturer. A collaborator.

I sat by myself on one of the smooth black rocks by the cove and let the waves lullaby my crescent moon sorrow. I watched skiffs and boats pepper the pier in the distance. The booming voices of leather-skinned men echo, their shirts open, their ebb and flow matching the waves. The breeze tickled me like an old friend, my arms, my legs, my ankles, grazing against the fabric of my clothes.

I had the waning light. I had the perfumed air. I had the songs of the howler monkeys from the canopied trees. I had myself.

Bel Air, California

The early 1990s

Mara, age twenty-six

chapter ten

IN THE EVENING OF KATHRYN'S LAST DAY OF RADIATION therapy, as if to mark the occasion, celebratory music drifted in from the tacky château across the street. I heard it from the kitchen, the whiplash of treble from the live band, the microphone echo.

I knocked on Kathryn's open door, as a courtesy, and stepped in.

"The noise, is it bothering you?" I asked, leaning against the doorframe, both my arms and legs crossed. "Should I go over there and ask them to keep it down?"

Kathryn smiled and shook her head. "No. It's a wedding. I mean, it's a wedding reception."

"Oh."

"And it doesn't bother me. I'm glad they're having a good time."

"That explains all the cars."

"I was invited to it," said Kathryn, a bit wistfully.

I sat down on the chair across from her. She was wearing a faded cream shirt with a black asymmetrical button line. She'd

rolled up the sleeves. She looked ready for a meeting at a hip coffee shop instead of convalescing at home.

"Do you want to go?" I asked.

Kathryn gave me a look of surprise. "A second ago you were
ready to shut down the party."

"That's before I knew you had been invited. I can see in your
eyes that you want to go."

"I'm too weak," said Kathryn, her smile betraying her.

I leaned forward on the chair. "It's just across the street. And
you don't have to dance or drink. You can sit around and listen to
the music."

"Do you think they'll mind?"

I furrowed my brows. "You *were* invited, yes?"

"I was. But the Kathryn Weatherly they invited was a different
person. If I show up like this, will they think I'm a fraud?"

"You're being ridiculous," I said, leaning my head to the side, as
though looking at a crooked painting. "Everyone's rooting for you."

She looked at me unhappily. "Times like this I wish Nelson
were here. He was good at parties. It was nice to have him by
my side," Kathryn said, noticing the sympathy on my face. "Sometimes when I'm honest with myself, I admit that it's not really him
that I miss. It's love that I miss. Love with a capital L. I've never
craved love more than I do now."

She made her hand into a fist and pressed it lightly against her
lips. "People think that when you're sick, you want pity. But it's not
pity, it's love. It's the only thing that makes it more bearable. I wish
people didn't say, 'I'm sorry,' or 'Oh, what a tragedy, I can't imagine what you're going through.' That just makes me feel bad for
you, actually, that *you* have to deal with *my* sickness." She looked

out the window where more people were parking cars, arriving to celebrate. "I wish people would say instead, *I care about you*, or *I love you*. That way, I get something to hang on to, something in return."

"Maybe someone will say that at this party," I said. "I'll come with you, if you'd like. You don't have to go by yourself."

Kathryn beamed. "Would you? You know, you've already won the Caregiver of the Year Award."

I shrugged my shoulders and helped Kathryn get up from her chair.

"You don't really want that award, do you? Do you by any chance *not* like being a caregiver?" asked Kathryn, looking at me with curiosity. "Because what a peculiar conundrum that would be, if you were so good at something you didn't want to do."

"It's not that I don't like it," I said, helping Kathryn stand on her own two feet. "I just feel like I never got to choose."

The neighbor's estate was far larger than Kathryn's, and had a pool and a tennis court he had transformed into a flower garden, with elaborate arrangements of roses and orchids adorning the tables, the entrances to the tents, and the trellised walls. The guests gossiped gauchely about the cost of everything; the budget of items seemed like public knowledge. They had spent ten thousand dollars on the flowers alone. We had missed dinner, but saw that they were served mushrooms as the appetizers and rack of lamb as the main entrée.

Kathryn sat down at the table we'd been hastily assigned to, with the other delinquents who hadn't RSVP'd properly. We were seated quite far from the wedding party's family, with a bunch of mismatched people, many of them there by themselves. Kathryn did not tell anyone about being sick, and no one asked. She looked thin, yes, but not dangerously so.

Soon after we arrived, a woman in a silk muumuu to the left of me took an interest in us and asked how the two of us met. She'd been a radio producer years ago and described herself as a "collector of stories."

"She's my adopted daughter," Kathryn explained almost light-heartedly. "I figured, I didn't want to raise a child, but I wanted one to take care of me in my old age."

"You consider yourself old? You look like you're in your forties," the woman asked, slowly and clearly, as if talking into a microphone.

"I'm not her daughter," I said, having to speak up a bit so I could be heard above the music. Kathryn watched us, and I made sure I directed a smile her way to take any sting out of my words. "I'm her caregiver."

"She's going through a rebellious period. Trying to get me to disown her," said Kathryn.

The woman let out a hearty laugh, getting the joke at last. "How long have you two known each other?"

"About four months, but it feels like a lot longer," I said.

I let Kathryn and the woman continue chatting. I felt a sudden warmth toward Americans as I watched them eat and drink. Americans were kind toward each other, trusted one another, did not have to worry about being cheated or lied to all day, every day. Their spirits were allowed to soar, unbound by the rapacity and hypocrisy of oppression. This party, filled with joy and celebration, was the very embodiment of the fruits of democracy—everyone free, smiling, unaware of how good they had it. How lucky I felt to be a part of it.

It turned out to be one of those evenings that had no end. As if night were a tall bottle of wine and because no one could find a cork, it kept spilling and spilling. The band gave way to a popular singer who'd been famous a decade ago and seemed overly excited and happy for the wedded couple. The party spread to the pool, the actual house, the endless slingshot-shaped gardens, transmitted by bodies contagious with curiosity and desire. Colored lights one-upped nature. I thought about my mother, what she would think of this party. She'd probably stuff her purse with chocolate truffles, down one glass of champagne after another. I could see her standing next to the staff area, so she could get first crack at the hors d'oeuvres.

Kathryn had not been out this late since her diagnosis. I looked around at all that she'd given up—festivity, merriment, the smiles of strangers. I could see the joys of life beckoning her back. She'd been sick in bed for so long, she'd forgotten all the things that she could do.

Like observe. Or take things for granted. Or waste time and space. Or walk around in the dark, arm in arm with her thoughts.

I wondered if anyone else at the party was like her—sick, but hiding it. Mistaken for healthy. I wondered if one of the people I'd recently honked at in traffic and given the finger to and cursed at had been a sick person like her. I wondered how many times I had stood in line at the grocery store next to a woman who only had a couple of years left in her.

What a pleasure it must be for Kathryn, to convene amidst the healthy, to pass herself off with the guile of a spy, to pretend with everyone else that they were immortal. It occurred to me that it cost her nothing to think like that, whereas being conscious of her impending mortality cost her, well, everything. What if, I wondered, Kathryn believed herself immortal until the very last minute, the minute right before it all came to an end? What if she saved her sorrows and her grief and her turmoil until then?

I could tell how much Kathryn wanted to stay at the party, how she had wanted to come, desperately, all along. She wasn't really doing much—not dancing, not drinking—just standing by the pool watching inebriated people, letting me take surreptitious trips to nearby tables for champagne and tuna tartare. But I could tell her mind was flush with the busyness of life.

Life is a party. I'd seen the cliché before, in a card sold in the knickknacks and novelties section of a clothing store, the words imprinted in a silly font, or maybe in the eleven o'clock number of some spirited Broadway musical. A party.

Some people had to leave in the beginning. Some people left in the middle. Some people got to stay until the end. But everyone got to be in it, at least for a part of it, and wasn't that what mattered? And maybe getting to stay to the very end, blissfully hungover, was a luxury rather than a right, a quirk of stamina and genetics and luck. Yes, it would be lovely to stay until the end, but even if you didn't, you got a chance to taste its flavors, to mingle with its strange creatures, to try out new tricks.

It wasn't that big of a deal. No need to cry, no reason to be mad. It was just a party that some were asked to leave early. My mother, Kathryn—they had been tapped on the shoulder, singled out for some unknown reason. We would linger, watching them go.

I brought Kathryn some tuna tartare as she rested on a leather cube by the pool, her eyes glazed. I sat next to her, following her gaze—the ripples in the water, the tiki torches, the colored lights reflecting purple and red.

"I don't want to die," said Kathryn, watching the light flicker across the pool's surface.

"I know," I said.

"I want to be here next year, and the year after, and the year after that."

"You will," I said. "I'm a witch. Didn't I already tell you that? I can see the future and I can see you in it. I see you alive. And healthy. And happy."

"Do you?" asked Kathryn, turning to me. She had spilled a pink dot on her cream shirt and her lips looked painted red from too much wine.

"I do. You're going to be fine, Kathryn."

"I don't want to go. I don't want to die," she kept muttering, on the brink of tears. I drew her closer to me and, for the first time since we'd known each other, I let her head lean against my shoulder. The physical proximity of comfort. She let her tears stream down her face, contour the curve of her chin, and fall onto the concrete in intermittent drops, oblivious to the party around us.

I ran my hand up and down her arm. "You're going to be okay."

"It's not because I'm still hoping to climb Mt. Everest," she murmured wistfully. "Or because I want to win Miss Universe.

It's not because I love to dance, or because I'll miss the music of Bono, or because I haven't been to Vienna yet. It's not because I'll miss my favorite flavor of ice cream." She dipped her hand into the pool. "There's no *why* I want to stay. I just do."

Even near the end, even during the worst days of her disease, my mother and I never spoke like this. But of course she must've ruminated on what it would've meant for her to stay alive. I thought now of all she did to keep herself—to keep *us*—alive, her nearly primal desire to survive.

"You don't have to have a reason," I said softly. "No one wants to die. And no one your age should ever have to think about it."

"I'm glad I'm still considered too young to die," said Kathryn, wiping her tears, and half hiccupping, half chuckling.

Then she got up, and, without excusing herself to me, faced the pool. She wasn't wearing a swimsuit, of course, just a cream charmeuse shirt she'd rolled up to her elbows, and a brown skirt. She put a foot in. Then another. She let the expanse of blue reach up to her ankles, then up to her knees. Finally, as people nearby started to notice her, she allowed the pool to wet her skirt, soaking from the waist down. I suspected she liked the feeling of wading through water, fighting its pull. All around her there were guests and none seemed to mind sharing the moon and the water with her. She didn't care about her low white blood cell count, or the risk of infection, or how it would take hours to warm herself up. It was so simple, to just let the water push firmly against her.

The next day, I watched as Kathryn sat on the edge of her chair, surprised by how hungrily—how suddenly—she clung to existence.

All of life's routines now felt precious to her. Like looking out the window and seeing the manzanita and snowberry trees brightly illuminated by the sun, feeling its warmth.

All she wanted was to be in a room, in a comfy chair, and able to breathe. That was enough. That was life. Those were riches. What could be more wonderful than to sit in a chair and say, *I am alive, I am here*.

Everything else was superfluous. The living focus on what they could gain, and pay no mind to what they could lose.

I watched as the sun made diagonal stripes on the floor, taking over more and more territory. The sun shone only in spots, as if drained through a sieve. The sun made objects shine as if the light came from within them. I could see the rays turning her hair into a torch, her skin ablaze with a pellucid glow. She was one of those objects, too, shining, shining—being loved by that rambunctious, boisterous star.

chapter eleven

IT WAS A THURSDAY AFTERNOON WHEN NELSON CAME BY
to visit Kathryn. I served them coffee and the lemon pound cake
he had brought.

"You look really good, by the way," said Nelson.

"I've lost a vicious amount of weight," Kathryn replied.

"I can't really tell. I'd never know you were sick just from looking at you."

"I'm not sick at all. This is a big, elaborate ruse for me to get
some attention."

Nelson laughed. I handed Kathryn her coffee, then Nelson his.

I didn't expect him to track me down an hour later, as I made a
grocery list in the kitchen.

"I just wanted to show you something quick," said Nelson.

"Where's Kathryn?"

"She went upstairs to watch TV," he said.

I did not move, and Nelson stroked his chin awkwardly as it dawned on him that the transaction would happen right there in front of the kitchen sink. He reached for his wallet and pulled out a clipping from a newspaper. He unfolded it carefully, the same way I imagined he'd folded it in the first place. I could tell Nelson had not torn off the article; he'd clipped it with a pair of scissors, the borders clean and even. I felt a fondness for the clipping, how it had sat in between the folds of his wallet for however long, waiting for me.

"Brazil is reopening the investigations of torture during the dictatorship," said Nelson, paraphrasing the headline I was now reading. "They're prosecuting the people responsible, releasing their names."

I was jolted. Were they really going to go after the guilty parties? I began to skim the paragraphs, trying not to let my shock unfurl against the neat black and white newsprint. That piece of paper seemed to contain the entire world—past, present, and future.

"Why are you showing this to me?" I asked.

"Just the way your face looked the other day." Nelson added, "I thought you might be interested."

"I *am* interested. But not in the way you're assuming. My mother wasn't . . . She wasn't tortured," I said, folding the clipping in his palm. "In fact, quite the opposite. She was a collaborator. With the military police."

Nelson furrowed his brow. "What do you mean?"

"She gave away names," I said. "She gave away information. Almost like a . . . like a spy? Like a double agent."

"Oh."

"Yes. *Oh*." I nodded bitterly. "You always figure you're talking to a victim. Or the family of a victim. But what if you're the perpetrator?" I sighed. "But it doesn't matter; she's dead now."

His face darkened and he put the clipping back in his wallet. "I'm so sorry, I didn't realize she was—"

I shook my head, touched by the genuine intensity of his concern. "It's because I still talk about her like she's alive. I like to think she still *is*, somewhere."

"Yeah, I thought she was still alive, just not near you," he said kindly, and I felt an overwhelming urge to wrap my arms around him.

"Yeah, it must be confusing, but I can't use the past tense when I talk about her. She exists to me, just on a different plane. I mean, literally, she *is*, not *was*, in her grave in Brazil. But she's all around me. In my thoughts. I know my mother, and I know that's what she wanted most. To be remembered."

"How long ago did she die?" he asked.

"I know. I'm in denial. But denial is not a bad place to be, contrary to popular belief. She's still around, I'm just not able to speak to her."

There was an awkward pause and then Nelson asked, "Do you want to . . . do you want to talk about what happened?"

"What's there to say? When she died, I felt so abandoned. I was so mad at her for dying. I used to worship her when I was little."

"How did she die?" asked Nelson.

"In infamy," I said. It was the first thought that crossed my mind. "But I shouldn't say that, should I? I mean, it's one thing to say bad things about her when she's alive, but I can't speak ill of her when she's dead. She can't defend herself."

I covered my face with my hands.

"Don't try to censor yourself," said Nelson, gently. "You feel how you feel."

Here, in front of me, was an educated, kindly man who wouldn't judge me or diminish my pain. "It's hard to say this out loud but . . . When I said that she gave away information . . . Well, that led to the deaths of six innocent people." A shadow crossed over my body. "I used to think she was an angel, but now I wonder . . ."

Nelson narrowed his eyes. "Either way you exalt her, make her out to be larger than life? What if she was just a person, and she made a mistake?"

"Did you hear what I said?" I asked, in agony. "People died because of her."

"I don't know the circumstances, but I know it must have been a violent and complicated time."

I wasn't sure how to even begin to tell Nelson how she had been responsible. I boiled it down to basic facts: She deceived people and they died because of it. When I was done, Nelson didn't seem to share in my antagonism.

"It sounds like your mother got caught up in matters that were out of her depth," said Nelson, scratching his chin for a second or two. "But that doesn't make her a murderer."

"People died because of her!" And besides Octopus, La Bardot, the others . . . how many more people—their relatives, their lovers—had suffered because of her? I wanted to forgive her. But how could I? She'd lied to me. When I felt charitable, I told myself that she'd chosen wrongly many, many years ago, and had already paid for it. But I often didn't feel like being charitable.

"You're making her so important. You're using her mistake to keep her on a pedestal. You're giving her a bigger role than maybe she had."

"Role," I scoffed. "That's ironic."

"What is?"

"Nothing." I sat down at the kitchen table. I felt like I'd waited years to talk about this with someone smart and educated enough to understand, and now that the opportunity had arrived, I no longer had the desire to do so. "Don't get me wrong. I love her."

"You love her but you don't forgive her for her mistakes?" repeated Nelson, as he sat down next to me.

"Sometimes I do. But lying to me was more than a mistake," I said, tugging my hair.

"I can see why she did, though," said Nelson, resting his hand reassuringly over my knee.

"No, you don't get it. Something this big, you never get over." As I pulled away from Nelson, he almost lost his balance. "And I think you should go, before Kathryn sees you."

He stood up and from the kitchen doorway said, "I think she didn't want to lose her stature in front of you." He paused, as if thinking this over. "But don't make a god out of her. It's hard to forgive God, but you can forgive a person."

Kathryn radiated an almost palpable sadness for the rest of the day after Nelson's visit. It was like a ghoulish cape. She created a silence between us, and into that silence I stepped, asking, "How was the visit with Mr. Nelson? Was it good to see him?"

She sighed and shuffled to a nearby stool, her slight frame making it look massive beneath her. "I wish I'd worked things out with him before it was too late," said Kathryn, looking wan. "I didn't know back then, that I might not have the years to waste. Everyone else, they can fuck around for ten, maybe even twenty years—they can afford it. But I can't."

"Are you sure it's too late?" I asked.

"Oh yeah, once you've poisoned the well, you can't drink from it. But I *did* love him."

Why wasn't love enough? Love was everything, but it wasn't enough.

"My God, what a waste," exclaimed Kathryn, looking up at the ceiling. Something in her voice made me think she was about to cry. "I used to think, we humans make so many mistakes, it takes so many tries to get it right, it's a good thing that life is long. But I was wrong. Sometimes you *have* to get it right the first time."

I nodded helplessly, trying to find the right words to comfort her. "I'm sorry, Kathryn."

"What a fuck-up. What a huge fuck-up, on both of our parts."

"You can't fix it?" I asked, wondering if mistakes could be erased, or redeemed.

"No," said Kathryn, wryly, running her fingers along her fine hair. "They make it seem so romantic in the movies. But who wants to kiss a sick person? Who'd want to be in a relationship with me now? What is the point of being with someone with an expiration date?"

"Don't talk like that," I said, shaking my head.

"It's not true? And I can't even complain, because it'd be weird if cancer *did* turn him on."

"You're not cancer," I said, reaching out to pat her lightly on her arm. "You're Kathryn."

Kathryn thought about that for a second and then said, "And it takes a lot of confidence to make someone love you for who you are. I don't know if I have that."

"Why're you talking like this?" I asked, gently.

Her eyelids hung low, exhausted. "I know. It's awful. This disease. I hate the bitterness that comes with it."

"You're not bitter. You're going to be fine, Kathryn. I know that."

"No, I won't. The ultimate goal is not to convince myself that nothing bad's going to happen. The goal is to know something bad will happen but still be okay with it."

"That sounds like a terribly difficult thing to do."

Kathryn laughed devastatingly. "It is *impossible* to do. But thank you for saying that. For trying."

Surely I'd gleaned some pearl of wisdom I could share with Kathryn after everything with my mother's death. But I couldn't think of anything, other than saying that losing a loved one was terrible and awful.

I realized then that I hated when people tried to find the silver lining in tragedy. There was no upside, none. I did not grow from it, or become a better person, or learn to appreciate life, or any such cliché. Kathryn's death would not seed some kind of beautiful legacy any more than my mother's had. It'd just make those she left behind feel sad and morose.

I didn't tell her any of this, but I moved closer to her, to let her know I was still there.

That night the lights went off, as though the universe was not the result of complex ongoing electromagnetic reactions, but merely reflected the moods of a single individual. Kathryn was already in bed, and I alone experienced the sudden disappearance of electricity, the TV and the lamp bulb dying together. I looked out the window and saw the streetlamp still shining its stubborn light, and the neighbor's house still glowing through its tiny squares. For a second it made sense to me that I was in the dark, the outside mirroring my inside.

I called Nelson for help. I was hesitant, but I couldn't go home with the refrigerator not running. I didn't want to wake Kathryn, and Nelson was the only other person who knew how the house worked.

He arrived ten minutes later and I greeted him by the back door.

"Have you tried the circuit breaker?" he asked, as he walked past me into the kitchen. He was wearing a worn-out white T-shirt stamped with the words *St. Louis 5K Run* and navy lounge pants. I was struck by his casualness, arriving essentially in his pajamas. This was his old house, though, so maybe his casualness had to do with where he was going, rather than whom he was coming to.

"I hope you're not afraid of the dark," said Nelson, a smile in his voice.

"Only if there's serial killers on the loose," I said, prompting a laugh from him.

I followed him in. Nelson had no trouble navigating in the dark. Like a pro, he had brought a flashlight. I held it and guided it to a corner of the room-sized pantry.

He easily found the circuit board and struggled, with both hands, to undo its tight latch and get it opened. Like most expensive things, it was built to look exquisite when it worked, but be totally inconvenient when it didn't. As the light illuminated both his fingers and his nearby face, I could see the attentive expressions forming around his eyes and lips, the gritting of teeth and furrowing of brows. My face was only a couple of feet from his, and there was something improbably romantic about the whole thing. Only a couple of hours earlier Kathryn had rhapsodized nearby, and maybe the molecules of her own desire lingered, waiting for a new host. There could be no other explanation for the closeness that I felt for Nelson at that moment, one that I immediately decided to stifle.

The L-shaped latch gave way to the circuit board and Nelson quickly flipped a series of switches, pausing a few seconds, and then flipping them again in the opposite direction. As soon as he did so, the sound of a cheerful TV jingle broke the silence and a small, washed-out light shone from the living room a few yards away. The rest of the house remained dark. The refrigerator, my main concern, began to hum quietly.

It was very anticlimactic.

The low light flooding in from the rest of the house was really not enough to illuminate our faces. I could see an overall shape of Nelson, and suddenly then, I could sense his head inch closer to mine. Slowly, tentatively, awaiting a pulling back. I moved closer, and our faces matched up by instinct, by memory, no different from Nelson feeling his way through the dark, familiar house earlier. Soon our lips touched, and I felt my body flood with the opposite of everything Kathryn had spoken of—not regret but fondness, not bitterness but joy, not disappointment but hope.

After that, maybe trying to escape the kiss, which we did not acknowledge, or seeing that he'd overstayed his reasons for coming,

Nelson took the flashlight back and left the house, moving a little more quietly than he had when he'd first come in. I followed him out, the way I would do with any guest, a pace or two behind him.

Before he went out the door, Nelson turned to me and said, "You're going to try to make yourself feel bad later. I advise you not to."

The next day tipped upside down and I couldn't figure out how to get it right side up. First, Kathryn had me drive her to Nelson's hospital without arranging to see him. A surprise, she said, to thank him for his visit. There, the receptionist said that Nelson was at lunch, but she was welcome to wait. Kathryn and I sat in the waiting room, which was screened off from the elevator area through a transparent, crystal-like hanging wall, the kind of wall that divided but did not separate.

Across from us sat an old man. He was an albino with prominent white eyebrows, and a head conspicuously large relative to his wiry frame. Next to him, a younger-looking woman with long hair read a magazine spread like a scroll over her lap. She could be either his wife or his daughter, and though they were sitting next to each other, her body language made no claim for him.

I reached for a *Time* magazine lying on the seat next to me. There was a gigantic sticker on the cover, which read: "Property of UCLA Oncology. Do not remove from the Lobby Area." The same white sticker was on all the magazines, and to me, they seemed a little dramatic and unnecessary.

"Could you go to the cafeteria and get me some coffee?" asked Kathryn, handing me a five-dollar bill. "You know how I like it."

At the cafeteria, I spotted Nelson at one of the tables in the back. I hesitated at first, but then walked up to him. It looked like he was finished with his food. I told him that Kathryn was waiting.

"Why? Is she not feeling well?" asked Nelson.

"No, she's fine, but she wanted to see you. I think she's feeling a little needy," I said.

"All right, I can help her with that," said Nelson, clearing the crumbs off the table. "And you? How are you? I've been thinking about you and your mother."

I sat down across from him on the plastic chair. "You know what I like about Americans?"

"What?"

"Your compassion," I said, smiling. "Like the compassion you offered my mother the other day."

"Everyone deserves compassion and kindness," said Nelson, as though this were his official diagnosis. I looked away, to a nearby window. I spotted a bird, imagined it chirping mellifluously. "You want to know what I think?"

"No," I said, shaking my head.

Nelson chuckled. "I'll tell you anyway. I think the anger is a scab you're afraid to pick at in case blood starts spurting out." Nelson reached for my arm and put his hand over it. "But maybe if you remove the scab you'll find that your skin has healed underneath."

I swallowed. If my mother was the flood, I wondered if Nelson might be an insurance adjuster coming to my aid. I reached for his face and pecked him on the cheek, a token of my gratitude. Nelson drew me in for a kindly embrace, and I let him envelop me. His body felt good against me. We stayed sealed like that for a while, without letting go. Behind him, I looked out through the window for the chirping bird. In the distance, I caught a glimpse of a woman standing haloed by the sun behind her.

I saw her expressions first, before I could fully designate their owner—confusion, followed by horror, followed by anger. It was Kathryn.

I drew away from Nelson. I felt a panic rise in my body. I looked at Nelson, trying to communicate without words what I had seen, but when I looked in the direction of the apparition again, it was gone. Kathryn wasn't there. There wasn't even a woman who resembled her. Had I just imagined it? There's no way Kathryn could've appeared and disappeared so quickly, within the blink of an eye. Either she'd been there and still was, or she'd never been there, to begin with.

Nothing about that day had fundamentally changed—the sun still shone too much, the birds were still chirping in tune—but just like that, nothing seemed the same, either.

Driving home, I tried to hide my nervousness. I focused on the traffic lights. The cars immediately in front of me, with license plates from as far as New York and Florida. The afternoon sun cascading down the asphalt.

Next to me, Kathryn kept her eyes straight ahead, out the window. She had not looked at me in the eye once since we'd gotten in the car.

When we arrived home, Kathryn did not get out of the car like she normally did. She hesitated, her right hand floating over the door handle. Her hands, it was hard not to notice, were as delicate and small as a bird's. It was clear: She could not look me in the eye.

I was parked on the curb by the driveway, and cars whooshed past us on the road. I remained fixed in my seat, awaiting Kathryn's lead. Kathryn finally took a deep breath and said simply, "You know you can't work for me anymore, right?"

She offered no further explanation. She did not say, *I saw this*, or *I know that*. She was not going to dive into the minutiae of it, the details, the narrative. The question allowed no discourse, no argument.

"I know. But—"

"What would you do in my place? In my condition?" Kathryn spat.

What could I possibly say? It felt like even if I explained to Kathryn what happened, she wouldn't believe me. I shrugged.

Kathryn kept going, as though she distrusted silence. "Is there anything worse you could've done to me?" she snarled. "Short of switching out my medication?"

I shook my head. "I'm not interested in your ex-husband. He was just—he was just helping me with something."

Kathryn scoffed. "And to think I was going to leave you this house—"

"You were never going to—" I interrupted her.

"Maybe I was!" she shouted, wringing her hands in exasperation. "You were like a daughter to me!"

Was I? Or had she said so to inspire my devotion? Her daughter. That wasn't a role that I'd asked for. If I'd accepted it, it had been out of habit or from a lack of imagination.

"I don't want to be anyone's daughter," I said, clutching the steering wheel. "I just want to be me."

Kathryn's eyes widened with anger. "Well, I don't want you to be my daughter, either. I used to think you must really love your real mother. If you treat her anything like how you've treated me today, I think, in fact, you must really hate her."

In the car, there was an excitable energy between us that could find expression in any number of gestures. I wouldn't be surprised if she slapped me, or started crying, or let out a scream.

"The truth is," she said in a tone of palpable asperity, "I know nothing about you. Or where you came from. Maybe this is all natural, back where you grew up."

With that, Kathryn left my Honda and slammed the door.

I watched as she headed back inside. I understood the unspoken procedure: I'd have to make arrangements with the new caregiver to come back for my things, preferably when Kathryn wasn't around.

As I put the key in the ignition, I gazed at Kathryn's back, knowing I might not see her again. I felt an unexpected ache, couldn't turn my eyes away. I wondered if it was possible to be exiled from my own heart.

chapter twelve

THE INVASIONS BEGAN ON A TUESDAY MORNING, ON AN
unreasonably hot summer day, a day so hot that the West Side
felt like East Hollywood, and East Hollywood felt like Brazil. I
woke to find three little ants roaming around the same spot on
the water-splattered sink, looking lost. Their black uniforms stood
out against the bright whiteness of the ceramic. I watched them
through the goggles of morning drowsiness, hoping they would
choose to go elsewhere of their own volition. Reluctantly, I recruited Bruno's help. He'd been going through an exercise kick
and I could hear him huffing and puffing as he lifted free weights
in the living room.

We stood over the sink, staring at the ants as they chased their
own behinds.

"It takes just one to venture into the wrong place, and pretty
soon we'll be overrun," said Bruno.

"Can we lure them outside, maybe with melted brown sugar?"
I asked.

"What if that just attracts more?"

"That's true."

"It's not enough to kill them. We have to get rid of the trace," said Bruno, furrowing his brows. "I wonder how they ended up here in the first place."

"They're probably thirsty," I said, looking out the window at the punishing morning sun. "I mean, you have to admire these little creatures. They're so selfless and cooperative, foraging for the collectivity. It proves that communism is actually endemic to nature. I wonder how they take water back to the colony."

"Maybe they carry it in their mouths and spit it out into this really large bowl once they get back to the colony, and the other ants drink from it."

Bruno's tendency to make light of things was something I was now used to. I hadn't left my room for days, and Bruno was really the only person I spoke to. It was so nice to speak Portuguese with him, after weeks of being trapped in Kathryn's English.

"There's probably lots more of them behind that wall."

"I'm gonna check in the kitchen and see if we have traps," said Bruno. "They'll eat the poison and take it to the queen. Matricide."

"Something about killing them feels wrong," I said, leaning forward slightly. "I don't mind killing predatory insects like spiders or mosquitoes, but ants, they're just going about their day, doing their own thing."

"I'd love to stand here all day and ponder with you, but I have to get back to my weights," said Bruno. "We gotta get rid of them."

He stepped forward and turned on the faucet. Without smashing them, he swept the ants with his fingers into the running water. They hardly resisted, dying the second they hit the stream. The ant that Bruno hadn't yet gotten to began to run faster, in a more disorderly manner, as if trying to escape. Bruno got to all of them. A few seconds later there were only blotches of water where his hand had been.

The next morning, I woke but did not leave the bed. It became clear by now Kathryn wasn't going to change her mind, wasn't going to bring me back to the house. I closed my eyes and when I reopened them, I found Bruno in the bathroom of my suite. He wore a torn-up yellow T-shirt he'd gotten from a secondhand store, the words *À Boute de Souffle* printed on it.

"Are they still there?" I called out, groggy with sleep.

When I heard no answer, I slowly pushed the blankets away and got out of bed. I joined him at the battleground.

The little creatures, small but ambitious, had taken possession of the sea of white that was my sink. Some of them ran in an orderly line, others circled around in their version of figure eights. I noticed two of them bumping into each other for a deliberate second, and they appeared to kiss, or relay, before heading in opposite directions. I sensed their busyness, their preoccupations. There was an unspoken logic to their actions I wasn't privy to.

"We should call our landlord," said Bruno. "He'll bring the pesticide guy. Those people who got rid of the cockroaches last year."

The creatures seemed harmless—tiny, unable to fly, running away when you weren't even chasing them.

"Maybe we should wait." I pondered. For a moment, I felt thankful for this distraction.

"What for? It's only going to get worse."

I sighed. "I'm just not convinced we have control over the matter. What if they call the pesticide guy and the ants just retreat for
a while and come back after a couple of weeks?"

"They will die," he said. "I'm going to spray Raid all over them."

"Some of them will die, but not all of them," I said. "God
knows how many ants live in that colony. God knows where that
colony is."

Bruno put out ant traps on the sink, right in their trail, but the
creatures brazenly ignored them, stepping around them, avoiding the gloomy dark hole. Bruno and I had never met such well-
trained soldiers before. We would have to restrategize.

"We need to find the colony," said Bruno.

"It won't be easy," I said.

Bruno twisted his face. "You know what the problem is? You
don't know what you want. Do you want them dead, or not?"

He was right. As if emboldened by my hesitancy, the ants had
begun to multiply. They were not only on my sink, but on the floor
as well. Even though Bruno had killed some of their brethren the
day before, the ants were acting as if nothing had happened, as if
they didn't notice me and were just minding their own business.
Unlike elephants or dolphins, the ants had no memories. They focused entirely on their own foraging, on making it to the next meal.

A few minutes later, I watched as Bruno came into my bathroom wearing oversized plastic goggles and a metallurgical worker's yellow mask over his nose and mouth. He leaned over the
floor, regarding the zone of kill with the intensity of King Lear
marking maps divvying up his kingdom and then, with great flair,
he sprayed the Raid in a straight Maginot Line. I watched as the
ants died instantly. Some, as if smelling the hint of toxins, began to

scurry wildly. Bruno, merciless, sprayed over them, too. He then wiped the area with a paper towel, restoring the tiles to their immaculate blanchness.

I returned to bed. The bamboo-slatted windows kept the light out. The red light of the answering machine on the nightstand remained dormant. No call from Kathryn. My heart sank. I let the weight of the comforter cocoon me.

Bruno left my door open when he crossed my bedroom to exit the bathroom and I could hear him finally heading back to the living room. I heard his footsteps as he walked by; I could hear him crossing the hallway, clearing his throat. Starting his weight lifting always made him do that.

Sometime later that afternoon, I received a call from Bruno. He was working more and more at Renata's restaurant, taking cash for shifts when the video store wasn't busy. He said that a man came in and asked him if he knew a woman named Mara Alencar. Bruno did not say he did, in case he was a stalker, dangerous in some way. He offered to take a message, in case said Mara Alencar ever came by. The man declined.

When I asked Bruno to describe him, I thought he'd conjure the picture of a fifty-something tall American man, in the manner of Nelson Weatherly. Instead, Bruno said he was our age, and, based on his accent and clothes, a Brazilian. Not an immigrant, but a tourist, someone only in town for a few days. Bruno could always tell when their feet were headed back. He could also tell he had money, in the way he made eye contact and wore ironed clothes.

The first thought that came to my mind was that maybe it wasn't me the man was looking for. Maybe it was another Mara Alencar. Maybe there were hundreds of Mara Alencars scattered around the world, each with our own secrets, our own stories.

Who in the world could possibly be looking for me? What Brazilian man could be after me, ten years after I'd left it behind? I had no ties to that country anymore.

There were only two men who might ever come looking for me.

One was my father. I'd only seen him once, fleetingly, in a moving bus, when I was eight, and after that, I'd never seen him again.

The other was Lazarus.

Bruno said this man was our age. But I hadn't seen him since my mother died. He had no idea I'd moved to America.

I took a deep breath, cut off the reverie. So much wishful thinking! The man looking for Mara Alencar wasn't Lazarus. The man looking for Mara Alencar wasn't even looking for me. But it was nice to think that the past could reach for me, and right itself.

I reached for the phone and dialed a fifteen-digit number, starting with the country code. It was our old number, in the apartment that my mother and me shared. It rang and rang, and this was the best part for me, the part that still made me do this, so many years later. While it rang, it was still possible to believe that Ana would answer, and I could hear her voice, the slightly annoyed voice she always deployed when she picked up the phone.

As usual, a woman answered. A housewife, I imagined, with curly hair and a shift dress, taking care of her own husband and her own children. "Hello?" she'd repeat, ever so patient. Hello, hello, hello. Finally, she said, as she often did, "Stop doing this. Why're you doing this? It's not funny. I wish I knew your mother so I could tell her how naughty you are." She probably pictured a boy in his early teens. "I'm gonna hang up now." She never did. "You hear me? I'm gonna hang up." And we stayed on the line, a few seconds more, the two strangers, until her tone softened. "You don't have to do this." She sighed. "You can find some other way to pass your time."

The next day, Bruno called me again from work. In the background, I could hear the clacking of metal pans in the kitchen, the furor of pizzas getting made.

"That man who asked about you yesterday is here again. He's having lunch."

I wondered for a moment if I had heard him right. "Are you sure it's the same man?"

"Yes. If you come right now, you can still catch him," he said and hung up.

I swallowed hard. Curiosity won me over. I slung my nylon satchel over my arm and grabbed my keys, adrenaline slowly building.

At the restaurant, within its white and blue tiled walls, it wasn't hard to recognize him, as he sat by himself at a table for two by the window, elbows resting on the checkered plastic laminate. His sandy brown hair, his slight frame, his poor posture. He looked like he'd been poured into his seat by an uneven hand. He didn't look that different from the last time I'd seen him. He matched the mental photograph I consulted once in a while, a portrait I'd taken with my irises. His waiter hadn't removed the second set of glasses and dishware. They never did—this wasn't a fancy restaurant— but for a moment I thought maybe he was waiting for someone.

Bruno saw me standing there. He was in the kitchen, an apron around his waist, placing a hot pizza inside a white cardboard box. He didn't say anything, as though he saw that I was in a trance and feared what might happen if I woke from it, in case superstitions were true. Bruno, looking very self-satisfied, just smiled and nodded, as though he'd given me a gift. I never mentioned Lazarus to him in explaining my life's history. All Bruno knew was that a good-looking, rich Brazilian man had come after me.

The restaurant was full of customers, a couple of large groups and a row of twosomes against the wall. It was almost two o'clock. Both Portuguese and English all around me, the crest and fall of mirth and laughter.

I walked over and stood by Lazarus's table. He was wearing a forest green shirt with the sleeves rolled up stylishly. It was tucked into his blue jeans and bunched up around his waist. He'd left most of the buttons unbuttoned, revealing a black undershirt.

He must've thought I was the busboy, because he gently pushed his empty water glass in my direction. Then he looked up and saw me and pulled the glass back toward himself. He didn't say anything at first and seemed genuinely shocked to see me, as though he hadn't summoned me at all.

"Do you remember me?" I asked, in Portuguese, putting my hands on top of the chair gently, as though it were a friend's shoulders.

Lazarus let out something between a cough and a chuckle. He held his hand out and pointed toward the empty seat. I lowered myself onto the wooden chair. Face-to-face, it was fascinating to see what time does to memory. He had expression lines I didn't remember him having, and his eyes were a newly darker shade of brown. He'd lost the amorphousness I'd attributed to him in my head.

"Mara Alencar," he said simply.

"In America," I added. "Is it a coincidence that we've run into each other?"

He shook his head like I expected him to. "I'm not here by chance. I've been looking for you," he confessed. "I'm in town for some business and I thought, why not give it a shot? How big can this country be?"

I smiled at the joke. But I was still surprised by his interest. As monumental as our brief time together had been for me, I expected it to be a mere footnote in his own life.

"How did you even know I was in America?" I asked.

"I went to your apartment after you left me." There was a halting quality to his voice. "They told me you'd moved to Disneyland, to Los Angeles. I said to myself, if I were ever here, I'd look for you."

"Los Angeles . . . *and* Disneyland are both very big and crowded," I said, without hiding my amusement.

Lazarus shrugged. "But there are only a handful of Brazilian restaurants in the city," he said, taking a sip of his nearly empty water, a gesture to hide his nervousness.

I nodded. "And how did you find my address in Rio? I don't think I ever gave it to you." I knew for a fact what my young sixteen-year-old self had and hadn't given him.

Lazarus hesitated, as though about to share something uncomfortable. "I found it in one of my father's notebooks on his desk. Your mother's name, her phone number, her address."

A chill rushed through me. Lima had had not only our phone number, but also our address? I felt immediately transported, remembered exactly how it felt to be in Lima's ghastly presence. Ten years could be ten minutes ago.

"He had our address?" I asked, in disbelief.

Lazarus looked at me unhappily and nodded. Bruno, carrying a tray of Margherita pizza, suddenly appeared next to us. Lazarus shook his head to Bruno, turning down the offer. I didn't look at Bruno or acknowledge him, too consumed by the conversation. Once Bruno moved on to the next table, Lazarus locked eyes with me and said, "After you left that day, I asked my father about what happened, and who you really were, and what he did to your mother."

Was there more to the story that I didn't know? The thought occurred to me: I had run away so far, so far out of reach, so that the shame of the past couldn't reach me, that perhaps I had made it so absolution couldn't reach me, either. But Lazarus had crossed an entire continent to find me, like a letter that had taken too long to find its destination, but finally had.

"And what . . . what did he say to you?" I asked, trying to hide my eagerness.

Lazarus cleared his throat and began. "He told me the story he told you. That's what it was. A story. He left some things out. And he changed some things."

"Like what?" There was a tense silence.

"It wasn't the case that your mother was the one who initially offered him information in exchange for money," said Lazarus, staring straight into my eyes for emphasis. "When he told me the story, he said that she did try, at first, to go along with the students' plan. But he could see right through her, and told her that he didn't believe her."

"And that's when he . . . he did torture her. Didn't he?" I murmured. "Didn't he?"

Here it was. The truth, at last. Lazarus would clear my mother's name. I had been waiting ten years for this. He would tell me, in no ambiguous terms, that my mother had been innocent. Lima had lied. Lima had lied. She'd told the truth. Lima had lied.

"No, he didn't torture her," said Lazarus, casting a quick glance around the restaurant. I felt myself deflating, my back sinking against the chair. "He could tell that she wasn't a true revolutionary. She was in over her head, he said. He'd tortured a lot of revolutionaries and she wasn't like the rest of them." He watched me carefully as he spoke. "She was just a civilian, and my father chose not to hurt her."

I must've given him a skeptical look, because he added, "Listen, I know that my father did terrible things." Lazarus leaned forward and lowered his voice. "But he really thought those revolutionaries were terrorists, and they were at war with him." He paused for a moment as he collected his thoughts. "He told your mother that the people she'd gotten involved with were bad, and once she was done with her mission, they still wouldn't leave her alone, and she would be stuck with them for the rest of her life."

I looked away, trying to quiet my breath. This was what I wanted, wasn't it? To hear what really happened? Somehow getting it felt strange.

I was just about to speak when Lazarus continued. "And then he offered her money. And she turned it down."

"Your father said it was the other way around," I repeated, "that *she* asked him for money—"

"No, no, he changed his tune when he told me the story," said Lazarus, shaking his head with conviction. "He wanted you and your mother to have the money."

"Are you sure? Are you absolutely sure?" I asked.

I looked at him, not knowing what to think. I felt shame for not having taken my mother's side. I'd taken Lima's words at face value. I'd chosen to believe a torturer over my own mother.

"She resisted," said Lazarus, his tone filled with a surprising admiration. "She resisted as much as she could. She didn't trust the revolutionaries, didn't like them, but she still didn't betray them. Maybe she felt guilty taking blood money. Who knows?"

I exhaled. "And your father told you this?"

Lazarus furrowed his brows. "He had no reason to lie to me, if that's what you're thinking."

I didn't reply, my mind still racing, and he added, looking annoyed, "And *I* have no reason to lie to you, either. I don't know why he didn't tell you the full truth. Maybe he wanted to rewrite his own history. Maybe he was just toying with you. He was complicated at best."

I leaned back against my chair, considering the ways parents can both protect and hurt their children with the truth. Outside the window led into an alley that served as a parking lot. There was no view.

"But she did, eventually . . ." I couldn't finish my sentence. Betray the students. Collaborate with the enemy.

Lazarus leaned forward. "Yes. When my father told her that the revolutionaries were going to harm her child."

It took me an endless second to accept that he was talking about me.

"He said that *he* would never hurt her daughter, but the revolutionaries would," Lazarus said, his voice filled with surprising sympathy. "And that's when she finally took a side. That's when she revealed what their plans were. She didn't do it lightly. My father said she cried."

And there it was, so clearly, so explicitly stated. It was so much easier to see my mother as some kind of monster or a liar, an opportunist collaborator, than to really own the obvious facts and accept my own part, my own responsibility as her motivation.

It was easier to think of her as a bad person than feel the guilt of being the reason she'd made that decision. I had been only a child, only eight years old. But children can be powerful and drive adults to commit mad, mad deeds. This was the truth I'd chosen to sidestep, but had always known: She'd done it for me; she'd done it for our love.

"I think I know now why the phone calls started in the first place," I said, tears welling up. I wiped them away with a napkin.

"What do you mean?" asked Lazarus, suddenly the recipient of information instead of the bearer.

"He wasn't calling her because he'd tortured her and wanted to torture her again, like I thought," I said, almost thinking out loud. "He was calling her because he *hadn't* tortured her and she was proof that he wasn't an entirely evil person." He had spared her, hadn't he? In his dying days, he liked the person he was when he thought of my mother, when he talked to Ana. That's where the attachment had come from. That's why he'd come back into her life so many years later.

I sat in silence for a moment, absorbing the meaning of my realization.

A waiter who wasn't Bruno came by to offer slices of chocolate pizza, the dark cocoa melting pleasingly over the warm dough. Once again Lazarus refused and asked for the bill, in Portuguese. The waiter reached into one of his many pockets and handed it to him. As this transaction occurred, I felt an unexpected surge of affection for Lazarus.

"The food here isn't so great, is it?" said Lazarus, stifling a belch and making a clear effort to change the subject. "I bet they're not using butter, but margarine instead. And that olive oil stuff, it's just not as good as corn oil." He stretched his arms a little, never giving up eye contact with me. "One thing I want to do before I leave is get a Big Mac. I want to see if it tastes the same as back home. I feel like it shouldn't. It should taste better."

I smiled gently. "You know, when I first saw you here, I thought you came back because of the night we spent together. Maybe you were still in love with me."

Lazarus chuckled, as a hint of sadness flew across his face. "You're overestimating the potential of a seventeen-year-old boy for romantic gestures." I nodded in agreement, and he continued. "I think when you left for America, I wanted, at the time, though not now, to escape, too, and that's why I never forgot about you. You weren't just Mara, a girl, you were also Mara, the girl who went to America."

Also, the girl whose mother his father hadn't tortured. He'd been looking for absolution, too, and he knew he could only get it from the daughter of the *one* woman his father had spared. Being

Lima's son must've been a terrible burden. I thought of that lonely boy by the gate. He desperately clung to the possibility that his father had not been a complete monster. Was it unkind of me to think that he hadn't come looking for me out of a pure and guileless desire for charity? By clearing my mother's name, he cleared his father's, too. We were not all on different sides of the line. We were the line itself.

Lazarus told me that he was flying to Miami later that evening, where he'd spend a week before returning home to Rio. I wasn't quite ready to relinquish him back to the world, though, a warm feeling that I'd had in almost every interaction I'd ever had with him. And so I asked him if he'd like to go for a walk. He agreed, wiping his lips one last time with his tiny, square paper napkin.

I took him to Runyon Canyon, a hiking trail only a few minutes away from the restaurant. We walked past the small, secluded gate, and found ourselves leaving the noise and traffic of Hollywood and being surrounded by canopies of trees and sandy hills in every direction. The park was pretty empty. The morning joggers were gone and it was too early for the late afternoon dog walkers. After twenty minutes or so, we reached the top of the cliff, and settled on an elevated concrete bench, staring at a view of the sun scowling over the thousands of tiny miniature buildings.

"Do you think we would've turned out differently if we'd had different parents?" I asked Lazarus, without looking at him. "That is, if you'd had a different father and I'd had a different mother?"

Lazarus thought for a second and then said, "Yes . . . and no."

We sat in silence for a while, weighed down by our respective burdens, our respective heirlooms.

"I don't hate my father," said Lazarus, shooing away a mosquito with his hand. When he brought his arm back down, his skin brushed against mine. "Even knowing all that he did. Knowing what people think of him now. What they say about him. I still can't hate him."

To not hate. That was a thing worth trying to do. To love instead, even if that love was a secret. One that glowed privately, shielded from scrutiny. Dictated by mighty forces. If Lazarus could forgive a monster, why couldn't I do the same for a woman who'd done a fraction of what he had done? So many good things in my life had come out of her.

I gave myself license to rest my head against Lazarus's shoulder. Together we enjoyed the extravagant view of the whole steaming city, without remarking upon it, without drawing attention to it. It would still be a few hours before that ball of fire in the distance even began to think about setting. What a luxury, then, to enjoy it without thinking of endings, a thing freed of any demands upon it, able to simply be itself for that moment.

The next day, the weather suddenly turned. The day was gray, with hints of rain. And just like that, the ants disappeared. I had no idea where they'd gone. Nature had its own logic, and though the ants had invaded our apartment, our apartment belonged to something larger, more complex and ignorant than them, too. All I knew was this: Once they were there and then they were gone; the humans tried to kill them and failed to do so before they succeeded. When they left, they obeyed a solstice cycle that prefigured me and my kin, but who was to say I couldn't take credit?

I took their absence as a good omen.

Bel Air, California

Two years later

Epilogue

SHORTLY AFTER RENATA BOUGHT HERSELF A CONDO AND moved out, Bruno and I found ourselves alone in the apartment and with that our dynamic changed. I learned more about him, and the more I learned, the more I cared for him. I discovered in him a humor and an adaptability and a resilience that I admired. He loved not knowing the names of things, or how to speak properly. His helplessness seemed to inspire everyone else's kindness. And being a foreigner gave him an excuse to be an outsider. It felt like a relief not to belong.

In the beginning of our relationship, we would treat each other as friends, as enemies, then friends again. He would rant about his work, how much he hated a female coworker who hadn't sided with him during an argument, and I would surprise him—and enrage him—by taking his colleague's side. All the things I'd heard described in the love sections of the women's magazines *Claudia* and *Capricho* would come true, but things I hadn't expected, either, like having a dream that something terrible happened to

Bruno and waking up in a fright, my fingers squeezing his arm and my heart beating fast until I was convinced he was really there.

At times, I would think of ways to escape the relationship and then how much I would miss the relationship, all in one breath. I would hold everything in, frustrated, mad that I'd lost control, that I had to surrender to a stranger's whims, until one day I'd explode at him about it and he'd mention—hurt, surprised—the fact that he'd been doing the exact same thing for me, too.

We would talk about marriage, though without making actual plans. We would make love looking at each other, and then at different points each of us would drift and conjure someone else's face. I would find out that he had likes and dislikes in bed, and more surprisingly, that I did, too, and those had less to do with positions or intensity than with the look in his eyes, how hungrily he needed me, how hard he tried to please me.

After a while I would grow used to almost everything about him, and accept the fact that Bruno would never really stop being a single man—he would now be a single man who happened to have a woman next to him when he did all the things he'd grown used to doing as a single man. He would be the kind of man who compartmentalized, who held things back from me, who eyed me with utter mystification at times. He would be the kind of man who knew that being around me was like being by himself, but a relief, without so much loneliness. Sometimes, I would see a man in the supermarket—a man who looked like Bruno, the same dyed blond hair and facial features, a younger version of him or him in ten years—and I would feel myself filled with an unexpected wave of longing, wanting to protect that person, staring at him until he turned the corner and disappeared.

Most evenings, our routines were the same. I would cook dinner—Brazilian food, or Italian food that was also Brazilian— and serve it, call for Bruno, and then be frustrated that he always took ten or fifteen minutes to finish transferring a video, or quit his game, or put away his cameras. By then the food would be cold—a source of irritation that I would never bring up with Bruno since only someone who cooked would understand it. I would try one day to trick him by saying dinner was ready when the Chicken Stroganoff still had ten minutes left on the stove. Bruno would choose that day to come sit at the table right away.

After being together almost a year, he proved to be a better boyfriend than he was a roommate, though now technically he is both. In fact, Bruno was the one who encouraged me to transfer from Santa Monica College to UCLA, which I am now attending on a generous Regents' scholarship that covers my entire tuition. That is a big deal for someone without a Green Card like me. My expected BA is in Latin American History, and even though I am older than a lot of my classmates, I do not feel out of place. In fact, I feel much more at ease with my professors and fellow students than I ever did with my former employers. With the exception, that is, of Kathryn Weatherly.

I think of her often. Especially lately. From what I knew about stomach cancer, and I knew a fair amount after my months with her, I knew it usually killed within the first two years after diagnosis. Sometimes my own stomach curdled as I wondered if Kathryn was still alive. When I mentioned this to Bruno, he suggested I simply call her. If she answered, I could just hang up if I didn't want to talk to her. He suggested I drive by her address. That's how, two years after I saw her last, loathing not knowing what had happened to her, I found myself going to Kathryn's house in Bel Air once again.

There, I remained in the driver's seat, unable to make myself get out of the Honda. I opened the window as a compromise. Outside, the shade and the breeze greeted me like a long-lost friend. The day tasted like taffy. I waited, watching the maids and gardeners trekking up and down the driveways. I recognized a couple of them.

A half hour or so passed, and I noticed a Jeep idling at the stop sign at the other end of the street. It was packed with rich teenagers on their way to school, all blissfully rambunctious, bobbing their heads and arms to the rhythm of a loud song blasting from the car's stereo. They acted as if they were on their way to a party. They didn't notice me, or how their morning had intersected with mine. They remained at the stop sign for a long time, and I couldn't take my eyes off them. As they drove away, I felt the afterglow of their happiness.

What was I doing there? I thought of the day I'd lost my mother, how suddenly she'd been taken from me, our final embrace brief and insufficient. I could try to understand the present moment only in relation to that day. I would spend the rest of my adulthood, I knew, trying to hear that echo from my past, slip into one of those faded notes. There were so many days, so many chapters in my life, and yet when it came down to it, if memories were objects to be saved from a fire, there would be only one or two I'd reach for before leaving the burning house.

I thought of myself at age five. Five-year-old Mara had been a skinny little thing, with a fat belly. When Ana had to leave home, even for the briefest of errands, I would wrap my arms around my mother's waist, hanging like a monkey. I'd look up at her, smiling, my head dropping back. My eyes were big and happy and adoring. Back then, my mother had been the sun and the moon and the stars for me. She was the water I drank when I was thirsty; the blanket that warmed me when I was cold. I could not survive without her; I knew that—as a little five-year-old—and I hung on to my mother with joy. *Don't go*, I would say, or *Take me with you*, or *I want to go with you wherever you are going*. I thought of my own big eyes at that age, bigger than the rest of my body. I would jump and fall and jump up again; make myself into a ball, then stretch out, all legs and arms. I would kiss my mother while smiling, and smile while kissing her, and I did think, innocent as I was in those days, that it was really going to be like that forever.

My mother's biggest gift had been to teach me how to be a good daughter. She'd taught me how to be mothered, how to find new mothers, how to be loved by a mother. So even without her, even with her gone, I might still be taken care of. It was as if she knew—of course she knew—that eventually we'd be separated. That I'd need somebody else to fill her place. Not one new person, but maybe many, a series of women, for the rest of my life. I would be loved again and again, and it was because she'd taught me how.

First, I had forgotten what she sounded like. Then, her smell, I had lost her smell. The last thing to go had been my memory of her touch. Each of these losses I bemoaned. But I would never, ever forget what she looked like, and with eyes opened or closed, I could see her, her luminous face, smiling mischievously at me. I had that image still. From the day I lost her, wherever I was, whenever I had felt particularly lonely, I had cradled the memory of my mother's face, the essence of her. I had wrapped her around me like a shawl.

I could see her shading her bright eyes with her flat palms, as wind chimes tinkled, pulsating with the knowledge of her own existence, this Ana who lived in all things and was a part of the whole world. There, in her eyes, all the beauty and loveliness of her. In my memories, there was neither time nor desire for admonition. My mother just kept smiling, loving me, and I finally understood—she was my joy, my joy and my curse. Flawed as she had been, I would be hers and hers alone for the rest of my life. And that knowledge widened me, made me feel unbound. An apotheosis. A pang in my heart.

The front door opened.

Kathryn emerged, wearing a silk chemise and a billowing beige skirt. I fought back a shiver. Right away, I could see just how different she looked from the last time I'd seen her. She'd lost her tan, and her natural complexion was a paler shade of ivory than I'd expected. Her blond hair, which once burned parchmentlike in the sun, resembled faded copper.

I felt my throat clench. I watched as Kathryn walked to the mailbox by the curb. There, she stood only a few yards away from me. Kathryn looked normal, not sick. I thought about calling out for her.

As Kathryn flipped through her mail, she finally looked up and noticed me. Our eyes locked. After an initial second of confusion and perhaps anger, Kathryn smiled. There it was, recognition. But more than that. A look both rueful and hopeful, embroidered with a hint of longing.

I realized then who she was and who she wasn't. As far as anyone knew, we were just two strangers whose glances happened to meet. What did the woman in the house see in the woman in the car? Perhaps the distance between happiness and melancholy was far narrower than people wanted to believe: It wasn't a continent; it was the diameter of a razor's cut. Happiness wasn't necessarily the result of hard work and decent character, but purely a by-product of choice. Did I know that? The stranger wanted to make sure.

And there, right at that moment, just by looking at her, I knew that I'd found my answer. I turned on the motor, set the engine to drive, and pressed my foot on the gas. I drove away.

We're all alive, I said to myself as I left the house in Bel Air. We're all alive.

The following was originally published in the *New York Times's* Sunday Review section on January 14, 2017.

I Had a 9 Percent Chance. Plus Hope.

BY SAMUEL PARK

Before I got cancer, I used to collect two-dollar bills. They were rare, and I thought that meant they were lucky, but rare and lucky are not the same thing.

For most of my life I associated low statistical averages with good fortune. I was one of the 20 percent of applicants admitted to my freshman class at Stanford in 1994. When I applied for my first job as an English professor at a liberal arts college, they told me I beat 700 other candidates. And after my second novel was published, one of the hosts of the *Today* show, Hoda Kotb, unprompted by my publicist, recommended my book on the air to her millions of viewers. I estimated the odds of my experience being something like 0.0001 percent.

With luck like that, I figured I should be playing the lottery. Soon I did win a certain kind of lottery, but the prize was something nobody wants.

In the beginning of the spring semester in 2014, I began suffering from severe pain and fatigue, which I originally chalked up to overwork. I had an endoscopy. A few days later, my gastro-enterologist called to tell me that my biopsies had tested positive for stomach cancer. The chance of getting this disease was approximately 0.9 percent.

The typical stomach cancer patient was a nonwhite man in his sixties and seventies. I was an Asian man in his thirties. While I found no hard data on the odds of getting stomach cancer in your thirties, it was certainly a fraction of a fraction of that 0.9 percent.

I immediately wanted to know my odds of survival. My oncologist wouldn't say, leaving me to perform the rite of passage of looking up survival rates on the American Cancer Society website. That speaks to an intrinsic characteristic of cancer: It does not kill right away. Cancer is death by promissory note, and the spaces for "when" and even "if," for those in earlier stages, are left blank.

It might be fair to say that after I became sick, I stopped thinking of myself as a person and began to think of myself in terms of statistics. I asked my doctors for numbers all the time. How would my odds of survival increase with radiation? And with chemotherapy? And by getting care in an academic hospital? Did I get bonus points for being young? (No, it turned out.) I pored over charts from clinical studies, examining survival odds based on various treatments.

My surgeon refused to predict my future and told me to ignore my survival odds, which were a low 9 percent. He pointed out a cognitive error that people make when looking at statistics. If you survive, he reminded me, you'll survive 100 percent. No one survives 9 percent. No one is 9 percent dead.

The numbers that matter are 0 and 100, dead or alive. To make an analogy to a commonly cited statistic, 50 percent of marriages end in divorce. There's a part of the brain that therefore mistakenly believes all marriages experience 50 percent worth of divorce, making that number seem relevant to all couples, when it isn't. For the happy couples, it is irrelevant. That meant that if I survived, it wouldn't matter, looking back, whether I'd beaten chances of 9 or 19 or 90 percent.

After I finished my treatments, months passed and my cancer did not return. According to my doctors, the longer I went without a recurrence, the less likely I was to have one. That meant my odds of survival were not a static 9 percent, as I'd thought, but actually increased over time. By November 2015, I had gone nineteen months with no evidence of the disease, and based on the calculations of a physicist friend of mine, my odds of survival were 70 percent. The chances were high—*very* high—that I would beat my cancer for good.

Around Christmas of that year, however, I began to have trouble eating. One night, shortly after a small meal, I started to feel the sensation of being repeatedly stabbed in the belly with a knife. I had to go to the emergency room for the first of several hospital stays. Soon, I was no longer able to eat solid foods, only protein shakes, and after a while I couldn't even drink those anymore. I was living on 700 calories a day, and at 5 feet 10, I saw my weight drop to 105 pounds. Walking took enormous effort, and my starvation coincided with a seemingly never-ending battery of CT scans, ultrasounds, X-rays, procedures, and biopsies, until my cancer's return was confirmed.

It had not returned when my chance of recurrence was high but when it finally became low. So the fact that my outlook had become rosy meant nothing in the end. My surgeon had been right to say that the numbers weren't predictive—neither when they were against me nor, unfortunately, when they were in my favor.

In retrospect, I'd used survival rates not as a piece of information but as a coping mechanism. I'd used them to measure the amount of hope I could give rope to. They'd allowed for my otherwise unjustifiable optimism to feel rooted in reality. Deep down, every cancer patient wants to believe he is going to make it, and the survival rate is the blunt, messy tool we use to convince ourselves.

However, cancer does not respect the rational nature of numbers. It operates within its own cruel logic. Nowhere is this truer than in the way cancer is treated today. Stage 4 cancer used to be pretty much a death sentence to all patients; the rise of immunotherapy has turned the battle against the disease into a wheel of fortune in which some people continue to die while others live longer and a few achieve seemingly miraculous long-term remission.

In one trial, patients with advanced melanoma who received immunotherapy had a response rate of about 50 percent to 60 percent. But that's not true for most patients with solid tumors. In a recent clinic trial for the drug Opdivo, for instance, only 14 percent of stomach cancer participants benefited.

My ten-year-old niece recently saw one of the two-dollar bills that I carry in my wallet. She'd never seen one before, and asked me if she could have it. I hesitated, wondering if I was going to have to either dispense with some good luck, or saddle her with the opposite. But the hesitation passed, and I handed her the note.

about the author

SAMUEL PARK was an associate professor of English and creative writing at Columbia College Chicago. He graduated from Stanford University and the University of Southern California, where he earned his doctorate. He is the author of *Shakespeare's Sonnets*, a novella, and the writer-director of a short film of the same name, as well as the novel *This Burns My Heart*. His nonfiction has appeared in *The New York Times*. Born in Brazil and raised in Los Angeles, he lived in Chicago. Samuel Park died of stomach cancer at the age of forty-one, shortly after finishing *The Caregiver*.